THESE THINGS
TAKE TIME

Steve and Julie Carter

ISBN-13: 9798326339997
ISBN-10: 1477123456

Cover design by: Steve C
Library of Congress Control Number: 2018675309
Printed in the United States of America

CONTENTS

Genesis 29:20: So Jacob served
seven years for Rachel,
and they seemed to him like
only a few days because
of his love for her.

FOREWORD

There's a famous story about the great songwriter Cole Porter. When he was asked who wrote 'Some Enchanted Evening,' Porter replied, 'Why Rogers and Hammerstein? If you can imagine it taking two men to write one song.' Well, you have to imagine it took two people to write this book because it did.

 I started this my third novel at least eight years ago and maybe longer. After an initial burst, I quickly became disillusioned with my plot and put it down.

They joke that the modern novel has a beginning, a muddle and an ending; that was certainly true here.

After several years, my wife picked the book up and began to sort the mess out selflessly, as she does in all her dealings with me. When she finally asked me to read through it, I was genuinely surprised at the opportunity that lay before us to finish it.

From that point, Julie took on large parts of the descriptive writing, using her talents on this while I stuck with narrative and characterisation. Julie then generally honed and encouraged me wherever we decided to go with it.

So here it is, 'finished.' If there's any such thing as finished. We hope you enjoy it.

It's a book that might appeal to working-class northerners, those of the Catholic faith, Smiths fans and those who like a story with a few twists.

 For anyone born in the '60s and who lived through the '70s, '80s, and '90s, the music scene in those years was unparalleled, and we hope this book will evoke great memories of those times.

At the heart of it all, though, there's no escaping that it's a love story. I don't sit down to write love stories; it's just what comes out. I'll leave it to the psychiatrists to figure out why that is.

Steve and Julie

1969

Man on the moon; Woodstock; Sugar, Sugar; The Love Bug;
The Beatles on the roof of Apple; Kes; Concorde.

The lens of time has a peculiar way of distorting memories. The long, hot, golden days of childhood summers slide out of focus, and we remember them as longer, hotter, and even more golden than they really were.

But whenever Brian 'Pele' Smith cast his mind back to the summer of 1969, and more specifically, the 2nd of July, his memory was as sharp as his mother's tongue was back then. For that was the day that he lost a jumper and found true love. Whenever Pele thought about it, the more he wondered if the demise of his favourite jumper and meeting his true love were in some way inextricably linked, as if they were bound together by some unseen but carefully woven fabric of fate.

Of course, the older you get, the more you realise that cause and effect is just how the universe rolls. But when you were only nine years old, well, you were still some years away from figuring out that simplest of truths.

As was the want of the universe in such matters, the day started like any other. The hot July sun had climbed above the estate's slated rooftops and tall factory chimneys. Heat radiated down on currents of hot air, not dissimilar to a blazing furnace. The clear, azure sky would form a perfect backdrop to the day's coming events, which began at around four o'clock. Despite the heat, three young boys with sweat-drenched hair plastered atop their foreheads were running around a patch of freshly cut grass. A dozen or so oak trees provided a welcome canopy of protective shade for a game of after-school football.

'That was never a goal!' Pele cried loudly while raising his lightly sunburnt arms above his head in protest. 'It was the wrong side of the post.' Pele was wiry and strong for his age; he had dark hair, dancing brown eyes, and a smile that could warm even the coldest of hearts.

Amid Pele's protest, his friends Mark and Peter began to argue. They were identical twins and had thin, ungainly arms and legs with an abundance of freckles. Their red hair was coarse and unruly, and both were prone to raucous laughter. 'You do know that wasn't a goal, Mark,' said Peter, his sweaty fists clenched on either side of his hips.

'Yeah, all right, Peter,' said Mark, shrugging off his loss with good humour before wrapping an arm around Pele's neck to wrestle him to the ground. They were in mid-tussle when they were distracted by running footsteps thumping in the distance.

'The Crosses are coming,' cried out Gordon, a boy who lived on the next street. He was running with an odd, gangly lollop. It only became clear why he had the gait of a three-legged giraffe when he was almost on top of them. The laces from one of his shoes were missing. In full panic mode, his feet became entangled in the pile of clothing that passed for 'goalposts,' and he fell into a heap. 'Where's your shoelaces, Gordon?' asked Mark as he picked up Gordon's shoe from the scattered pile of clothing.

'They...The Crosses took it,' Gordon replied breathlessly, taking the shoe from Mark's outstretched hand. His eyes were brimming with tears. 'And they burst Martin's football with a penknife!' He sobbed, then sniffing, he set off toward his house, calling loudly to anyone within earshot that 'the Crosses are coming!'

Pele and the twins exchanged knowing looks. The Cross boys were the estate's version of the Kray twins, although some argued that the Krays were much nicer lads. 'Let's go back to yours,' sighed Pele, picking up the football. His head swivelled anxiously to check for their imminent approach. The boys then jogged across the green to the sanctuary of the twin's house.

From there, they peered out of a large bay window with bated breath.

Three or four nail-biting minutes later, the Crosses appeared, swaggering around the corner, less with malice aforethought than it being their only thought. Accompanying them, as usual, was their chief partner-in-crime, one Slug MacDonald. The Cross brothers, who would all see the inside of a prison cell within the next six years, were at least three years older than Pele. Slug, though, he knew from personal experience. They were in the same year at school. As Pele and the twins ducked down below the windowsill, Pele whispered a question, 'Hey, do either of you know why Slug's called Slug?'

'No. I thought it was just a daft nickname?' Mark replied, fixing his eyes on Slug. Slug was tall for his age, with closely shaven blond hair and piercing blue eyes that were striking yet coldly indifferent. He wore a slim-fitting, white t-shirt under red braces attached to blue jeans. These were rolled up above cherry-red Doctor Marten boots. But nothing about his appearance shed any light upon his nickname. 'I give up,' said Mark, frowning. 'Tell us then. Why?'

'His sister bet him he couldn't eat a slug when he was four, so he did.'

'Ewwww! That's disgusting,' Peter said, followed by a huge guffaw. 'You sure? You mean, he actually ate it??'

'Yeah, well… Erm… That's what I heard. His sister Niamh bet him a shilling,' said Pele, not quite knowing where the line between fact and fiction lay. 'Well, nobody really knows for sure, I suppose. But anyway, he's been called Slug ever since.'

As the Crosses and MacDonald approached, the boys continued to peer over the windowsill. That was when Pele noticed he'd left his jumper. 'Noooo!' Pele groaned, giving an involuntary cry of dismay as Slug strode purposely towards it.

Slug MacDonald was a boy with a naturally destructive disposition. Being completely incompetent in any area of creativity, he was instead hugely adroit at breaking anything he could lay his hands on. Pele watched helplessly as Slug jumped up and down in mock triumph, swinging the jumper around his head. 'I'm sorry, Pele,' Peter said sadly. The twins placed their warm, grubby hands on each of his shoulders and peered wide-eyed over his head to observe the events play out. Extracting a penknife from the back pocket of his jeans, undoubtedly the same penknife Slug had used to burst footballs down at the canal earlier, he bent to hack at the fabric and removed the sleeve in its entirety.

Pele heard the Cross boys' loud shouts of approval from their side of the window. Slug strutted across the green, swinging the detached sleeve above his head. The last sighting of it was of Slug setting it on fire with a Bic lighter before throwing it over Mrs Hennessy's garden wall.

When the coast was clear, the three boys picked themselves up from the floor and, one by one, traipsed into the kitchen in quiet formation. Pele sat forlornly at a yellow Formica kitchen table, his two small hands on either side of his face cupping his chin. Mark pulled out a glass bottle of Dandelion and Burdock and filled an orange plastic beaker, handing it to Pele, who stared miserably into its dark, fizzy depths. He wondered just what he would say to his mum.

Eventually, Pele made his way home to face the music. His mum had interrogation techniques that the CIA would have done well to employ. So, there would be no way of explaining the jumper's absence or its current one-armed state without her getting to the truth.

Pele found her in the back garden scrubbing paving stones with a yard brush and a bucket of hot, soapy water. Marvin's 'I Heard It Through the Grapevine' was playing on the radio, and she was humming along between the push and pull of the brush. Its tinny sound was turned up high, and she was seemingly unaware of his presence. A soft, pink scarf was tied in a loose knot under her dark hair, holding back her damp fringe. She was slim, pretty, and with no shortage of admirers. Not that she sought any: 'No one could ever replace my Kevin,' she'd declared after he died.

And nobody ever had.

Pele stalled. His hands were burrowed deep into the pockets of his shorts. In his right pocket were four of his favourite marbles and a dobber he'd won off one of the twins that morning. His fingers absently twirled the glass balls around the inside of his pocket, making soft, clicking noises. Meanwhile, his mum vigorously attacked the path with the brush. Her headscarf flopped over her left shoulder as she worked. Finally, she noticed him.

'Oh! Hello, love. What are you doing back so early?' she asked. She walked to the radio to turn down the volume and pushed a cheap pair of tortoiseshell sunglasses onto the top of her head. A white bra strap was showing a little below her stripey, sleeveless t-shirt.

Then she noticed the remains of the jumper.

Pele decided he might as well get it over with, so he gave her chapter and verse of the day's events. Her response was exactly what he feared it would be. 'Oh? He did, did he now? Well, we'll see about that. We're going over there right now to sort this out,' she said angrily. She dropped the yard brush onto the floor with a clatter and stretched her back into an arc with a groan. Despite the expected belligerence, Pele was still alarmed. So, he began to plead.

'Mum. I don't think you understand. It's the MacDonalds! Don't you know *who* the MacDonalds are?'

'Of course, I know who the MacDonalds are. Don't you worry about them, Brian,' she exclaimed, using the name he was christened with and not the nickname his father had given him. 'And let me tell you something else, just so you know: I don't care who they are!' She thrust two soapy hands on his shoulders and bent down towards him. 'Your Aunt Bricey got you that jumper for your birthday, and a little thug like him isn't getting away with this sort of vandalism.'

It was the final word on the matter. Pele knew it was pointless to pursue any further discussion. Though she was only seven and a half stone soaking wet, and Seamus MacDonald was eighteen stone of bulging Irish navvy, it would still be a fair match. His mother pulled what remained of the luminous, mud-covered jumper from the crook of his arm, gripped his wrist, and took off in the direction of the MacDonald 'castle,' which was situated in the most run-down part of Cedar Avenue.

She strode purposefully through the estate with Pele traipsing a few calculated steps behind, cutting a very forlorn figure. Though the day was cooling quickly, his sun-parched face was still burning as heads suddenly appeared at doorways to watch them. The inhabitants of the estate had a sixth sense where trouble was concerned, and as long as they weren't involved, they rather enjoyed it.

Mrs Jacobs, a middle-aged harridan who knew everybody's business within a two-mile radius of her house, was in her usual position at the front doorstep. An Embassy Regal hung from her thick bottom lip, and as she sucked on it, a stream of smoke curled upwards into grey, lopsided eyes. Mrs Jacobs squinted uncomfortably, causing her creased face to wrinkle like a deflated balloon. She was cradling one of her offspring's offspring against an obese protruding hip. 'Everything all right, Katy love?' she enquired, throwing the question out there without really expecting an answer. As she spoke, ash fell off the end of her cigarette, and she glanced down to where it had landed, brushing it off her protruding belly with the back of nicotine-stained, sausage-shaped fingers. As expected, Pele's mum didn't reply. Instead, she turned to see where Pele had gotten to and discovered that he was now languishing some ten yards behind her. She motioned at him to catch up and, putting her arm around his drooping shoulders, propelled him briskly forward.

On reaching the MacDonald's front door, a few minutes later, Katy lifted the decrepit, tarnished metal knocker and brought it down sharply with three successive raps. Pele had slunk more than a few yards behind, being, as he was, utterly mortified at the myriad of faces that were quickly appearing.

A gaggle of housewives spilt onto the street, sensing

trouble like hounds sensing blood. There would be severe disappointment on the estate tonight if there weren't any. The estate's great dames stood at a respectable distance, arms folded, nudging one another and exchanging conspiratorial glances. They collectively grumbled about another disturbance, yet another involving the MacDonalds, a clan of seven children, all of whom resided with their father.

After a few seconds, Katy knocked a second time. The door opened just wide enough for a pair of timid, cornflower eyes to appear. They belonged to a scrawny-looking girl of around 12 years old who Pele recognised as Caitlin. As far as the MacDonald clan went, Pele considered Caitlin to be okay, even more so as she shared the same general antipathy towards Slug as he did. 'Is your father in?' demanded Katy of the puzzled face peering around the door. It was a well-known fact on the estate that there had not been a Mrs MacDonald in residence for quite some time now.

'Who is it?' boomed an irritated voice from the room at the end of the dark hallway.

'It's Pele's ma, Da,' shouted back the MacDonald girl, without once taking her wide eyes off Pele's mother. She had flawless, alabaster skin framed with wild, auburn hair that didn't look like it had seen a hairbrush in weeks.

'Who? Who is it?' the voice boomed again, but even louder now, as if to show whoever was at the door that it couldn't be intimidated. Katy spun around and thrust the remains of the jumper into Pele's chest.

'Put that on,' she commanded.

'What!!?' replied Pele, alarm shooting up to his brain. 'Mum, please! You've gotta be kidding?' But he knew full well that she wasn't.

'I said, put it on,' his mother hissed. Pele's mum said this in the *She*-who-must-be-obeyed voice so there would be no discussion. Instead, Pele stared dismally at the dirty, grass-strewn, green bundle and began to pull it over his head. He pushed his right arm through the one remaining sleeve, now almost twice as long as it had been. His left arm merely poked through the gaping hole. Gasps stifled laughter, and murmuring started up from the crowd that had gathered on the other side of the street. Pele could feel the shame spread across his cheeks and up to the very tips of his hair follicles. He bit down hard on his lip and fixed his gaze firmly on his feet where the cuff of his green jumper dangled limply above his shoelaces. This was, without a doubt, the most embarrassing moment of his life. 'Come on, Brian,' his mother said resolutely. Pushing firmly against the door, she knocked poor Caitlin off balance and into the wall. Katy strode down the short hallway and burst into the front room while Pele loitered behind, still trying to maintain as much distance as he could between them.

In a grim hallway mirror that hung on the wall, he stared in dismay at his reflection. His one-armed, luminous-green jumper was covered in grass, muddy footprints, and stretched beyond recognition. The left side of the jumper resembled a weird poncho. Still, Pele's 'poncho' was naught compared to the scene that greeted Pele's mother as she arrived in the living room. There, she encountered a string-vested Mr MacDonald shaving into a broken mirror over an unlit fireplace and five other MacDonald girls sitting on a brown, threadbare sofa, squashed up like World War Two evacuees on a train. They all had the same luminescent skin, red hair, and sharp, piercing blue eyes, which had been passed down through their mother. She'd been something of a beauty in her youth, and all the evidence to confirm this could be seen in her female progeny.

The girls had been watching a small, black and white, coin-operated TV with a very poor picture. Horizontal waves of white interference pulsated across the screen. Pele could see that Blue Peter was on. A baby elephant was running all over the set and had made a right mess of the studio floor with what Pele's mum would have called 'number twos.' Had he been watching this under any other circumstances than the ones he found himself in, he would have found it as entertaining as the MacDonald clan.

Mr MacDonald had been scraping a razor down the left side of his face, which was smeared with thick, white shaving cream. Distracted by Katy and Pele's sudden, unannounced entrance into his living room, the blade slipped. A large droplet of blood appeared on his cheek and dribbled slowly down onto his double chin. He cursed and turned around to face Pele's mum, the shaving brush and razor held out in what might be construed as an intimidating gesture.

By now, the girls had stopped squealing with delight at the small TV's entertainment as the elephant dragged its pitiful keeper off stage and turned their attention to the bigger and better show unfolding before their eyes. They whispered and giggled at the sight of Pele. Then they hushed as their eyes turned to their father and back to Katy. Redheads bobbed from left to right like they were watching a tennis match. 'Do ya usually burst into people's houses like this, Katy Smith?' MacDonald demanded to know as he dabbed the edge of a grey cloth that may once have been white against his face. His voice wasn't as menacing as it might have been.

'My name's Katherine to you, MacDonald, as well, you know. And I do when their spawn has been damaging my property.'

'Damaging your property, you say?' His face was deadpan as he turned to put his shaving kit on the fireplace. He brushed his hand through a mop of thick, greying hair, revealing a scar underneath the hairline at least six inches long. Pele shuddered when he thought about how he might have gotten it and hid behind his mother.

'I do say so. Now, take a look at this,' she said, turning to one side and dragging Pele in front of her where MacDonald and the gawping girls could see him. MacDonald looked at Pele's sad state and smirked, revealing an incomplete set of front teeth.

'Well, isn't he a sight for sore eyes?' He laughed a deep belly laugh, prompting the girls on the sofa to join in. Pele's head sunk even lower. He wanted the floor to open up and swallow him whole.

'He is indeed,' agreed Pele's mother. 'And there's nothing

funny about it. It was your Stephen, out with those good-for-nothing Cross boys, I might add, that led him to this sorry state.' At this revelation, a thunderous look crossed MacDonald's face. He snapped his braces up over his broad, hairy arms and shoulders whilst hollering even louder than before,

'Stephen, you little shite! Get yerself down here.' Pele looked behind him to see that Slug was already at the foot of the stairs. Like Pele, his head was bowed, and his shoulders slumped. He wasn't embarrassed, though; he was terrified. He edged slowly over to his father, who bent over him. Large hands like shovels gripped Slug's upper arms in a vice. He pulled him close, his wet, half-shaven face nose to nose with Slug's. His fat gut hung over his leather belt as he leant down to hiss into Slug's ear, 'What have I told you, boy?' Before Slug could formulate an answer, MacDonald's backhand struck out at lightning speed, making contact with the boy's face and knocking him clear across the room. As he lay crumpled and dazed on the floor, Slug began to fight the tears that were starting to well up in his eyes, and he was shaking with fear. This was MacDonald's equivalent of giving your kid a clip around the ear. Pele's mum was horrified.

'You'd no need to hit him that hard on account of the jumper!' MacDonald turned his back to her and resumed his position at the fireplace. His eyes met hers in the mirror as he picked up his shaving brush and thrust it into a pot of cream. When he spoke, he spoke evenly.

'That had nothing to do with yer jumper Katie. I've told the little shite time and time again to keep away from those Cross boys.' Pele looked over to where the stunned boy was now rubbing his jaw and slowly hauling himself up from the floor. His left cheek, smeared with a mixture of shaving cream and blood, was already badly swollen. He would wear the black and purple bruise that was starting to form for some weeks. If Slug's eyes were dazed, they weren't so dazed that Pele couldn't see the dark hatred in them as they made contact with his own. The girls sat holding their breath in passive silence, their eyes as wide and terrified as Pele's. Katy realised there was nothing to be gained by pursuing the matter any further with MacDonald. She stared pitifully at Slug.

'Go and put some ice on that lad, and if you haven't got any, use cold water,' Katy told him. Placing a slightly shaking hand against Pele's neck, she guided him out of the living room, but not before shouting, 'Yer a waste of space, MacDonald. Always have been.' Then, they both walked out of the house and up the path as quickly as they'd come.

The women assembled outside on the pavement stepped aside in hushed anticipation as Katy pushed through. Pele spotted Mrs Jacobs arriving on the scene and eager to glean what information she could. She patted him heavily on the head as he passed and tut-tutted at the sorry mess he was in due to those terrible boys. He recoiled from her clammy, smoke-stained hand and the stench of stale sweat that saturated her clothes.

When they were away from the crowd, Pele's mum stopped suddenly by the telephone box on the corner of Acacia Avenue. 'Brian, I'm calling in to see your Aunt Bricey for a cup of tea. I'll only be half an hour. Here's the key. You go home, and I'll see you back there. I'll make some dinner when I get back. Okay?'

'Yeah, okay, Mum,' he replied miserably. The anxiety he felt for Slug's future retribution vied with the guilt and sadness for what Mr MacDonald had done when he'd hit him. His mother, who often said she could read him like a book, gripped his chin in her hand and tilted his head back until she could stare directly into his eyes.

'None of this is your fault, Brian,' she said in a firm voice, her soft, brown eyes penetrating his. 'Do you hear me? None of it.' She examined his face, waiting for him to acknowledge her. Pele tried to say yes, but as his chin was in the grip of her hand, he could only give a muffled reply. Satisfied with his response, she let go of his chin and gave him a crushing hug, which he sensed was as much to comfort herself as it was to comfort him. And it was why he didn't try to disentangle himself before any of his mates saw him being hugged in the street by his mother.

After they parted, Pele set off in the opposite direction and cut through the park to go home. As he walked, he mulled over the various revenge scenarios that he would almost certainly face when he saw Slug again. He was weighing his options, and currently, the least popular choice of jumping off the garage roof to break a leg was vying with contracting a serious illness that would keep him off school for the next six months. He began to wonder just how you might acquire a bad, but not necessarily deadly, illness when an amused voice from the swings behind him disrupted his thoughts. 'Hey! Why are you dressed like that?' Pele, to his surprise, realised he was still wearing the one-armed poncho and had walked nearly half a mile through the estate looking like an even bigger idiot than usual. He turned to see a slight, pretty girl leaning back against one of the swing seats, holding it in a vertical mid-air position. Her slim, tanned legs were braced against the floor, and she was gripping the chains above her head.

'What? Oh! This? It's a long story,' he answered, shrugging his shoulders and sighing as he looked down at himself. It occurred to him to pull the jumper over his head, but the truth was that he was well past caring how he looked.

Meanwhile, the girl was observing him in frank appraisal. She had a straight, dark fringe and two long plaits that hung down her back with small, blue ribbons tied at the ends. Pele's eyes were drawn to the girl's face. He had no idea what it was about her flushed, pink cheeks and ever-so-large, deep, blue eyes, but the whole effect made his stomach ratchet into weird knots. She stepped forward, letting the swing drop suddenly, and walked confidently towards him. 'My name's Angela. Angela O'Brian. What's your name?' He began to feel a tad breathless and more than a little stupid, though he had no idea why.

'I'm Pele Smith,' was all he could mumble in return, picking at the edges of his jumper.

'That's a funny name,' she giggled.

'It's not my fault,' he said, feeling self-conscious. 'My dad was mad on Pele. You know? The football player? Anyway, it's been my nickname since I was a little kid. My real name's Brian, but everyone calls me Pele. Only my mum ever calls me Brian.'

'Brian's a nice name,' the girl said, nodding. 'But I really like Pele. It's different.' Her eyes locked onto his. Then, without any warning and much to his consternation, she plucked lightly at his hair with her fingertips. 'Where do you live?' she asked, clearly indifferent to his obvious alarm.

'Larch,' he told her in a trance. 'Number...err...what are you doing?' She produced several blades of grass that she had removed from his hair and tossed them into the air. Her proximity to him felt like an electric charge. He stood rigidly, examining every detail of her face as she gently brushed her fingertips across the top of his head. Finally, she stepped back to inspect her work.

'That's much better, although I can't do anything about fixing your jumper,' she said with a grin and lightly touched the ragged edge where the sleeve had been ripped off.

'Thanks,' said Pele, no longer even slightly concerned about the jumper. He lamented that he didn't have a few more blades of grass in his hair so that she might touch his head for a little longer.

'Will you give me a push, Pele?' she asked enthusiastically and tipped her head in the direction of the swings. 'I like being pushed really, really high.' Without waiting for an answer, she spun around and climbed back onto a seat in anticipation.

'Yeah. Okay. But I've got to get home for my tea soon,' he told Angela. Pele removed the jumper and stood behind her, placing both hands firmly on her back. She was wearing a pale blue, thin cotton dress adorned with big, white, and yellow daisies. He pushed her gently at first, but she insisted he put much more effort into it. So, he shoved the swing seat so hard he was suddenly worried she might fly out of it. Her long plaits and the skirt of her dress were airborne for a second. Her laughter filled the air, and it seemed to him that it was the most wonderful sound he'd ever heard. As the swing rose and fell, he was utterly captivated.

He had thought he was too old to play out with girls now that he was nine. But he knew with absolute certainty he wanted to play out with her very badly, and the game that sprang to mind was the kissing game. He'd seen some of the older kids play it in the fields at the back of his house, and until today, he'd thought it was truly disgusting. Now, all of a sudden, it didn't seem quite so disgusting after all.

The swing slowed a little, and she slid off it, dropping nimbly to the ground. She stepped towards him and looked into his eyes with a poise that belied her years. 'How old are you?' he asked, feeling nervous as she drew near. The beat of his heart increased in pace and was now thudding loudly in his chest. Her dark eyelashes framed large eyes that he would like to gaze into for a very long time.

'I'm nine next week,' she replied, looking very pleased at her advancing years. Her mouth broke into a winning smile as she added, 'My da's taking me to the zoo for my birthday.'

'That will be nice,' Pele replied. He kicked his toes into the soft earth. 'If you want to play out tomorrow, I could call for you?'

'Oh,' she said, a frown creasing momentarily across her forehead. 'I'm visiting my aunty, and she doesn't like boys calling for me. But I could call for you tomorrow if you like?' Pele wondered if it was a good idea if his mates or his mum knew that an eight-year-old girl was going to knock-on for him.

'Tell you what,' he said, rubbing his temple with his fingers. 'Why don't we just meet here at two o'clock tomorrow?' She nodded at this, like it was the best idea she'd ever heard.

'Yeah. I'll meet you here at two tomorrow then,' she confirmed.

'Okay,' he smiled back. 'I gotta go, but I'll see you tomorrow. Yeah?' She nodded again and, with that, turned away, picked up her bike, and cycled off in the direction that he'd just come from. She waved at him with one hand while expertly steering the bike with her other. He watched her go until she was out of sight, and then he picked the green jumper up from the floor where he'd dropped it and tucked it under his arm. As he made his way home, he had to keep suppressing an urge to swing the jumper above his head in exactly the same way that Slug had done earlier that afternoon.

Maybe it hadn't been the worst day of his life after all.

Later that night, despite feeling exhausted, sleep eluded him. Around ten, he switched on his 'Ever Ready' torch, tiptoed over to the set of drawers at the bottom of his bed and pulled out a box. Inside were keepsakes, including an old wristwatch of his dad's that no longer worked. He picked the watch up by its faded, brown-leather strap and held it in front of the beam of light. Engraved on the back was an inscription that read: '*Happy 21st Birthday, Kevin, all my love forever, Katy.*' Pele's fast-fading, ultimate memory of his dad was of him kicking a football in the garden when he was only four.

Pele picked up a photograph album and opened it. The first photograph was of him as a newborn baby. His doting parents were smiling down at him as he lay in his pram, their arms encircling each other's waists as they leant forward.

His favourite photo was of him and his dad kneeling on the grass. They were looking at something, their heads locked together in earnest, as the sun shone warmly on their backs. His mum had taken that one four months before his dad died.

It had been an accidental fall on his way home from work. Nothing but a slip on a grassy embankment. Something so very ordinary that it didn't seem fair it had resulted in his death. It wasn't anybody's fault; it was just one of those things. Everyone said what a great man he was. They said that God always takes the good ones first.

People said a lot of things that didn't make any sense to Pele.

The following day, he got to the park early. It was one-thirty when he sat down on the same swing where he'd first seen her. He held the chains and rocked backwards and forwards from his heels to his toes while he waited. The feeling of excitement began to grow as the minutes ticked by.

By two-thirty, there was still no sign of her, but he kept willing her to appear on her bike. He imagined Angela cycling towards him one-handed and dazzling the world with her wonderful smile and sheer exuberance.

When he eventually left the park at four, he walked aimlessly around the streets, trying to find her.

But he couldn't.

And it would be five years before he saw her again.

1974

Three-day week; Bagpuss; The Towering Inferno; David Essex; Godfather Part II; Watergate; Lord Lucan.

The muddy football spiralled through the air. Pele was unmarked inside a crowded penalty area, and his eyes were fixed on its trajectory. As the ball plummeted towards him, he calculated that there wasn't enough time to take it down and control it, so, trusting his instincts, he leaned slightly backwards on his heel and swung his right foot as hard as possible.

From the moment his foot drove through the ball's arc, sending it off toward the goal, Pele knew it would end up in the net. He watched it rise and sail above the goalkeeper's outstretched arm, where it careered into the top right-hand corner of the goal. Pele felt the elation of living up to his exalted nickname for one of the few times in his life. He threw his hands into the air and ran towards his teammates, who immediately jumped on top of him, pushing him to the ground. Through the multitude of limbs embracing him, he could hear Father O'Malley's booming voice on the sidelines shouting, 'A wonderful goal, Pele! That's the Saint Jude spirit. You'll be on United's books for sure next month.'

Pele walked back to the halfway line for the restart and looked along the St Jude's line, where parents, friends, and visitors were loudly cheering and clapping. Pele noticed that not everyone was celebrating, though. Stood apart from the supporters was the miserable countenance of St Jude's under 15's substitute, one Slug MacDonald. And he wasn't celebrating in any shape or form.

Pele sighed.

The game ended in a hard-fought 2-2 draw, with Pele's goal being the standout moment. Afterwards, in the changing rooms, the boys sang songs and shared good-humoured changing-room banter. Pele emerged from the shower to find the changing room had quietened down. Dressing quickly, he looked around for two of the lads who lived on his part of the estate. They were waiting for him outside, and as soon as they saw him, they began to recreate Pele's goal moment by moment. While reconstructing the greatest goal of the season so far, Pele heard Father O'Malley call out to him, 'Have you a moment, Pele? I'd like a word if you don't mind?' Pele told the lads to walk on and that he'd catch them up.

'Yeah, Father?' he asked, jogging over and wondering what he might want. 'What's the matter?' The priest's head tilted slightly to one side.

'Well, to be sure, I didn't say anything was the matter, did I? But since you mention it now, I'll get straight to the point. It's Stephen I want to talk to you about.'

'Stephen?' replied Pele, forgetting for a moment who the priest was referring to.

'Stephen MacDonald. You do know him. He's your teammate?' Pele's shoulders slumped with recognition when he realised the priest was talking about Slug.

'Oh, yeah, Stephen. What about him, Father?' he enquired glumly.

'Well, he quit the team before. Do you know why he'd go and do that?'

'Maybe because he's not very good?' Pele said, not particularly caring one way or another. Slug was the least talented footballer on the team, and consequently, he was a substitute more often than not.

'Now then, Pele, that's not a very nice thing to say, is it? And here I am thinking that it's most unlike you. You're better than that, to be sure. Because we all have different gifts, don't we?' Pele could feel one of the priest's infamous sermons coming on and interjected quickly,

'But I don't know anything about why he's left, Father. We're not really friends. Honestly, I have no idea.' The priest nodded thoughtfully.

'Well, isn't that a sad state of affairs?' he said. 'Don't we try to instil team spirit into you boys? Isn't the team more important than the game, more important than one player? All the better then that you be the one to go around to his house and get him to change his mind.' Pele was instantly horrified. He'd only ever been to Slug's house one time, and that particular memory wasn't filed away in the same cabinet as Easter eggs, Christmas presents, or playing football in the back garden with his dad. But when he heard the next few words trip off his tongue, he couldn't believe he was actually saying them to the priest.

'I'm sorry, Father, but I can't do that. He's not my friend, and, if anything, he's...really, well...' He looked up at O'Malley's kindly face, peering down at him, and felt the wind go out of his sails. '...not my friend.'

For the briefest moment, Pele thought he might have wriggled off what seemed to him, at least, a nasty hook. The priest scratched his head and appeared to muse over what Pele had said before replying, 'But don't ya see Pele? Stephen's a big worry to me. No mammy at home and surrounded by all those girls. And his da is, how can I say this? Often busy. Can ya just imagine all of that? He's the sort of lad that could easily fall into trouble if we don't occupy his mind.' Pele nearly laughed out loud: '...could easily fall into trouble.' It was clear that O'Malley wasn't yet aware of Slug's many exploits around the estate.

'But what's all that got to do with me?' grumbled Pele. 'It's not my fault he's only got sisters and that his mum left. I've got no brothers or sisters, and my dad died when I was four. Don't you always tell us that we've all got our crosses to bear?' The priest's chin dropped towards his large, barrelled chest, and he gave a tired-sounding sigh, which seemed to confirm Pele's analysis of the situation.

'You're right, Pele, of course you are. I'll see if one of the other lads will do it. Go on, then. Off ya go. I'll see you in church on Sunday.'

Pele thought he'd netted another winning goal with this argument and inwardly celebrated his victory. But as O'Malley walked away, he felt a guilty gnawing pang in his guts. O'Malley hadn't implied that he was upset with Pele, but it was the first time he had sensed any disappointment from him.

Pele ran back to his friends heading down Heath Road. He didn't know why the priest's disappointment should bother him so much, but it did.

A week later, Pele found himself scanning the lower school corridor. Thankfully, it was empty, and the coast appeared clear. He breathed an inward sigh of relief. Pupils attending secondary school from his estate had a strict unwritten code. Only essential contact with teachers was acceptable; anything more than that was unequivocally viewed as fraternising with the enemy. And so, for the sake of self-preservation, if you were going to fraternise, you didn't let any other kids see you do it.

Pele cautiously knocked on the door to classroom E4. A friendly voice called out loudly, 'Come in!' He pushed against the door and stepped inside. Mr Cooper was sitting behind his desk at the bottom of the classroom. Looking over his glasses at Pele, he smiled warmly.

Pele didn't like many of the teachers at the school. Some of them were dismissive of pupils, like they were annoying flies that needed to be swatted away. Cooper was different; he was engaging and looked at you like you mattered. If you put your hand up in class, and even if you said something stupid, he always tried to place some value on what you had said. Pele was glad to have had him for the last two years for English. 'Hello, Mr Cooper,' Pele said. 'I'm sorry to bother you. I wondered if you had a minute?'

'Yes, Pele. What can I help you with?' replied Cooper, putting his marking pen down on the desk and waving him in. Pele closed the door and made his way towards the teacher.

'It's about the homework you set, Sir.'

'Glad to hear that you intend to do it,' Cooper teased him lightly, though not without good reason. The plain truth was that, of late, he'd become a bit too interested in girls, music, and football, and those distractions had led him to a point known within educational circles as 'coasting.' Like all good 'coasters,' he could get away with it to some degree because he was so bright, but his mum had noticed this lack of commitment and serious 'words' had been had the other day. Pele was left under no small illusion of the consequences if he didn't improve quickly. He figured he might as well start 'improving' with his favourite subject, English. So, Pele happily accepted the jibe and grinned.

'I do, Sir,' he replied. 'And I want to do my best on it, or else my Mum will have something to say.' Cooper tipped his head back and laughed; his brown eyes twinkled with understanding.

'Yes, indeed. A very formidable woman is your mother, Pele. Not a lady I would want to upset either. So, how is it that I can help you?' Pele tugged at his English book, which was firmly jammed into his jacket pocket. He unfurled it from its tight cylindrical shape, turned to the back page, and read out the question he'd written from Cooper's direction earlier that week.

'Which is the most important character in Moby Dick, Ahab or the Whale?' Pele looked over at Cooper, who had rocked back on his chair and was fixing Pele with a 'go on' look. So, he did. 'Well, Sir. I don't know how to answer the question because it seems I have to choose one or the other.' He shrugged at Cooper, hoping his dilemma would be obvious to him, but Cooper did what he always did: he asked Pele a question.

'And why exactly is that a problem?' Pele thought carefully about how to phrase what he wanted to say because he didn't want to appear stupid in front of his favourite teacher.

'Well,' he began slowly, 'I was thinking that neither character is more important than the other. I mean, it's like they both have to be as important as each other for the story to make any sense…' Cooper leant forward in his chair and clapped his hands to Pele's surprise. Pele was puzzled by his teacher's behaviour, but Cooper smiled.

'Very good, Pele! I've been setting that question to third years for five or six years now, and very few realise that you can answer it like you did. As you correctly point out, the choice isn't a simple one or the other, as both are crucial to the story. So, my advice to you is to go and write it based around your conclusion.' Pele thanked him and began to roll his book up, intending to leave.

At the last minute, though, he had a change of mind. Instead, he looked up and said, 'Mr Cooper, I've got another question about the book. One that's not been set. But erm... well, I wanted to ask you about it anyway.'

'Oh? What's your question, Pele?'

'Does Captain Ahab want to die? He must have known that he was going to die in the end if he kept chasing the whale. And it just doesn't make any sense that he didn't stop before it was too late. Why would someone throw their life away like that?' Cooper sucked in air as he thought about his reply.

'Well, Pele. I think that Ahab was probably incapable of ever giving up his pursuit. In some ways, the whale was the only thing that made him feel alive. It gave him a purpose and, therefore, a reason for living. If he gave up on the whale, he would be giving up on life itself. So maybe, for him, the quest was worth risking his life, as the alternative was not really living at all?' Cooper watched Pele's face scrunch as he attempted to take this in.

'Well, it sort of makes sense now that you've explained it. But it's still a bit crazy if you ask me.' Cooper laughed; his arms were folded across his chest, and he seemed to be contemplating something.

'Pele, what do you want to do when you leave here?' Pele stopped trying to force his book into his pocket and thought about the question.

'Well, I know what I'd like to do, but it's not likely I'll ever do it.'

'Oh?' said Cooper, raising an eyebrow. 'What's that then?'

'If I could do absolutely anything, I'd love to be an English teacher, Sir. It's my favourite subject and probably the one I'm best at,' Pele said, re-curling his book tighter and forcing it once more into his pocket.

'Well, if you wanted to go into teaching, then to start with, you'd have to sit your A-levels, which would mean doing some extra work in Mrs Crabtree's O-level group. That's well within your ability, Pele.'

'The thing is, Sir, I'll probably need to get a job when I leave school. My mum's been working since I was little, so I'll have to earn some money to help out.' Cooper gave a small sigh and nodded his head in understanding.

'Maybe you could think about night school when you leave then? Keep up your English studies, as you have a real talent. You just need to sharpen up your grammar and vocabulary a little, so those big ideas that you have in that head of yours can get out onto a page where they belong.'

Apart from leaving and getting a job, Pele hadn't given much thought to his future. Some of this was because his mother did enough thinking about that for both of them. She had always told him there was no way he would work at the ICI or join the Army like the other kids: 'Not that there's anything wrong with that,' she would tell him, but it wasn't for him. Yet further education had never been discussed as an option. It was implicitly understood that working-class people went and got jobs at sixteen. They didn't have the luxury of going to college when bills had to be paid at home.

In the end, Pele looked back and simply said, 'Thanks, Mr Cooper. I'll definitely think about that.' But by the time he'd walked out through the school gates, he'd forgotten any crazy ideas of becoming an English teacher.

Pele knew that timing was everything at these moments. From a young age, he'd learned that sometimes, when his mum said no, it was no, and then, sometimes, it wasn't. He was pretty sure that this was one of those times when it wasn't, especially as he'd shown her the 'A' that he'd gotten off Mr Cooper for his Moby Dick essay. Nothing brought a smile to his mum's face quite like a good school grade. When he judged the moment to be right, he spoke again, 'Aww…come on, Mum. Everyone's going. All of the kids on the estate will be there.' His mum was standing by the sink, peeling vegetables for a stew. She pursed her lips before replying.

'I don't care what the other kids are doing, Brian. It's a school night.' With that, she bent her head and resumed peeling a carrot while he hovered at her elbow.

'But Mum, I'm doing really well at school! When you went to parent's evening, every one of my teachers said I was near the top of my class in almost everything.' Pele examined his mum's face, and it seemed to him that it had softened. He took this as the moment to press home his advantage. 'I'll be back before ten. I've done all of my homework this week. And I promise: I'll get up the first time you shout me in the morning.' His mum didn't seem very impressed by his argument. Instead, she put the peeled carrot and peeler on the chopping board, wiped her hands, and turned to face him. He waited, holding his breath for her answer, and blew out a loud, exasperated groan as she gave it.

'I'm sorry, Brian, but the answer is still no,' she told him. 'I know that you're doing better now in school. You've been trying hard again, and that's because I'm on your case. I have to be. You don't realise it now, but your education is everything.' At this, she picked up a carrot and, pointing it at him, said firmly, 'It's your way out of here.' Pele could never work out what was so bad about 'here' that he needed a way out from it. Trying to think quickly on his feet, he had one last card up his sleeve to play.

'Well, you know Father O'Malley's going to be there? He's running it with some woman from the Labour Party. So, think about that, Mum! The Catholic Church and the Labour Party? They can't both be wrong!!?' He grinned as he saw his mum's head drop in mock defeat. The beginnings of a smile emerged on her face. She shook her head wearily as she washed her hands at the sink with a bar of green Palmolive soap.

'And how often a week is it going to be Brian?' He didn't complain that she hadn't listened to a word he'd said.

'It's just twice a week,' he told her. 'Tuesdays and Thursdays. And then maybe more nights in the school holidays. Everyone's going to be there. The twins are going, and their mum will be there too, and she'll keep an eye on me,' he added, just for good measure. Pele stared pleadingly into her face. She slowly lifted the hem of her white and orange striped apron, then dried her tiny hands on it.

'I want you back by ten, Brian. If you don't get back by ten, I swear, it will be the last thing you ever do.'

'Yes!! Thank you, Mum!' Pele whooped and gave her a bear hug. 'I'll be back by ten. I promise. I won't let you down.'

With that, he burst upstairs, put '*Ziggy*' on the record player, with the volume halfway, which was as high as he dared if he didn't want to push his luck, and began to change out of his school uniform.

Pele got to the 'youthie' ten minutes after its doors had opened at seven. It seemed like half of the estate had already arrived by the time he got there. The club was an old hall attached to the Church where Pele had been an altar boy a few years back. There was table tennis, a pool table, table football, a few board games, and a small refreshment area where the twin's mum was swamped, serving juice, teas, sweets, and crisps to a throng of noisy teenagers. Towards the back of the hall, a group of girls had gathered around a record player. A few of them were dancing together, their long, black skirts swishing from side to side as they moved in time to Dean Parish's Northern Soul classic '*I'm on My Way.*' Pele's eyes continued to circle the hall to see if he recognised anyone that might be 'trouble.'

Over on the far side, he spotted a potential danger area. One of the Cross boys was sitting on the edge of the stage with Slug MacDonald, but they seemed happy enough just watching the girls dance. Then Pele saw the twins waving at him from behind the refreshment bar, and he wandered over to meet them. They were almost six feet tall and towered above everyone else in their year. They both wore metal braces on their teeth and were eagerly counting down the days before they would be free of them. Their red, wavy hair was worn below their ears, a bone of contention between them and their mother. Their 'look' reflected bands like Led Zeppelin and Deep Purple that they played on repeat, much to their mum's dismay and disapproval.

As Pele approached, they greeted him with the usual double pinch to the arm and a headlock. Being slightly smaller and outnumbered, the twins had an advantage over him. On finally breaking free, Mark grinned a metal-toothed smile. 'So, you made it after all. How do you always get your own way with your mum?'

'It's called charm, and you've either got it or you haven't. In your case…' Pele stepped back to avoid an arm being wrapped around his neck again. Peter offered him a moist-looking kola cube from a scrunched white paper bag that he pulled out of his denim jacket pocket. 'Nah, thanks,' said Pele as he ran his fingers through his roughed hair. 'I've got fifty pence off my mum, so I'm going to get some chocolate. I'll see you at the table tennis in a minute. Put my name on the board, will you?' The twins jostled with each other as they manoeuvred towards the table tennis, causing any teenagers in their path to get out of their way. Pele waited his turn to get served and began to walk over to where the twins were.

That's when he saw her.

The girl!

The girl from the park!

She watched him with a shy smile, and he stopped dead in his tracks. He felt mildly light-headed and wondered if she was an apparition he'd conjured up. Then she waved and broke the spell. Pele stole a sideways glance at the twins, who by now were forcibly taking bats off the younger kids. Their game had apparently finished, although there seemed to be some disagreement about this state of affairs. They beckoned for him to come over and play. 'No. You play the first game. I'll…I'll be back in a minute,' he called out to them. With that, he turned and walked towards her.

'I knew it was you!' she exclaimed as he approached. 'As soon as you walked in, I recognised you.'

'It must be the sweatshirt,' Pele joked as he stopped before her. 'It does have two sleeves this time, I suppose.' He raised his arms, and she giggled. Pele's stomach was beginning to churn in that anxious, lurching way that felt similar to a ride on the fairground Waltzers. He was usually adroit when talking to girls his age, but he was uniquely tongue-tied.

'I haven't seen you around since…'

'The park?' she interjected with a smile. 'Yeah, I'm sorry I never came that day. I wanted to, but I had to go home the next morning because my mum came early for me. Then, my dad relocated with his job two months later, and we all moved back to Ireland. That's where I've been living for nearly five years.'

'Oh! Are you living back in England now?' he asked hopefully.

'No. We're still in Ireland. We're visiting my aunty on our school holidays. We're going back home next week.' Pele's heart sunk at the news.

'Oh… well. That's a shame,' he replied, trying not to look as deflated as he felt. 'So, who are you here with tonight?'

'I've come out with my cousin, Susan,' she explained, looking around the crowded hall to find her. Pele took advantage of the moment to secretly observe Angela. The dark plaits had been dramatically replaced with a short, wispy hairstyle cut over her ears. A jagged fringe was visible beneath a cerise beret, and she looked the epitome of cool. Her style was so cool, and her dress sense was very different from that of the local girls on the estate. She wore a small, floral-print dress with flat, lace-up ankle boots. It shouldn't have worked at all, but somehow it did. He was so engrossed in watching her that everyone else in the room might as well not have been there.

Angela suddenly pointed to a strawberry blonde, pony-tailed girl he vaguely recognised and who was stepping about to the

Northern Soul music near the stage. 'There she is,' said Angela, turning back to Pele and catching him watching her.

'Oh, right. Err...I think I've seen her around,' he replied, somewhat flustered and feeling a warm flush cross his face. Then suddenly, a familiar voice boomed in his ear.

'Who's this Smith?' Pele turned to see Slug McDonald standing there. Though he'd addressed Pele, his eyes were fixed firmly on Angela, who seemed a little embarrassed under the intense scrutiny of his gaze. Pele was taken off guard by the interruption but figured the best way to get rid of him would be to get the introductions over with quickly.

'Erm... This is Angela, Slug. Angela, this is Slug. He's...err... someone I know from school.' Slug still didn't look at Pele and didn't seem inclined to say another word either. In the awkwardness that ensued, Angela broke the painful silence.

'Hey, you're Stephen, aren't you? Stephen Macdonald? I used to play with your older sister Niamh when I was little. She was always very sweet about me hanging around. But you don't remember me?' she said teasingly. Slug's face creased as if some vague recognition began to dawn. He looked down at the floor.

'Oh, yeah, Niamh,' he muttered almost inaudibly.

'Well...it's been really nice to meet you both,' Angela said, breaking another silence. Hooking her thumb over at the table tennis court, she told Pele, 'I think your friends are calling you? Anyway, I should get back to my cousin. Maybe I'll see you a bit later?'

'Yeah, sure,' Pele agreed brightly. Only too pleased to bring an end to the painful exchange that had just taken place. Angela turned to give Slug a radiant smile and walked over to the stage, where she sat down next to her animated cousin, who seemed to be peppering her with questions about the two boys she'd been talking to.

After she'd gone, Pele became acutely aware that he was standing in the middle of the hall next to a besotted Slug MacDonald, who was too close for comfort. Unsure of what to say, he didn't have to worry. Slug opened his mouth and stated,

'Oh, she's as fit as a butcher's dog!'

'Yeah, I suppose so,' Pele muttered back before walking over to the twins, where he played the worst game of table tennis that he had ever played.

It was a bittersweet evening for Pele. He'd followed Angela's movements from his side of the hall, and even though he was desperate to go over and talk to her, he was painfully aware that Slug was intensely watching her, too. Slug was territorial. If he perceived that Pele was muscling in on what he'd already decided was his, trouble would ensue. This would be catastrophic if his mother found out, as he would be banned from attending the youth club ever again. As far as he could tell, he wasn't on Slug's radar as a potential threat and was glad to keep it that way. He glanced over to see her laughing with her cousin and exhibiting a self-assurance enough to send any 14-year-old boy weak at the knees.

Sometime later, Angela stopped Pele on her way back from getting a lemonade and whispered in his ear, 'I'm leaving in half an hour. Meet me outside if you want to walk me home?'

Twenty minutes later, Pele was waiting outside, his heart beating furiously. This was partly due to the anticipation of walking Angela home but also because he was half expecting Slug to come out and give him a kicking.

When Angela joined him ten minutes later, he was relieved that Slug wasn't in tow, but neither was her cousin. They set off together toward her aunt's house, a fifteen-minute walk away. 'Where's Susan? Is she not walking back with us?' Pele asked her whilst looking over his shoulder.

'Oh! She's getting a ride back with a neighbour's kid in half an hour. So, it's just me. Don't you feel safe being alone with me?' she grinned.

'I think I can manage without a chaperone if you can,' he replied amiably.

'Are you staying at your aunt's house with your mum and dad?' he asked. Her eyes dropped a little, and a shadow darkened her face.

'Oh… no. It's just me, my da, and my sister. Ma passed away a couple of years ago… from the cancer.' She turned to look at him, and he saw that her eyes were moist with tears. Pele reached out and touched her hand.

'Oh… I'm really sorry. That's horrible, Angela.' They walked a few steps in silence when Pele added, 'I lost my dad, you know? I was only little when it happened, but I still miss him.'

'Thanks, Pele, I miss her…' Her voice trailed off, and she shrugged lightly as they walked quietly together. 'But my da's held us together. We're closer now than we've ever been. I can tell he misses her a lot, but he says we have to play with the cards we're dealt because that's all we have.'

'He sounds like a wise man,' replied Pele with a smile, and she smiled back at him.

At some point during the conversation, Pele realised he was holding Angela's hand. He was pretty sure that he hadn't worked up the courage to slip his hand into hers, but he couldn't remember her doing it for the life of him but it felt like the most natural thing in the world.

She began to chat animatedly as they moved on to lighter topics, and he noticed that her accent had the hint of an Irish lilt to it these days. But Pele's mind was now consumed with only one thought. His mind was conjuring up the many different scenarios of an impending kiss and how such a kiss might come about. Should he wait until they were nearly home or ask her on the way? He wanted to kiss her more than anything and hoped the feeling was reciprocal, but how could you be sure of anything where girls were concerned?

In the end, he decided to wait until they were nearer to her aunt's.

At the last left turn, just before going into a small cul-de-sac, a car rolled up slowly beside them and parked just past the junction. Angela groaned and turned to him. 'It's the next-door neighbour Pele. You'll have to go now, or she'll tell my da I was walking home with you. And he won't be happy if he finds out. Can we meet on Saturday in the park? At the swings?'

'Err…yeah, sure,' replied Pele, feeling very disappointed at this sudden turn of events. His hopes of a kiss were shattered, but at least he would have another opportunity to see her again.

'Two o'clock then,' she said abruptly, then scurried off, leaving him somewhat bewildered in the shadows. She walked briskly over to the car, and as the driver's window rolled down, the rich, velvety voice of Barry White filled the night air, singing, *'Can't get enough of your love, baby.'*

'Hello, Angela. I thought that was you. Who's that you're with?' called a female voice from inside of the car.

'Oh, nobody. It's just a friend who's walked me home. He's gone now. How are you doing, Mrs Thomas? I love your new haircut; it looks very glamorous!' she gushed, turning her back on Pele as if he didn't exist.

Pele slipped away while Angela chatted to the neighbour through the car window. He walked home slowly, reliving the evening's events, all of the highlights as well as the lows. And, despite the disappointing ending, excitement rose inside of him whenever he thought about meeting her again on Saturday.

It was only two days, but they were the longest two days of his life. He barely slept on Friday night, and when he woke up bright and early at 8:00 am on Saturday morning, his mother stared at him wide-eyed in the kitchen. 'And what are you doing up so early?' she asked incredulously.

'Oh, no reason, I just couldn't sleep,' he replied, scratching his belly and looking in the cupboard for some cereal. This was the truth but not the whole truth.

'And since when can't you sleep?!' his mother asked suspiciously, putting her hand on his forehead. 'You could sleep on a clothesline. Are ya not feeling well?'

'I'm fine, Mum, honest.' He ducked under her arm, holding on to a box of Shredded Wheat, and went to find a bowl.

'Well, I never thought I'd see the day. I never did,' she muttered to herself. 'Up before lunchtime at the weekend, and it's not even Christmas day.' She shook her head in disbelief. 'Wonders will never cease.'

Pele smiled to himself as he thought of the wonders he might experience that afternoon. He scoffed three Shredded Wheat and then got up to make a fresh pot of tea with a slice of peanut butter and toast. He poured a cup for his mum, who was still looking at him with narrowed eyes. Her hair was in curlers, so she must have planned to go to the social club later with his aunt. He cleared the dishes, asked his mum if there was anything else she needed him to do, then went upstairs to make his bed and got dressed.

By nine o'clock, he sat back in the kitchen, drumming his fingers on the kitchen table. The problem with getting up early, he decided, was that there were too many hours in the day. How were you supposed to fill them all? But then, nothing could have kept him in bed this morning. 'Do you want me to hang that washing up on the line for you?' he asked his mother, nodding at a basketful of laundry waiting to go outside. He was trying to think of something to do that might pass the time a bit quicker.

'I'd like to know what you've done with my son,' she retorted. 'Did aliens abduct him in the middle of the night?' She got up from the table and silently passed him the laundry basket.

After he'd hung up the washing, Pele decided he'd better find something to occupy himself with that didn't further arouse his mother's suspicions. He figured going for a run might help with his adrenaline and calm down his nerves. He'd joined the running club at school a few months back and loved it. He pulled his running shorts and vest out of the laundry basket and got changed. 'I'm off for a run, Mum,' he called out. When she didn't reply, he entered the dining room to find her polishing the dining table.

'Well, if you bump into my Brian while you're out, ask him to come home, will ya?' she replied, wafting her duster at him.

'Hilarious mum,' Pele laughed, shaking his head at her.

The rest of the morning intermittently dragged on and sped up. Time seemed to be standing still. Then, before he knew it, the hands on the clock were pointing to 1:30 pm, and it was time to leave. His stomach lurched at the thought of seeing Angela again. He went to brush his teeth for the third time that day and combed his hair for a record fifth. When he came out of the bathroom, his mother was putting clean sheets into the airing cupboard. 'I'm going out now, Mum. I'll see you later. I probably won't be back until teatime.'

'Well, have a nice time, Brian. What's her name, by the way?'

'How did you-?'

'Ach! You'd think I was born yesterday. Away with ya lad,' she chortled.

It took Pele less than ten minutes to reach the park. He was a few minutes early, but it was relatively empty. A newer, bigger one had been built a couple of years ago, so most of the younger kids on the estate hung out there. He perched himself on a swing; waves of excitement rose and fell in his chest as he waited. It wasn't long before he heard a voice call out to him, 'Hey! Do you need a push?'

Even though he'd been expecting her, his heart leapt at the sound of her voice. He looked up to see Angela strolling over a grassy knoll, exhibiting the carefree confidence she seemed to have been born with. She was wearing a tight-knit black polo jumper and a pair of flared bell-bottom pants that looked like they'd been made from orange and yellow curtains, yet she looked incredible. 'No thanks,' he grinned at her. 'I don't like heights.'

She smiled, completely unaware of the effect she was having on him, as she sat in the swing next to his. Holding onto the chains and twisting the seat from side to side, she said, 'Sorry about the other night. My da's always been protective of us girls, but since Ma died, he's got worse. And if he got wind that I was with a boy, I'd never hear the end of it.'

'Hey, don't worry about it,' replied Pele. 'If I was your dad, I'd probably be just the same. You have no idea how dangerous hanging around teenage boys can be.'

'Oh really?' she asked, leaning in towards him with wide eyes, 'If I hang around for a bit, will I get to see what all the fuss is about?' She set off giggling and started kicking her legs up, making the swing go higher than he thought possible.

If the time had passed haphazardly in the morning, the afternoon was a time warp. They left the park and spent three glorious hours whiling away their time along the canal. They walked and talked and shared stories about each other's family. When they stopped to skim stones in the canal, Angela's competitive streak came to the fore. 'You don't like losing, do you?' Pele laughed as Angela hunted around for a flat stone to try and beat his last throw. Looking up from her kneeling position, she beamed at him,

'Never give up; that's what my da always tells us. Ma used to say that I take after him and that it was like watching a battle between the unstoppable force hitting the immovable rock.' She smiled wistfully as she spoke. Pele sat on the grass beside her and plucked up a dandelion that had gone to seed.

'I can't remember hardly anything about my dad,' he said, blowing on the silvery, white seeds and scattering them into the atmosphere. 'I was only four, so I don't remember very much. I've spent most of my life not knowing him.'

'Is that easier or harder, do you think?' Angela asked him solemnly, staring into his dark eyes. He flopped back into the long grass and stared at the clouds floating by.

'Is what easier?' he asked her.

'Losing your dad when you were small like you did, or me losing my mum when I'm older,' she replied softly.

'I dunno, really. I think it's probably more difficult for you because you grew up knowing your mum. So that's harder, I guess. Maybe.' Pele said. She lay beside him, her shoulder pressed against his as she watched the clouds drift above them.

'Yeah, maybe it is. My da told us that love, real love, means you'll feel pain at some point. You can't have one without the other. So, it might be harder now that she's gone, but I'm glad I got to spend those years with her.' He turned his face towards her and smiled.

'It's a good job we don't get to choose; it's a difficult

choice when you think about it.' Angela turned onto her side, leaning her head on her hand. She looked into his eyes with a mischievous glint, and he wasn't sure what was going on in that beautiful head. She slowly stretched out her arm, plucked up a handful of grass, and, without warning, scattered the blades over his hair.

'I'm just recreating how you looked when we first met,' she laughed. He brushed his fingers through his hair and then lay still as she pressed the length of her body against his side. History repeated itself as she slowly picked out the strands of grass. His heart was beating so loudly in his chest that he was convinced she must be able to hear it. Her face was close to his, and he could feel her sweet, warm breath. Their eyes met, and he wondered if he should try to kiss her.

Out of nowhere, a young spaniel dog came bounding over to them, yapping excitedly. Angela squealed with delight as it clambered over her and licked her face enthusiastically. Its owner was shouting furiously at the dog, which couldn't have been more than six months old. 'Jack, you bad dog, come here!!' But Jack was having none of it, so eventually, Angela gently pushed the dog off her, and they both walked towards the apologetic owner with the puppy in tow.

'Shall we go and get an ice cream?' Angela suggested after Jack had been firmly scolded and put on his lead.

'Yeah, sure, why not,' said Pele, who wanted to go and lie back down in the grass and pick up where they'd left off.

They bought two 99 cones from the ice cream parlour and walked to the old town suspension footbridge. Standing elbow to elbow, looking over the rails, they watched the ducks waddling and quacking in the water as Angela dropped tiny pieces of her cone down to them.

When they realised it was time to go, Angela bounced along the bridge, enjoying the sensation of making it sway while Pele held onto the handrail, watching her with an ache he'd never known. 'Are you going to the youth club on Thursday again?' Pele asked her as they roamed the streets of the estate, walking towards her aunt's.

'Yeah, I'll be going with Susan,' she replied sadly. 'It's my last day, we're leaving Friday morning.'

'Well, I guess I'll see you on Thursday then,' said Pele as they stopped at the junction where they would part ways. Shuffling his feet and feeling awkward for the first time that afternoon, he put his hands in his pockets. His shoulders were hunched over in the cool evening air. He didn't feel the moment was right to try and steal a kiss from her. They'd had a perfect afternoon together, but he feared he might ruin it.

'I'll look forward to it,' she replied, her eyes twinkling. She started to head off in the opposite direction, and as the gap between them widened, she called out, 'Maybe I'll finally get to hang out with one of those terrible teenage boys me da's so terrified of me meeting.'

And with that, she blew him a kiss before turning the corner.

Pele arrived later than he'd hoped to on the Thursday. His Aunty Bricey's voluntary work at a local charity shop meant that she had the pick of the best stuff before it went on the shelves. Consequently, when an almost new pair of Adidas running shoes were donated in his size, she bought them for him. His mum had made it clear that he wasn't to run off to the youth club in a hurry, so he stayed a while to show his gratitude.

At about quarter past seven, Pele wondered if he would ever escape. In the end, his mum bailed him out, saying, 'Brian's going out now, Bricey, to the youth club. He's been sat so far forward on that chair that I've been worried that he might fall out of the door any minute now.' His mum and Aunt both erupted in laughter. Pele took the jibe with a mild eye roll and got up to kiss his aunt goodbye. His mother winked at him as he kissed her cheek before sprinting out the door.

On entering the church hall, he scanned the room until he found Angela near the stage, where her cousin was dancing. She raised her palm and waved him over. Then, she returned to watching her cousin move wonderfully to 'The Night' by Frankie

Valli. Thankfully, Slug was nowhere to be seen, which was some relief.

Pele headed to the snack bar, where the twin's mum poured orange juice into polystyrene cups. The twins were on a coach trip O'Malley had organised to Altrincham Ice Rink. They'd pleaded with Pele to go, and although he loved ice skating, there was no chance he was missing Angela's last night.

He bought a couple of drinks and a bar of chocolate and carried them over to Angela, who was sitting on the stage. 'Hey,' she smiled as he passed her a polystyrene cup.

'Hey,' he smiled back. She sipped the juice from the polystyrene cup. Her ankles were crossed, and she leaned back with her free hand on the stage as she surveyed the room. Her eyes returned to meet his, dancing with inexplicable amusement.

'So, I hear on the grapevine that you're pretty bad at table tennis? You know, I'm a fairly good player, and I could teach you a thing or two. I promise to go easy,' she said, maintaining a straight face.

'Oh yeah? Bring it on, but you should know I don't take any prisoners, even good-looking ones,' he laughed. And he held out his hand to help her off the stage.

He discovered Angela was actually very good and, unsurprisingly, very competitive. She whooped with glee for every point that she scored against him, but the final score was 21-16 to him. 'Well, of course, I had to let you win,' she laughed after the game while handing their bats to an eager pair of younger kids waiting for the table. 'But you did pretty well, considering.'

At around nine, Angela suggested they should leave, so Pele said goodbye to the twin's mum and stepped outside into the chilly evening air. Their hands found each other's without either speaking a word, and they walked together in silence for a minute or so, just enjoying the moment. Pele spoke first, 'How long do you think you'll be living in Ireland for?'

'I don't think me da's got any plans to come back,' she replied glumly. 'He says he doesn't want any more changes for us until we're older. He thinks we need some stability after Ma passed. So, not anytime soon, I suppose.' She glanced over at him. He squeezed her hand in response, as there wasn't anything left to say when all was said and done.

When they eventually reached the road leading to the cul-de-sac, Angela turned to him and spoke in a low voice, 'It's probably best if we stop here to say goodbye.'

Pele's heart pounded in his chest as he realised the moment had arrived. The moment that he'd thought about so many times this week, and if he wasn't mistaken, she seemed to sense it too. Why else would she suggest that they said their goodbyes here? It was private, hidden amongst dark shadows, and far away from streetlights, windows, and any slow-moving cars that might happen to be passing by. The scene suggested the promise of a kiss, even though it appeared to be a goodbye kiss.

He was about to pull her towards him in what he considered would be a romantic but passionate embrace when she started fumbling around in her skirt pocket for something. 'I've written down my address in Ireland, so you can write to me if you want?' she said, holding out a piece of paper. Pele was thrown off-key a little by this. Her address? Her address was fantastic, but he wanted to kiss her more than anything else.

'Oh, great!' said Pele, trying not to sound in any way impatient. He took the paper from her and pushed it deep into his Oxford Bag's pocket. 'I'll definitely write to you, Angela. I really, really want to keep in touch.' He turned to face her, tentatively holding both of her hands and moved towards her slowly. She was so lovely, he thought. Her eyes were dancing, and he noticed her mouth parted slightly in anticipation of his. As he drew near, he could feel her warm breath on his face. He was close enough to smell apple shampoo from her hair. In the park across the road, an owl was hooting. The moment seemed just perfect, and he thought he might die of happiness. He was about to press his mouth upon hers when a deep, gravelly voice spoke from the darkness.

'Well, well. Is that you, Angela? Is that you out at this time of night, hiding in the dark and with a strange, wee fella?' Pele spun around to see a prominent figure looming a few feet behind him. Angela let out a long groan while Pele couldn't believe his bad luck. Looking at the man, it was evident he was her father. The neighbour must have told her dad about the boy escorting Angela home after all, and he had been waiting for them. He realised very quickly that it would be very bad for his health and any future prospects of living if he didn't release Angela from his embrace as quickly as possible. The man continued to stare at him, although he addressed all his words to Angela. 'Cat got yer tongue, girl?

Despite the brooding goliath opposite him, Pele was relieved to see that Angela at least was relatively calm and unmoved as they extricated themselves and faced her father. 'No, Da. Of course, the cat hasn't got my tongue. And this isn't a strange fella at all! It's Pele, Pele Smith. He's a friend of mine, and he kindly agreed to walk me home. I'd have thought you'd have welcomed him looking out for me?' Her dad laughed at this as if amused by Angela's front and as if he'd expected nothing less from his daughter. He didn't mention that she could have gotten a lift back with her cousin and that he knew as well as she did that Pele wasn't walking her home for any protection.

'Well, I'll give you that, girl. You've got yer ma's blarney. Listening to yer then you could have been her.' After a brief pause, it seemed as if his demeanour went serious again. 'But you know the rule, Angela. Tell me now. What's the rule?' Angela held her father's face with her piercing eyes set like flint. Both of them were engaged in a battle of wills that neither seemed prepared to back down from. Pele shuffled around awkwardly until, after what seemed an eternity, Angela's dad broke away and turned to Pele. 'Pele? What sort of a name is Pele? What's yer real name, son, and who's yer family?' Pele took a deep breath, held his shoulders straight, and looked him squarely in the eye.

'Brian Smith, Sir. My real name's Brian Smith, but I got the name Pele from my father, and now everyone but my Mum calls me Pele. My mum's Katy Smith.' The man's gaze softened slightly, and he rubbed his hand across his chin.

'Ah! ... Sure, I know Katy. She's a fine woman, and I knew yer da too, God rest his soul. I always found him to be a man of his word and as straight a man as can be.' Pele nodded at him. 'Now then, Brian, as a father myself, left to bring up my girls alone. I have to be...How shall I say this? A cautious man. And I've been a boy myself, so I know how they think and what they think about. My girls are raised to put their family first, school second, Church third, and boys, well, they just don't enter into it at all, you see? When they're eighteen, or when they're no longer living under my roof, then they can do as they please. But I will keep them out of trouble with boys until they are old enough to look after themselves. You understand me?' Though Angela's dad had softened his tone, Pele had the good sense not to disagree with him.

'I do, Sir, yes. If you don't mind, I'd just like to say goodnight to Angela, and then I'll be on my way. My mum is expecting me home soon, too.' He looked up at the man, who nodded and folded his arms, watching Pele turn back toward Angela. She was grimacing apologetically under the scrutiny of her father. Pele felt awkward but needed to say goodbye, even if he had an audience. 'It was great seeing you again, Angela. I'm sorry you're going back to Ireland, but...' Angela impulsively lunged forward and hugged him. As she did so, she looked over his shoulder at her dad.

'Don't forget to write to me,' she said into his ear. Surprisingly, her dad said nothing, and Pele let go of her.

'Bye, Angela. See you again sometime.' Pele was about to leave when her dad spoke.

'Now run along, Angela, while I speak with Brian.'

'Dad?!!' she shouted, letting loose a horrified cry and blushing furiously.

'Run along,' he repeated slowly. It was said in a way that indicated it would be a very stupid thing to do if she didn't. And whatever Angela was, she was far from stupid. So, she indignantly turned on her heels, gave an exasperated groan, and walked away.

Pele turned to face Angela's father, uncertain what he might want from him. A small, sad smile cracked the side of Angela's dad's face as he spoke, 'I'll get straight to the point, son. You can't write to her. This is not your doing. I can see yer a good lad from a good family. But see, the time's wrong. She's got a few years of growing up to do before she gets distracted with boys. Sometimes, as you go through life, you'll think that something should be, just because you want it to be, but it doesn't work out because the time's not right. That's this now. Nothing more: nothing less. It's nothing personal.'

He held his hand out to Pele and waited. Pele dug into his pocket and located the paper with her address. He realised that even if he didn't give it to him, it would only cause problems for Angela, as her father could easily intercept any letters, so there wasn't anything else left to do. He held the paper out to him and gave away his only tentative connection with Angela. 'Good night to you, son, and get yerself back to yer ma safe.' With that, his large hand patted Pele's shoulder. He brushed past him and walked back to the house. Pele watched him for a second or two before turning around to walk back home.

As he wandered down the dark, quiet streets, his mind kept returning to what Angela's dad said: '...you'll think that something should be, just because you want it to be, but it doesn't work out because the time's not right. That's this now.'

1979 (I)

Mrs Thatcher; Alien; Lycra; I will Survive; IRA bombings
Beanbag chairs; Inflation; Atari 400; Superman the movie

Pele awoke to a soft gnawing on his left eyelid. Somewhere in his deep-sleep-addled brain, he deduced that his mum had been in the room and had let the budgie out. He felt its tiny claws prick his forehead as it hopped across his brow. It pecked sharply and pulled out a hair from his right eyebrow. 'Ouch! Get lost, Pip,' he cried and swatted his hand to shoo away the bird, but Pip dodged it easily and went airborne. Little wings beat above him like the sound of a tiny Chinook helicopter. Pip landed effortlessly onto the sidebars of its cage, where it clung, screeching with enthusiasm, 'Get up, Brian. Get up, Brian,' mimicking his mum's perennial early morning call with an unnerving accuracy.

The old, worn springs on his bed creaked loudly as he raised himself up and shivered in the cold air. The bird flew off the cage, circling above his head. 'Get up, Brian. Get up, Brian.' Pele looked at his reflection in the full-length mirror on the wardrobe door. He had dark, slightly wavy, collar-length hair; regardless of the time of day, it always had a 'just-got-out-of-bed' appearance, angular cheekbones and a broad, confident smile. However, girls had often said that his best feature was his eyes, which were dark brown, slightly hooded, and framed with dark eyelashes. A previous girlfriend had commented that they were 'brooding,' whatever that meant. He opened the wardrobe and found his black work pants lying crumpled on a stack of old NME magazines. He sighed and stepped into them. He noted an inch of space between the fabric and his flat-toned stomach. Maybe the impoverished look would catch on, he thought.

He went into the bathroom to brush his teeth. A loud voice came from the foot of the stairs as his mum exercised her considerable lungpower. He wondered, not for the first time, how so much noise could emanate from such a tiny frame. Pele answered its call, 'Yeah, I heard you the first time, Mum. I'm up!'

'That wasn't the first time, Brian. I've been shouting you for half an hour!'

'Why? What time is it?' he asked, panic beginning.

'It's nearly eight,' she shouted, more than a little exasperated.

After rinsing his mouth, he searched for the rest of his clothes. He tied his shoelaces, bounded down the stairs and tucked a half-buttoned-up shirt into the back of his creased trousers. He could hear his mum in the kitchen putting dishes into the sink. Every morning, she'd boil a large kettle of water on the gas cooker for their pot of tea and use what was left for the breakfast dishes. Pele wasn't entirely convinced of the economic advantages, but he didn't argue them with his mum. The Boomtown Rats' *'I Don't Like Mondays'* was on the radio, capturing Pele's mood. Why was it always harder to get up for work on Monday mornings than any other day of the week?

A cold mug of strong, milky tea next to a plate of cold peanut butter toast was waiting for him when he got downstairs. He gulped it down with a grimace, but he knew that beggars couldn't be choosers, and raising the issue with his mum was likely to result in an ear-bending of biblical proportions. He picked up his breakfast and went into the kitchen. His mum was smoking at the back door and chatting with Edna, their next-door neighbour. Even though it was cold enough to see your breath, Edna was on the other side of a low, wooden fence hanging her husband Eric's overalls out on the washing line. As long as it wasn't raining, Edna and his mum hung their washing out no matter what time of the year it was. Some nights, ice-cold clothes would be brought inside stiff and unyielding after the sun had gone down. Then, towels had to be folded like cardboard. After a bath, Pele thought those towels dried almost as well as any cardboard box, except they probably weren't as soft. Despite having a couple of clothes pegs in her mouth, Edna was gushing about Katy's hair, 'Away with ya, Katy! You're definitely not too old for it. You look fantastic if you ask me.'

Katy was now in her early forties and had finally taken the plunge to get herself the *de mode* Purdey haircut, which was perfect for her waiflike face. Pele had always thought she might meet someone else, but her mantra never faltered over the years. There was only one man that she would ever love, and he was dead. 'Well, I agree with Edna. It suits you, Mum,' Pele remarked, bringing a warm smile to her lips as she turned towards him. 'Thanks for the toast, Mum,' he said, dropping his empty mug into the warm soapy water of the washing-up bowl. He lifted his jacket from the back of the kitchen door and pushed his arm through the sleeve. He leant over to kiss her on the cheek. Looking into her clear, brown eyes, he thought her smooth face could easily pass for mid-thirties. He felt a pang of regret for her. Regret that her life, in many ways, had stayed still since the passing of his dad. Digging around in the pockets of his denim jacket to find change for the bus, Pele glanced up. 'I'm off mum. I'm late again; the bus is due at quarter past. Will you put Pip back in the cage for me?' He shouted this out over his shoulder as he jogged down the path. His mum muttered something derogatory about the budgie that he didn't quite catch.

Two minutes later, Pele was sprinting around the corner, and to his relief, he saw a middle-aged woman waiting at the graffiti-covered bus shelter ahead. This meant that the woman was either ridiculously early or, much more likely, the bus was thankfully late. He observed the catholic kids jostling to board a bus on the other side of the road and began to muse about his school days. They seemed like a lifetime ago, even though it had only been three years since he'd left.

Pele had achieved high grades in all of his subjects. And when Mr Cooper told him to follow his dream and return to education when he could, Pele said he would seriously consider it without ever giving it another thought. His mum, on the other hand, had been doubly proud. Not only had he done so well with his exams, but he'd managed to get a job that wasn't in the army or ICI.

Pele looked down the road towards the Cherry Tree pub and saw a distant, bonny figure tottering down the street in high heels and a tight-fitting outfit. A faint smile appeared on his lips. He recognised the movement and attire as those of Caroline Green, a girl who'd been in his class at school. She had a job working for Cousins the Bakers on the cake counter, and like Pele, she too was late for her bus. Caroline sprinted inelegantly, her heels clacking on the pavement and her handbag swinging wildly off one shoulder. Her above-the-knee, tight skirt was riding higher and higher up her shapely thighs as she ran.

A minute or so later, she stood slightly breathless alongside Pele, pulling at the hem of her skirt. She looked up and grinned at him. It was a lovely strawberry lip-gloss smile. 'Alright, Pele. Please tell me the bus is late!'

'Yeah, I think so, Caroline,' he replied, trying not to make it obvious that he was eying her up and down. He recalled a gawky, skinny, bespectacled girl in their second year of high school. He'd found it very disconcerting that she always seemed to be grinning at him through her braces whenever he looked up from his desk. Most often in Mr Cooper's English class. But that was a while back now. Caroline had undergone a transformation in the last few years that would have left the Ugly Duckling feeling short-changed.

Firstly, her gangly frame had taken on an hourglass figure that had caused a meteoric rise in her popularity with the boys on the estate. She had little interest in most of the local boys her age and tended to date slightly older, more mature lads from out of town.

Secondly, she'd lost the braces and changed her prescription glasses for contact lenses. She also wore semi-light make-up that accentuated her pretty face. Many of the girls on the estate wore heavy make-up that wasn't unlike that of a geisha gone nutty in the Chelsea Girl concession counter.

Last but not least, she had developed a great taste in clothes that seemed to emphasise and accentuate her figure, especially if you considered the long, shapely legs that had her towering above her school peers years ago. Pele couldn't help noticing that all the changes were gelling together perfectly. He had always liked Caroline; it was just that now he realised he was starting to like her in a different way.

Anyway, today, as her breathing returned to normal after the short exertion to the bus stop, she fixed her large, brown eyes on Pele. With a reverence that suggested he worked alongside James Bond in MI5 instead of the wages department of a small manufacturing company, she asked, 'Are you still working in the offices?'

'Yeah,' he replied. Finding it impossible to hold her penetrating gaze, he glanced down at his shoes before asking, 'You still at Cousins?' She nodded enthusiastically, and then they stood in amiable silence, waiting for the bus to arrive.

After a few minutes, she broke through his daydreaming, twirling a strand of hair between her fingers. She asked him, 'Are you going anywhere this weekend?'

'Oh, err... dunno,' he replied, unsure. 'I might go to the Cherry on Friday or Foxy's on Saturday. Depends on what's on and what everyone else is doing. What are you up to?' She twisted a silver oblong-shaped catch on the flap of her white Topshop handbag and pulled out a packet of Wrigley's spearmint gum.

'I'm not going anywhere on Friday, but I'm going to Foxy's on Saturday with Cheryl. It's Grease night.' She beamed with obvious excitement while Pele cringed at the mere thought of this and immediately ruled out Foxy's for his Saturday night out. She must have seen it in his face and backtracked a little. 'Yeah, I know. I know. It's not cool. You like all that Roxy and Bowie stuff my brother's into, don't you?' In an effort to make up for her teenage *faux pas*, she offered him the packet of gum.

'Thanks,' he said, removing a stick. They both turned and looked down the road to see a red double-decker bus ploughing its weary way up Laburnum towards them. Pele stole a sideways glance at Caroline. She had dark chestnut hair and soft curls that cascaded around her face and shoulders, creating a very pretty effect. He realised that he was rather attracted to her, which was a bit of a shock, considering he had done his best to avoid her whenever possible at school.

When the bus pulled up alongside the kerb, the door swished open. After the middle-aged woman had embarked, Pele gestured for Caroline to go ahead of him, and a trail of her light perfume wafted past as she stepped up. Caroline fumbled around her purse for change and paid the smiling driver. Then she waggled up the stairs. As she did so, Pele noted that practically every male set of eyes, and more than a few females, followed her as she climbed the stairs. He gave the driver a twenty pence coin that he'd previously taken out of his pocket, collected his ticket and followed Caroline's path - without the waggle - to the top of the bus. There, he surprised himself by going and sitting down next to her.

In all the times they'd talked to each other at the bus stop, Pele had never previously sat next to her. Caroline seemed to sense the shift in the tide. 'My Mum's staying out on Friday night,' she said matter-of-factly while looking out of the window at the council estate houses floating by. She paused and lightly twisted an oversized, gold-hooped earring under her wavy hair. When he didn't reply, she went on, 'And our Mark's working down south for a few months. So, I've got the house to myself.' She glanced over to gauge his reaction, wondering if maybe she was being too forward. 'I was gonna ask Sharon to come around and listen to the Grease soundtrack, but you could come over...? If you're not doing anything?' By this time, Pele's mind was already made up.

'Err...yeah. I suppose that sounds...okay,' he agreed, trying not to sound too enthusiastic. 'What's your -'

'Five, seven, six, five, five,' she chanted while placing her hand unexpectedly on his arm. 'Only two different from yours.'

That put a brief cap on proceedings, and they sat in silence for the next two stops. Pele wasn't sure if he was relieved or disappointed when they alighted at the town centre. It had been the most pleasurable agony sitting in silence next to her, what with the smell of her scent and feeling her thigh lightly pressed against his. He couldn't help taking sideward glances whenever she turned her head to look out of the window. 'Well, give us a ring before Friday if you're thinking of coming over. We can even listen to some Bowie if you want,' Caroline blurted out, her cheeks flushed self-consciously as if realising she might have been a bit forward. Pele's gaze settled on the silk knot of her blouse at her neckline. It was easier to focus on that than Caroline's brown eyes, which he was finding dark and somewhat hypnotic. A hint of sensual promise was barely concealed in those eyes, and it was one that he found disconcerting. For no reason that made any sense, his heart had started racing in his chest.

He cleared his throat and attempted a nonchalant, 'Yeah. Okay. Will do.'

'Promise?' squealed Caroline and did a cute hop in excitement.

'Yeah, promise,' he laughed, feeling the tension ease between them. Then, glancing at his watch, he knew he had to get a move on. 'So, erm... I'll see you around then?'

'They might be making me supervisor on the cake counter,' Caroline gushed unexpectedly.

Not really knowing how to react to this piece of news, he replied, 'Oh! Brilliant! Well done, you.' At this, her face seemed to glow. She grinned, gave a little wave, and then walked towards the Bakery. The smell of grilled bacon drifted out the door, making Pele's mouth water. He watched as Caroline squeezed between two workmen coming out of the shop with their readymade breakfasts. At the door, she turned to give him a final, frantic wave, and he walked off in slow motion, feeling strangely elated.

It took Pele five minutes to walk from the escalators to the office, and he couldn't recall a single step by the time he arrived. He flashed his cheap, plastic pass at Johnny, the security guard, who had his head firmly buried in The Sun. Johnny briefly glanced up before consenting to give him an 'Alright, Pele lad,' before resuming his full attention to Samantha Fox, who was adorning page three.

Fuelled with the adrenaline of a date with Caroline, Pele avoided the lift, which was known to be a bit temperamental, and he skipped up the four flights of stairs leading to the second floor's payroll office.

A quick look through the office door window confirmed that his supervisor, John O'Leary, was already in. He was clowning around with someone on the phone, and his infectious laughter could be heard from the corridor. As Pele entered, John looked up and tapped his fake Rolex, gesturing to Pele that he was fifteen minutes late. Pele shrugged and silently mouthed, 'Sorry, the bus was late.' John rolled his eyes, but a smile tugged at the corner of his lips, confirming that Pele wasn't in any real trouble. Pele hung his head in a penitent gesture that only made John shake his head at him. He waved him away with a smooth, sun-tanned hand and returned his attention back to the phone call. Judging by his banter, it was clear that the person on the other end was female. John was a man of taste, designer clothes, high-end, fake jewellery, and the kind of women they attracted.

John's sense of humour in the factory was legendary, and as a kind of male initiation ceremony, Pele had roamed the factory floor on his first day there when John had sent him to find the 'verbal agreement stamp.' Even more elusive had been the 'box of short-circuits.'

Pele shrugged his jacket off and dropped it on the back of his chair. He was pulling it out and about to sit down at his desk when a shrill, nasal voice whined at him from behind. 'Forgetting something, young Brian?'

He slid his chair back under the desk and, without looking around, wearily answered, 'No, Alf. How could I when you remind me every morning?'

'So, what are you waiting for then? You're already 20 minutes late,' Alf grumbled. Pele wandered over to tackle a stack of unopened letters near the pigeonholes. Opening the post was one of the tasks given to the most junior worker, so the application of 'Young Brian' was a non-too-subtle reminder of his subordinate position. When he thought about it, his mum, the budgie, and Alf were the only ones to call him Brian.

Alf Johnson, the owner of the voice, was a gaunt grey-haired man with a thick moustache and tiny rounded spectacles that were permanently perched on the end of a narrow, disjointed nose. He had small, stuck-out ears, beady eyes, and a permanent frown, which gave him the air of someone who lived in a perpetual state of disapproval. As the office's acting 'deputy supervisor,' he lauded his position at every opportunity. Any mistakes or oversights by Pele would be duly noted and reported to John, who was painfully aware of Alf's difficult personality. He would placate him with a solemn nod and promise to 'talk to young Brian,' which more often than not meant a pint in the pub after work and a game of pool.

Alf and Pele shared a mutual antipathy from the moment Pele entered the office. 'Don't think those CSEs mean anything here, lad; they don't. I've got a degree from the University of Life. That's worth more than all your CSEs put together, so don't you forget it.'

Pele slid a knife under an envelope flap and pulled out the contents. He checked the name on the top and filed it in one of the sixteen pigeonholes available to him. Above his head, the mellow voice of Dave Lee Travis was emanating from one of the office speakers. His voice faded out as the intro to Costello's 'Oliver's Army' slowly increased in volume. Pele's office-induced mood brightened considerably. Costello was the perfect antidote to lift his spirits. A door abruptly slid open at the other end of the room, and Newtog Neil sauntered through it.

No one seemed to know why Newtog was called Newtog. Even Newtog didn't really know. Some in the factory thought it was because he was always dressed in new clothes or togs in local speak, despite the fact that he only earned minimum wages on the shop floor. Other people argued it was because he was very often drunk whenever you saw him outside of work. Whatever the truth of the matter, he and Pele got on very well.

He was a tall, heavyset lad with light-brown hair styled in a Rod Stewart feather cut. He possessed a pair of small, mischievous blue eyes, and his cheek dimples were deep-set in a round, cheerful face. He had the demeanour of a jovial, easy-going lad, and his endearing hamster-like features often meant he was erroneously judged as being a bit soft. He was anything but. 'Alright, Pele, my son,' he said, grinning affably and leaning his thick elbows on the small wooden counter that separated the factory workers from the office staff. 'How's it going in the big, bad world of office management?'

'Okay, Señor Neil. Mustn't grumble. A little birdie told me you were a little tipsy last Saturday night at the Cherry Tree.'

'All lies, young Pele. All lies.' They both snorted at this. Then, a throat cleared loudly behind them. Pele sighed, blowing his cheeks out for effect, and Newtog raised an eyebrow in commiseration. Alf's miserable countenance was also renowned amongst the shop floor workers. So, Pele brought them back to business.

'What can I do you for?'

'I'm just checking if my overtime has gone through. It got missed last week, and I need the money big time this Friday.'

'Hang on a minute,' Pele told him. 'I'll go and check the printout.' He walked over to a large folder on the desk opposite John, who was now off the phone. His head was buried in a cup of coffee and the latest copy of Autotrader. 'Is it okay if I let him know if his overtime is in John?' asked Pele.

'Only if he buys me a pint in the Cherry on Friday,' John teased.

'It's a deal,' Newtog called out from the counter. 'It's not every week a guy gets married.' Pele and John jolted around, surprised. John spoke first.

'You're joking, mate! Who's the unlucky lady?'

'Sheena from the warehouse. She is, as they say, with child. We were keeping it quiet that we were seeing each other.'

'Probably at her insistence,' John butted in, and Newtog grinned at the quip.

'Yeah, who'd want anyone to know they were going out with me,' Newtog agreed amiably, with a pan-faced nod. 'Anyway, we're made up about it, and the good news is we'll shoot up the council housing list.' His chubby face flushed with self-conscious pride. However, the news of the impending nuptials and little Newtog-to-be produced a snort of derision from Alf. It was one that John and Pele were all too familiar with, but the snort seemed to get Newtog's back up. 'What's that supposed to mean?' he demanded. His blue eyes had now turned as cold as ice as he glowered at Alf. His hackles were raised, and he stood tense, ready for a verbal fight. Although he was a good sort, Pele knew he could be quick-tempered and not someone you wanted to get on the wrong side of, as a few lads in the local pub with black eyes could testify to. Like most bullies, though, Alf was a coward when challenged, and he quickly backed down to the young man's macho posturing. The palm of his right hand was stretched out in front of him in defence. His eyes darted between Newtog and Pele before protesting with a high-pitched whimper.

'It's not supposed to mean anything. It's just that the council hands out houses like they're confetti these days. Not like when I was your age.'

'Not for much longer,' Pele interjected. 'Haven't you heard? Thatcher's selling them all off.' This produced loud cheers of approval from John and Newtog, if not from the old, working-class Tory Alf, who shook his head in abject misery. He shuffled over to a filing cabinet in the corner of the room, turning his back on everyone and avoiding any further conflict that might ensue.

After that, Newtog leant forward and pressed Pele about the information again. 'Anyway, sorry mate, but I've got to get back. What's the score with my overtime?' Pele looked at John, and he passed the printout to him.

Pele scanned through it and said, 'Yeah, it's all in for Friday. You should get about sixty after tax and insurance. Not a bad week.'

'Get in!' shouted Newtog, punching the air. 'Look, it's all been a bit of a rush, but my stag-do's this Saturday, which was the other reason I dropped in. Fancy it, Pele? John? There's a coach leaving for the Wilderspool at six from the town centre. Pick-up's near yours, Pele.'

'Yeah. You can count me in,' Pele said, doing some quick maths around his wages due this week. If he went around to Caroline's on Friday, that would mean he'd have enough money for the stag do. He would buy the new Blondie album on his next payday.

'John?' Newtog looked hopefully at John.

'I dunno. It might be tricky,' John mused, rubbing his fingers lightly against his cheek in contemplation. 'I'll have to run it past the missus. I'll ask her Saturday afternoon after she's had her hair done. She's usually in a good mood after a visit to the hairdressers. It's all about timing, lad. You'll learn soon enough.'

Newtog turned from the counter with a wink at Pele and said, 'See you Saturday then. Pick-up by the shops at your end, six thirty.'

'Gotcha,' Pele replied.

On Thursday evening, Pele found himself standing in front of the blue trimphone in the hall, which was a relic from the early '70s. His face was scrunched in contemplation as he recalled Caroline's number. 'What was it she'd said on the bus?' he muttered to himself. 'Just two different from yours.' Eventually, he worked out which two numbers were different, picked up the phone and dialled. He was amazed to see a slight tremor in his hand. If you had told him that Caroline Green could produce a nervous reaction in him in high school, he would have laughed. But here he was, feeling more than a little intimidated.

The phone started to ring, and it was answered almost immediately. 'Hello,' a cheery voice said.

'Can I speak to Caroline, please?' he replied.

'It's me, Pele,' she giggled. 'Who'd you think it was?'

'Dunno? I thought it was your mum,' he said, feeling slightly embarrassed. 'You sounded really old.'

'So did you,' she laughed again. 'Everyone says I sound like my mum on the phone.' He felt a little less self-conscious at this and wondered if he should mention tomorrow. Fortunately, Caroline had no intention of letting him off any hook. 'So, are you coming round tomorrow, then? How does eight o'clock sound?' Pele's admiration of Caroline was growing exponentially. She was much more self-assured than he'd initially realised, which he decided was a good thing; it stopped him from having to overthink things. Bizarrely, he quite enjoyed having someone else make decisions. The complex minefield Pele associated with dating was already much easier with Caroline. Straightforward and steady as she goes seemed to be her style, and he liked it.

'Yeah, that's great. Do you want me to bring anything?' he asked.

'No, just yourself,' she told him. 'My mum's left some vodka in the drinks cabinet, and she said I could have some if I wanted. And there's four cans of Skol in the fridge that my brother's left. He's not back for months, so he won't be bothered.'

'Great,' Pele replied. 'I'll see you at eight then. It's number 20, isn't it?'

'Yeah, it is,' she said chirpily. 'Okay then, Pele. See you tomorrow.' And with that, she was gone. Pele hung up with some relief. In truth, the conversation hadn't gone anything like he'd imagined it would.

With a bit of help from Pip and his mum, Pele made the early bus the following morning and, in doing so, got an extra hour's overtime in. The downside was an hour alone with Alf before John arrived at eight-thirty. In that time, Alf had criticised Pele at every opportunity and had given him two of the worst jobs in the office: cleaning the giro cutter and sweeping the machine room floor. Pele took it all in his stride as his thoughts drifted off to Caroline and their meeting later that evening. He tried not to imagine what tight dress she might be wearing or the effect that could have on the physiology department.

Once John appeared, Alf gave up badgering Pele. And the rest of the day sped by on the wings of the good news that John had managed to get a pass-out for the stag-do on Saturday. Janey had already made arrangements to go out with the girls, which meant he had a free night.

1979 (II)

When Pele got home that night, the first thing he did was turn the immersion heater on. His mum had gone out and left a note to say that mince stew with dumplings was in the oven, one of his favourites. Despite the fact his stomach was in knots at the prospect of the night ahead, and he wasn't sure if he could eat anything, he removed the casserole from the oven, and before he knew it, he'd eaten two full bowls and half of a loaf of bread to soak up the gravy.

When the water had heated enough to run a bath, he enjoyed a long hot soak whilst Bowie's *'Heroes'* blasted out of the downstairs stereo. Over Bowie's pronouncements that even Pele could be king just for one day, he ran a comb under the tap water. The seventies equivalent of gel: copious amounts of Brylcream allied with his mum's Harmony hairspray. He spent the next twenty minutes trying to fashion his tousled hair into a centre parting worthy of a Roxy Music fan.

Pele left the warm, steamed-up bathroom and entered his much colder bedroom. There, he spied the alarm clock next to his bed. To his surprise, it was seven-fifteen. Feeling his stomach flutter, he closed his eyes, picturing Caroline in a tight-fitting dress. He swallowed hard at that thought and decided it might not be a good idea to let his mind wander further.

Although still fiercely loyal to Bowie and Roxy, Pele had recently embraced the burgeoning New-Wave scene. Naturally, his clothes, or rather his granddad's old clothes, reflected this choice of music. The first time he'd worn drainpipe trousers on the estate, the older women had stared at him like he was the reincarnation of Elvis. The younger boys jeered, shouting out insults pertaining to his sexuality. The varying reactions and creating a stir were something that Pele quite enjoyed.

After examining himself in the mirror and marvelling at his granddad's excellent taste in clothes, Pele put 'Plastic Letters' on and checked he'd switched off the immersion heater for the third time.

Before leaving the house, at a quarter to eight, he left his mum a note saying he wouldn't return until midnight. Although he was nineteen, she still wouldn't allow him to stay out later than twelve unless it was a social occasion like tomorrow's work's do. He closed the door behind him and double-locked it with his key. He looked up at the black sky. The primary star constellations were peeking through despite the estate's hefty light pollution. Pele smiled, put the key in his top pocket, and thought tonight just might be a stellar night.

The ten-minute walk to Caroline's house took him past the young Kane brothers, kicking a football around in their usual ferocious manner. As they sped past and saw him, they started chanting. 'Oy! Punky boy, where are you going dressed like that, ya big daft punkhead?'

I'm going to meet a girl,' Pele replied gamely to the pre-pubescent boys. 'And you need to get your facts right. I'm no longer a big daft Punkhead. These days, I'm a big daft New Wavehead.' The boys looked at each other, momentarily confused, and then began to laugh whilst pointing and shouting in unison.

'Big daft New Wavehead. Big daft New Wavehead.'

Pele turned the corner a few seconds later, and their mocking voices faded into the dark night. A few minutes after that, he entered a cul-de-sac. He stood outside Caroline's front door and knocked lightly on the metal rapper. From inside, he could hear John Travolta screeching, 'You're the one that I want...'

Though there were lights on in the house, no one answered the first knock. He wondered briefly if she could even hear through all the racket and then almost had second thoughts as a wave of awkwardness washed over him. But the thought of Caroline's lightly make-uped face and heaving bosom spurred him to knock louder.

Eventually, he heard the sound of footsteps scurrying down the stairs, which were followed by a fumbling noise at the latch. The door flew open, and Caroline stood there with a wide grin. She had a metallic clip holding a lock of her chestnut hair while a tumbling avalanche of curls surrounded her face and shoulders. A delicate silver necklace adorned her slim neck, which was exposed as she wore an open-necked blouse that accentuated her curvaceous figure, a knee-length pencil skirt, black tights, and no shoes. Her cheekbones were lightly brushed with pink blusher, and she had a touch of mascara on, but apart from that, she was au-natural, and Pele thought once more how very pretty she was. 'Well, come in,' she said, motioning with her hand. 'Don't just stand there.' Pele guessed right there and then that she'd probably visited the drinks cabinet while she'd been getting ready. On beckoning him in, she promptly gave him a brief kiss on his cheek as he stood awkwardly in the hallway, then she closed the door behind him, saying, 'I won't be a minute. Get a can from the fridge and wait in the living room for me. If you like, you can change the music.' Then she bounded back up the stairs and was momentarily gone.

Like all houses on the estate, the house was remarkably similar to his, so he had little trouble finding the fridge or following the sound of the music to the front room. Inside, Travolta's friends were now imploring him to tell them more. Instead of sitting down, he cracked open the can and went over to the stereo. An album case was lying next to it, which, judging by the stickers and felt pen adorning the red leather, belonged to Caroline's older brother. A minute's perusal of the case confirmed it had some very decent recordings inside. He couldn't find any New Wave but pulled out a copy of Lou Reed's *'Transformer.'* He pulled the needle off *'Grease'* and flipped it back into the cover, which had been flung unceremoniously on the floor. Then he sat down on a large, green, comfortable sofa, took a long gulp from the can of Skol, and listened to Lou tell him to take a '*Walk on the wild side...*' His stomach churned once again, as that was precisely what he hoped Caroline had in mind for them both.

Looking around the room, he saw the gas fire held centre stage with a large mirror above it. There was a small Telefusion TV, rented, he guessed, that was switched off in the opposite corner. A cream sheepskin rug lay in front of the fire. His mind was so engrossed in what he wanted to do with Caroline on that rug that he didn't even notice when she appeared at the door. 'You managed to get yourself a drink then,' she said and switched off the ceiling light, instantly changing the atmosphere of the lounge. The only light in the room now was from the gas fire and a small, oriental-themed lamp on a side table in the corner. She settled down next to him, tucking her legs underneath and resting her arm along the back cushion. She smelt of Coty le Monte, SR minty toothpaste, and Babycham in no particular order.

'Err...yeah, thanks,' he smiled. Feeling nervous, he put the can to his lips and took a large gulp.

'That's good,' she said, sliding in closer and pushing her considerable assets onto his arm, where they pressed against him like a small inflatable dinghy. 'Who's this racket? It sounds a bit depressing.'

'It's Lou Reed,' he replied, shifting the can into his other hand to place it on the table before him. When he sat back again, she continued the full-court press on his arm. 'He's supposed to be depressing, I think.' She thought about this for a minute.

'Oh, alright then. Well, leave it on if you want. So, what do ya wanna do?'

Pele was unable to decipher what she actually meant. It was more than likely that Caroline was propositioning him somehow, but she was doing it in that ambiguous way girls sometimes did. He wondered if they were ambiguous on purpose. It would be a few years further down the line before he worked out the answer to that particular conundrum. 'I don't mind. Whatever you want,' he said rather hopefully, putting the ball firmly back into her court.

'Well, I know what I want to do,' she said, placing her warm hand on his thigh and sending a tingling sensation that radiated up into his groin.

'What's that?' he asked.

'Get another drink.' She giggled at her own joke, then got up and disappeared for a few minutes before she returned with a rather large-looking vodka and lemon in a plastic tumbler.

The next hour passed pleasantly by as they sat in semi-darkness, all the while Caroline leaning in against him and occasionally saying slightly suggestive things. Pele wondered if the moment was right to pounce or if she even wanted him to pounce. But in the end, he decided against it. The way Caroline kept leaning over and looking deeply into his eyes, he figured it wouldn't be much longer before she pounced herself anyway.

As he waited for that to happen, he had two more cans of Skol, and Caroline partook of another large vodka. Pele was more than happy with the way things were panning out. The gas fire glowed, making shadows dance across the wall in the darkened room, and even if Caroline had flipped the music over to the Stylistics, despite his groaning, it was all very pleasant indeed.

Somehow, during their time on the sofa, Caroline had managed to sit even closer to him than he would have thought possible unless you were actually Siamese twins. Her right leg was pushing against his left, and he could feel the taut fabric of her C&A tights. 'Can I ask you something, Pele?' A slightly tipsy Caroline said, as the Stylistics warbled, '*You make me feel brand new...*'

'Yeah, 'course,' Pele said, looking into her eyes that were on the point of devouring him.

'When are you gonna kiss me? Cos I've been waiting since high school for you to do it, you know?' Pele laughed out loud at her candour and quickly put his almost empty can down. Caroline's face was tilted towards his, and she looked extraordinarily pretty in the half-light of the glowing fire. Her big brown eyes locked onto his, and her tongue briefly slid out to moisten the corner of her mouth, seemingly anticipating his next move. Pele carefully put an arm around her and pulled her towards him. When they kissed, it wasn't the frenzied, passionate embrace he'd imagined it would be. Instead, he kissed her tenderly, pushing his fingers through her long, silky hair and planting light kisses on her eyes and nose. Then, finally, he rested his lips on her full mouth, at which point he felt her shudder.

She tasted of a wonderful mix of Polo mints with a strong vodka twist. She snaked out her tongue and sought his, and he was immediately aroused. He responded more fervently, and her fingers pressed hard into the small of his back. Without breaking their kiss, they somehow managed to lie down on the sofa, and he found himself on top of her, something she didn't seem to object to.

Pele now asked himself the same question that teenage boys in his position, as well as Antarctic explorers caught in poor weather conditions, always ask: how much further can I possibly go? To Pele, at that particular moment, the 'South Pole' itself seemed within reach. He'd only ever reached the 'South Pole' on three previous occasions, and two of those times had been with his first girlfriend. It suddenly seemed that there was a distinct possibility that he could plant his flag once again, as Caroline was now, very slowly, using her left hand to unbutton her blouse, which he had absolutely no objection to.

Pele couldn't help noticing that Caroline seemed to be enjoying the turn of events every bit as much as he was. She was breathing out soft moaning noises and moving her hips against his. All of this was bringing Pele to a point where he thought he might explode with very much unwanted premature pleasure. Taking a moment to control himself, he raised himself slightly away from Caroline's writhing body. Her mouth was open, and she was breathing very heavily, their eyes locked together in a fevered passion.

This was it, he reasoned. Caroline was clearly as aroused as he was, and he was very, very aroused. So, he bent to kiss her again whilst reaching down to his zip and, after some fumbling, pulled out what he presumed would be the object of Caroline's desire. It was just as his hand was leading said object of desire towards the general direction of Caroline's skirt that she suddenly stopped making moaning sounds and coldly said, 'Pele! What do you think you're doing?'

At this particular turn of events, the alarm bells in Pele's head went off like a fire drill in Woolworth's department store. Clearly, he'd badly misjudged the situation and made his move way too early. All this must have been before he was sure Caroline had reached what the lads in the factory called the 'up for it' stage. It now appeared Caroline wasn't anywhere near that stage. So, he quickly thrust his slightly-less-pulsing-than-a-minute-ago object of desire back into his pants and blustered out, 'Err...I'm sorry, Caroline. I just thought-'

'You just thought what?' she said, now sounding very offended. She jerked up into a sitting position and started to fasten her blouse back up. 'Well, Pele? What did you think?'

'Err...Well...' He didn't think right then would be the best time to tell her precisely what he had just been thinking. Neither did he judge it any wiser to tell her that he'd been sure that it was her that had led him to believe that. To Pele, it was all very confusing. One minute, they'd been in the very throes of passion, and now here she was talking to him like a policewoman arresting a Peeping Tom. 'I...I thought you wanted to,' he said lamely. At this point, what tripped out of Caroline's mouth only added fuel to the fire of his mounting confusion.

'Of course, I want to do things with you, Pele. But you have to understand I'm not some slag. I mean, it's not like we're going steady or anything, is it?' She was now sitting bolt upright at the other end of the sofa and looking very composed. Her eyes found his, and it suddenly dawned on him that what he'd thought initially was a statement was actually a question, albeit a very clever one. As the full extent of the question dawned on him, he realised he really would have preferred a few weeks to think about it. But somehow, Caroline had managed to put him in a very tight spot. If he said yes, then he'd be going steady with her, and it was clear that he'd get to do it with her right there and then.

But then it would be all very official.

If he said no, then he would look like a horrible person. The sort of lad that thought she was good enough to have sex with but not good enough to go steady with. His head spun around while Caroline continued to fix those big, brown eyes of hers firmly on his. His breathing became more rapid, and he wondered why she didn't even seem to be the faintest bit tipsy anymore.

No. She looked…well…in total command of everything?

How had this happened? It couldn't be that she'd manipulated events all along, could it? Or was it that he had simply gotten himself into what was fast becoming to him anyway, a trap? The philosophical questions and moral guilt conundrums were enjoying a raucous tour around his head, yet Caroline was nothing less than composed and silent. Her eyes continued to be fixed upon his own. He couldn't be absolutely sure, but she seemed to be making her breasts heave up and down, a bit like the Oxford boat crew with five lengths to make up on Cambridge. 'Well, Pele?' she asked softly. 'What's it to be?'

And he knew it was his last chance to say something.

So, he gave her an answer.

When Pele hit the sack at around midnight, although he was exhausted, he found it hard to sleep. Sex with Caroline had turned out to be amazing. He had finally gotten to know what the phrase 'a great lover' meant. She'd done some things to him that neither of his previous two girlfriends had, and those things had made him scream out loud with unadulterated pleasure. It was obvious from the start that Caroline had way more experience with the opposite sex than he did. But when he thought about it, the budgie probably had had a lot more experience than he did. He wasn't overly concerned, though. He'd been well aware of the older lads she'd dated in the past. Still, he figured, if that's what she'd been doing, then it had been time well spent. He knew he'd paid a price for his pleasure, and it hadn't come without a strict addendum. They were now 'official' and 'going steady.'

After she had brought him to a climax for the second time, Caroline had lay next to him, lightly panting and smiling with something approaching a very knowing look on her face. Her head rested on his shoulder, her right leg snaked around his, and the heel of her foot hooked under his calf like a lasso. Her body somehow fit every contour of his. She stroked his chest as she told him how happy she was to be going out with him finally and how she now not only had a blossoming career at Cousins but the right man befitting this new career status: a man who worked in the offices, no less!

Pele was more than a little flattered about how pleased she'd seemed to be about their newly acquired 'official' status. There was no way he'd ever go back on his word to her either. He simply wasn't 'one of those lads': the kind who promised things in the passionate heat of the moment only to renege on promises made after the girl had made good their side of the bargain.

Besides, he really liked Caroline. There was much to like. She was pretty, she had a great personality, they got on really well together, and there was undoubtedly loads more great sex to be had.

It was all looking good.

So?

So, what was it that was bothering him so much about it all?

Why was he lying there wondering if he'd done the right thing? Wondering if he'd made the right choice when faced with her ultimatum. Something was lurking deep down in the dark recesses of his conscience, and it was nagging at him like his mum did when she wanted his room cleaned. Yet he couldn't quite work out what it was.

Eventually, he dropped off into an uneasy sleep and didn't

wake up until the budgie stood on his head nine hours later.

1979 (III)

His mum left the house to go shopping the following day, and Pele decided to call Caroline. After a few minutes, and with some trepidation, he told her he was going out on a work's do that evening. 'So, erm… just to let you know that I'm going out tonight on a stag-do with some of the lads from work.' He waited uneasily, expecting her to make a big deal of this news, but to Caroline's credit, she didn't seem even remotely upset. This was a welcome relief as his last girlfriend had been the jealous type. So much so that Pele had once returned to his bedroom from a visit to the toilet to find her pulling out his undies from the wash and examining them for signs of infidelity. It was somewhat reassuring then that when he'd told Caroline about the stag do, she hadn't demanded a root through his washing basket in return.

'Oh, that's nice,' she told him. 'I hope you enjoy yourself, Pele. I'm going to Foxy's with Cheryl for that Grease night I told you about.' A sense of relief washed over him, but it was short-lived. Without any warning signs of where she was leading the conversation, she said, 'I was thinking you could come over on Sunday night, Pele, after you've had your dinner.' And before he had time to mull it over or reply, she continued, 'Mum said she'd like to meet you. I've told her we're going steady now. We can watch *The Professionals* on TV together.'

He recognised that she was calling in his promise to her, and there weren't any exit routes available to make a detour while he got used to the idea. Although he was slightly nervous about meeting her mum, it wasn't because he was afraid of the encounter; it was the idea of publicly committing to their new relationship when he hadn't had time to adjust. 'Yeah, yeah. That's fine, no problem,' he said, adopting a positive approach and squashing the negative thoughts screeching inside of his head. 'And will we have some time alone, do you think?' Despite the trepidation, he was looking forward to a possible heavy petting session, which he hoped would inevitably follow.

She giggled and said, 'You'll have to wait and see Pele. All good things come to those who wait!'

After he'd hung up, he reflected on how excited Caroline was about 'going steady.' To him, their new relationship felt akin to trying on a beautiful new coat that was too small. Even though it looked great on the hanger, it was uncomfortable and didn't quite fit when you put it on. He decided it was because he wasn't yet accustomed to the idea. He needed time to get used to it, that was all.

Saturday evening came around quickly enough, and dinner was their traditional ham, egg, and chips fry-up. He wolfed it down and finished with half a portion of Bird's Eye Arctic Roll. His mum was sitting at the kitchen table reading an out-of-date Woman's Own magazine. She was onto her second cup of tea and had just lit a cigarette, held between her fingers as she turned the pages. Her other hand supported her head as she pored over the latest fashion icons. Pele was also reading and scanning the local free newspaper to see if there was anything about enrolling for the marathon event that was coming up next spring. As he did so, his mum glanced at her wristwatch and said, 'Brian, you'll miss your coach if you don't get a move on, love. Your internal clock needs some new batteries.'

'Even a broken clock is right twice a day,' he quipped, scraping his chair back as he stood up and began folding the paper. She ignored his remark, then, as he started to clear the table, she informed him,

'The immersion's been on for an hour; it should be hot enough for a bath now.'

He beamed and affectionately kissed the top of her head, saying, 'Thanks, Mum.'

'Well, don't get used to it. It costs an absolute fortune to heat up,' she replied, raising her eyes from the article she was reading. Pele noticed it was entitled: *'The Positive Woman - becoming a New Woman with Attitude and Confidence.'* He decided there and then that he'd keep that magazine's article well out of Caroline's reach, as that was one she definitely didn't need to read.

Pele lay in the hot bath for as long as he could make it last without being late for the bus. His mum was right about his timekeeping; it wasn't the best. When it came to time, he always thought he had more of it than he actually did. After unwillingly exfoliating with a cardboard towel, he dressed and entered the lounge where his mum had curled up on the sofa. She'd had her allotted number of cigarettes for the day and was sucking on a sherbet lemon while she waited for Larry Grayson's Generation Game to come on the TV. She only smoked three cigarettes a day: one in the morning with her cup of tea and another two after dinner. He never understood why she bothered. 'I'm off, Mum. Don't stay up because the coach won't get us back until late.'

'Well, what time will you be back?' she asked the same question as always.

'Dunno? Late. Sometime after midnight,' he replied, moving to smooth his hair one last time in the mantelpiece mirror. 'So don't wait up, or you'll be cranky tomorrow if you don't get your sleep.'

'I don't get cranky!' she retorted.

'Yeah, right, and I don't have a dodgy internal clock,' he smiled. She got up and, taking his leather tie, straightened the knot. Satisfied with the adjustment, she flattened the tie against his chest with the palm of her hand.

'I'll be in bed well before you get back, so don't make any noise on the way in.' Then her voice changed to a lower decibel as she emphasised, 'And - don't - drink - too - much.'

'I won't, Mum. I never do,' he said, pulling a face at her. She brushed away some imaginary fluff from his shoulders and stepped back to look at him. She had a distant look in her eyes, and he knew she was remembering his dad, who, according to his Aunt Bricey lately, he'd become the spitting image of.

'Ahh, you'll do. Away with ya,' she told him, patting his cheek and turning away.

It was drizzling when Pele arrived at the pick-up point five minutes before the coach was due. He sat down on the wall opposite the Church to pass the time. The sun had gone down two hours ago, and the estate looked like a pirate ghost town in the mist that hung over it. He looked over Festival Way to the shops where a gang of youths were milling around aimlessly. Occasionally, voices echoed from the group, shattering the silence of the otherwise quiet and desolate-looking streets. Hearing the shouts from the youths took him back to the long, cold winter nights when he'd done the same thing in the name of teenage boredom. They were in-between times when nights after school stretched ahead with nothing to do but hang around outside pubs and shops with friends. The only viable alternative was sitting in the living room with your parents and watching one of the three available channels on television or reading a book.

The coach arrived on time, and the doors slid open, revealing an already the worse-for-wear Newtog. He sprang out, throwing his arms open wide, and gave him a crushing bear hug, lifting him off the ground. 'Peleeee! Yer alright, mate?' he said, breathing a mixture of Newcastle Brown and cheap whiskey into his face.

'What Sally Army shop did you get the shirt from?' Pele teased once Newtog had released him. Newtog feigned indignation as his fingers and thumb rubbed the collar of his Dayglo shirt.

'This,' declared Newtog, twirling around like an unsteady catwalk model, 'is something you'd know nothing about Pele, my son: it's called style.' With that, he slapped Pele on the back, and they trundled onto the small coach to loud and raucous cheers. Pele pulled himself down the aisle past the usual suspects from work. He moved down the bus to where it was less rowdy. Jason Smith raised his hand and pointed to a seat next to him.

Jason was a year younger than Pele and also worked in the offices. Emulating John Travolta in Saturday Night Fever, he wore a light-coloured three-piece suit with an open black shirt. Pele had to smile at his self-assurance. It was a look that most lads would find difficult to carry off, but it didn't faze Jason despite his rotund shape and a whiter-than-white chest. 'Jay,' Pele said, nodding as he sat down.

'Pele, mate,' Jay replied. He reached into a plastic bag under the seat and produced a can of Skol that he generously offered with an outstretched arm.

'Cheers, Jay. Don't mind if I do,' Pele grinned, pulling the tab off and swallowing a mouthful of cold lager. 'Where's John?'

'Picking him up outside the Unicorn,' Jay replied, fishing into the bag for another can. Pele was glad to hear that. John's seniority in work and on the football pitch had a calming influence on most of the younger lads. Fights tended to be an occupational hazard around Newtog, who at that very moment was tipping a small bottle of Bell's whiskey into his mouth.

A few minutes later, the coach made a lazy stop outside the Unicorn pub car park to pick up John, who looked as smooth as Richard Gere. He was dressed in a designer suit that would have exceeded everyone else's price range. He stepped onto the coach, accompanied by cheering and jeering in equal measure. Unfazed, he did a theatrical bow, which produced further heckling and a few welcome slaps to his back as he stepped along the coach. He made his way to the seat in front of Pele and Jason and sat down. 'Pele, does your mum know you borrowed her shirt?' remarked John.

'I'll have you know that real men wear pink,' Pele laughed. 'Only someone uncomfortable with his sexuality wears designer suits.'

'Touché,' declared Jason, throwing John a can which he caught adroitly.

'Look at him,' John saluted Jason with the can by tilting it back at him, 'speaking French when he hasn't even mastered English!'

Jason roared with laughter, then raised his can of beer.

'Cheers, old man.' This was a reference to the fact that he was the oldest in the group, even though he was only 29.

'So then, you got a pass-out from Janey easy enough?' Pele asked, pulling himself forward on his seat and leaning over to John.

'Well, sort of,' said John evasively. 'Janey thinks I'm in the Unicorn having a pint with our Davie.'

'Oh, John,' Pele groaned dolefully. Whenever John lied to Janey about his whereabouts, Pele's heart sank. That was because he liked Janey a lot. She was a witty, attractive, blonde scouse girl who always fussed over Pele whenever he visited their home. Pele often wondered why John got off with so many different women when he had a fantastic wife like Janey. He'd asked John about it when they were in the Unicorn one night, and what John had said stuck in his mind: 'Life is complicated, Pele. Sometimes you do things you know you shouldn't, but you do them anyway and then finish up hating yourself afterwards.'

Pele couldn't see how things would ever get so complicated that you had to cheat on your wife, or anyone for that matter, only to be miserable afterwards. 'Don't worry; she's out with her mates tonight,' said John, sensing Pele's discomfort. 'I told her I'd probably go for a game of cards at our Davie's house. She's expecting me to stay at his.'

'What dressed like that?' Pele asked incredulously, pointing at John's suit.

'Calm down, Sherlock,' John told him. 'I got changed into the suit in the Uni toilets. Our Davie brought it in a holdall. Do I look stupid or something?' Pele didn't know whether to laugh or not, but it was so typical of John. 'Come on!' he cried, reaching over and tapping Pele on the arm with a fake punch. 'Let's enjoy ourselves instead of worrying about what Janey might or might not find out. Besides, I haven't even mentioned how camp Jay looks in that outfit.' Jay jumped up like a jack-in-the-box, his fists raised in mock anger. The awkwardness of the moment was broken, and they laughed. Pele sat back and looked out of the window; he wasn't going to get heated up about something that had nothing to do with him.

No, it was going to be a great night.

The party of around twenty lads piled off the coach at the Wilderspool Causeway to orders from John to 'Quieten down. Or the bouncers won't let us in.' They lowered their voices and broke into smaller groups of two or three.

Pele stayed with John, who was a local amateur football celebrity and knew all the bouncers working the doors. As they joined the queue, moving slowly towards the entrance, a loud voice boomed, 'Alright, Johnny boy! How's it going, mate?' John hustled Pele out of the queue with his arm, and they walked over to a huge, shaven-headed doorman standing by the entrance. His arms unfolded from their customary position across his chest like a daddy gorilla keeping watch over its young.

'Alright, Paddy! Still attempting to play the great game?' John said, reaching out a hand. Seconds later, it was engulfed in a big paw and pumped brusquely up and down.

'Can't play these days, mate,' said the bouncer, releasing John's hand. 'Dodgy knee finally gave in, probably from chasing your backside around the field too often.'

'Don't tell the wife that,' John joked while slapping the big guy on his huge bicep. The bouncer smiled amiably, then nodded to the side.

'Through there, mate, and don't do anything I wouldn't do.'

'Cheers, Paddy,' John said, leading Pele by his shoulder through the door. 'Take it easy, big guy.'

'Yeah, I will. I will.'

Once inside the club foyer, Pele could hear the music's bass pounding from the dance floor inside, and if he wasn't mistaken, it sounded very much like 'Good Times' by Chic. The room was already starting to fill with cigarette smoke, and it wasn't even at maximum capacity yet. John went to sit down with a couple of the lads while Pele made his way to the bar, where one of the bar staff came strolling over to him. 'What'll it be then?'

'Two lager tops, please,' Pele said, holding a five-pound note. 'And take one for yourself.' The bartender nodded and almost smiled a thank you. He poured a drink, handed it to Pele, and then put the fiver in the till as the second drink poured from the tap into a glass. Pele was lifting the pint to his lips when it lurched in his hands; he'd felt an unexpected tap on his shoulder and had spun around in surprise to answer it.

'What? John...'

There she was. She stood in front of him like it was yesterday.

Like it was 1974 again.

Though it had been nearly five years since he'd last seen her, she was instantly recognisable. Those large, blue eyes that had taken his breath away all those years ago in the park were right before him. 'Angela!' he spluttered, shaking the lager from his wet hand. He put the glass back on the bar and stared at her in disbelief.

'Well, I did wonder if you'd remember me,' she laughed. Pele was, for once, almost speechless but quickly tried to recover his composure.

'Of course, I remember you. I'd recognise you anywhere!'

'Well, that's a relief,' she smiled.

He stared at her, somewhat transfixed. Her hair was cut into an impossibly straight-edged bob. She wore a black and white printed, halter-neck dress with a fitted waistline, flared skirt, and black high heels.

'What are you doing here?' she asked.

'Oh, I'm on a stag do from work,' he replied. 'And what about you? Have you moved back to England now?'

'Sort of. Not really,' she replied, then giggled at herself and his puzzled look. 'I'm studying art and design at uni back in Ireland, but I spend the rest of my time here. So, it's split. I still can't believe I've bumped into you here, of all places!' She grinned with unmistakable pleasure at seeing him again.

'I know. It's weird, eh?' he echoed. But he was slightly distracted by a girl who had appeared out of nowhere and was now standing directly behind Angela. Pele didn't quite know what to make of it. She was shuffling around behind Angela's back, hoping from one gold-footed pump to the other, occasionally peering over Angela's shoulder at him. His face must have given away enough to indicate to Angela that something behind her was distracting him.

Angela turned around and broke into a wide smile at the young woman. Now that Angela had stepped to the side, he had a better view of the intruder. He saw she was petite and wore a lightweight, white jumpsuit with a broad, gold lamé belt around her tiny waist with matching gold pumps. Her dark hair was cut into a short pixie style, offset with long turquoise feather earrings. Her eyes were unmistakably from the same gene pool as Angela's, and from this, he deduced that she was almost certainly Angela's sister. She stood awkwardly, painfully self-conscious, as Angela introduced her to Pele. 'Karen, this is Pele. Pele, this is my younger sister, Karen.' Karen looked down at the floor and nodded so imperceptibly that the only evidence of any response was the movement of her earrings. Her eyes somehow could not lift themselves away from the bright, orange, and brown swirls on the carpet where they were utterly transfixed.

'Hey, Karen! So nice to meet you,' Pele said, making a quick decision not to initiate a handshake as it might cause further unease to this painfully shy girl. 'Angela hadn't told me she had such a pretty sister.' Karen's lips twitched into something that could have been a smile, but her eyes remained downcast, so he wasn't sure. She leant forward and said something into Angela's ear, which Pele couldn't hear because of the music. Angela said something in return and pointed towards a group of girls sitting on the other side of the dance floor. Karen looked distinctly unhappy about whatever Angela had said, but Angela repeated it with hand gestures and nodded toward their friends. After a moment or two, Karen reluctantly turned around and set off towards the group of women without saying anything further to either of them.

'She gets a bit anxious if we're separated and it's her first night out with a group of girls,' Angela said, by way of explanation, while watching her go. Pele didn't think it was any of his business to enquire any further. She lifted her glass of wine to a pair of beautifully painted red lips and took a slow sip while she stared at him quizzically. 'I wasn't sure if you would be happy to see me. I mean, after my dad gave you the third degree for walking me home and all that. I never blamed you for not writing, but I really wished you had...' She took a large gulp of wine. Pele rubbed the side of his face and tried to find the right words.

'Your dad was only protecting you,' he said.

'Yeah, I know he thought he was.' She frowned, looking over at her sister Karen, sitting almost in isolation at the edge of the group. Karen was clutching what looked like a glass of coke with both hands as if it were a lifeline. 'So, is that why you didn't write Pele? My dad? I waited every day for months, hoping for a letter.' Her eyes fixed on his as she waited for his response.

'Kind of...' he said slowly. She studied his face, and understanding finally emerged in her eyes.

'He took the address off you, didn't he?' Pele sucked in some air and blew it out again. He'd had a long time to think about what happened that night, and the words that came out of his mouth were the words of Pele, the young man and not the 14-year-old boy who couldn't sleep for months five years ago.

'Yeah, he did; he took it from me. I was gutted when I couldn't write to you. I didn't sleep for months, never knowing if you would work out that he'd taken it or if you'd just think I didn't want to write. It seems you thought the worst of me.' He gave a shrug of the shoulders.

'You've no idea how many times I sat waiting for the postman to come, Pele,' she replied. 'And when nothing came, I asked my da if he'd taken the address off you. He told me that if something's not meant to be, it won't be; if something is meant to be, nothing will get in the way of it. You can never get a straight answer from my dad if he's not in the mood. So, I never knew for sure. But you could have asked my cousin Susan for it; you knew where she lived.'

'You're not thinking that through Angela,' he argued. 'Your dad would have intercepted any letters I sent. And even if one miraculously got past him, can you imagine the grief he would have given you if he'd found out about it? In the end, I couldn't see any way around it without causing problems.' Angela sipped her wine as she considered what he'd told her.

Then she said with a wry smile, 'Well, it seems that not even my dad can keep us apart forever. And maybe there's some truth in what he said after all... If something's meant to be?' Pele's heart leapt in his chest, and their eyes locked as though something was pulling them together. They stood in a comfortable silence until Pele realised that he should do or say something.

'Would you like another drink?' he asked, but she shook her head.

'No thanks, Pele. The girls have already got the next round in. And to be honest, I don't drink that much.' She began to laugh when he raised his eyebrows and gave a pointed look at how quickly she'd emptied her wine glass. Then, to Pele's surprise, she placed a hand on his arm before lifting it to his cheek. 'You could ask me if I wanted to dance, though?' Pele smiled at that.

'Well, I guess you are over eighteen now. So, ahhem...Would you like to dance, Angela?' She nodded.

'I would love to dance with you, Pele. I thought you would never ask.' Pele leant past her to pick up the two pints from the bar.

'Well, just wait here a second while I make a quick but important delivery. And DON'T go anywhere!'

He sprinted over to where John was seated with his back to him. He put the drinks on the table and said to John, 'I'll be back in a bit.' John turned away from his conversation with Newtog and was about to criticise him for the length of time it had taken him to get the drinks, but Pele was already making his way back towards Angela.

'Go on, Pele, lad. You don't waste much time!' John shouted to the back of his head. Pele found Angela's hand and held it tightly as he led her onto the dance floor and the growing crowd of gyrating bodies. Donna Summer's *'Hot Stuff'* blasted out of the smoke and strobe lights. Angela picked up the beat, and with her arms lifted into the air, she turned and twisted to the music. Every part of his body responded to hers in the most familiar way, like they'd danced together a thousand times before.

Thirty minutes later, they were both laughing, breathless, and hot from dancing. Angela was panting a little and had a thin layer of perspiration on her face. Pele was catching his breath as she leant slowly towards him and spoke into his ear, her hand resting lightly on his shoulder. He felt her warm breath tickling his ears. He leant into her, placing his hand on her uncovered back, and inhaled her perfume; she smelt of musky, exotic flowers. 'Thanks for the dance, Pele,' she said and pulled back to look into his eyes to check he understood her over the noise. Then she leaned forward again, her smooth cheek pressed against his. 'I don't want to spoil Karen's first night out, though, by making her anxious. She finds new situations stressful. Can we dance again in a bit?'

'Yeah, sure,' said Pele, nodding his head to show he understood when, in fact, he was utterly deflated and didn't want her to leave for the world. He hooked his thumb towards his rowdy mates. 'I'll be over there with the lads.' Angela glanced in the direction he pointed and burst out laughing as they were making 'Get in, my son!' gestures of approval from the side of the dance floor. She kissed his cheek softly, sending them into a wild frenzy, cheering and whooping loudly. Pele felt elated and embarrassed at the same time.

'Okay. Great. I'll see you later,' she said. He reached for her hand and pulled her back until they were stood face to face.

'I'll be waiting. And not for the first time.' Then he reluctantly let go of her and stepped backwards. She smiled and wiped at his cheek where she'd put her lips, presumably to remove her lipstick mark. Then she turned again to go, walking over to the now thronging bar area. He didn't move from where he stood; he watched her until she disappeared into the ever-increasing crowd.

Pele walked back, as if in a dream, to where the lads from his coach were chanting, 'Pele! Pele! Pele!' Newtog hooked his arm around Pele's neck in a vice-like grip and hollered into his ear, 'Pele, you've got more jam than a jammy dodger!' he roared. 'How did you pull her? She's gorgeous!' Pele wrestled Newtog's sweaty arm off his neck just as John returned from the bar and put more drinks on the table. Newtog was the first to pick up a pint. In a drunken gesture, he saluted Pele, swinging the glass upwards and sloshing lager down the front of his Day-Glo shirt. He took a big gulp and staggered back into a chair with a larger-than-life, cheesy grin aimed at Pele, who was shaking his head at his antics.

John handed a pint of lager to Pele and said, 'Well done, Pele lad. She's a real beauty.' Pele took a mouthful.

'Oh, she's much more than that, John.'

'How did you pull her so fast? We've only just got here?' Pele turned away, his eyes searching for her.

'Nah, John. It's not like that. We, sort of... go back a bit.'

Pele spent the next couple of hours with the lads, but most of the time, he was so distracted by Angela's presence that he almost felt like a bystander. Occasionally, their eyes would meet across the room, and she would hold his gaze and smile. He was irrationally afraid that she would disappear and he would lose her as he had five years ago. Determined it wouldn't happen again, he put his drink on the table and tapped John on the shoulder. 'You got a pen?' he asked, knowing that John always carried one. John removed a small ballpoint from the inside of his jacket pocket.

'Phone number time already?' John laughed, handing it over to Pele. 'You're quick off the mark.'

'I'm getting her number, and this time, no one's taking it off me,' said Pele, turning in Angela's direction.

When he got to the far side of the bar, his panic was alleviated when he spotted her seated at a table with her sister and a group of girls. Normally, Pele would have baulked about charging headlong into the 'enemy' camp in such a rash way. But now he was a young man on a mission, and he'd had a few pints, which only helped to boost his confidence. He picked a beer mat up from a nearby table and ripped a white piece off the corner. Resolutely, he strode over to Angela, where, upon noticing his approach, one of the girls nudged Angela and giggled. Angela beamed a smile at Pele that made him feel dizzy.

Pele's heart was racing in his chest as he stood awkwardly before the group of smiling faces, although one was distinctly unreadable. But the truth was he could only see one of those faces. 'If you don't mind, I really would like your phone number,' he exclaimed, holding the pen and torn beer mat out towards her.

This produced a sort of coo-ing noise from the table, and a voice said, 'Ohhh! He wants your phone number, Ange. All masterful, like.' Shrieks of laughter followed. Angela ignored the giggling and took the pen and beer mat from Pele's slightly shaking hand.

'Shut up, Marie,' she spoke to the girl on her left. 'Just because no one ever asks for your number, there's no need to get jealous.' The girls all shrieked again, and even Karen looked like she might be slightly amused, though it was hard to tell. 'I was just coming over to see you,' she said to Pele, who continued to stand like a lemon while she scribbled on the mat and handed it back to him. 'Our coach is going soon. Can we have another dance before I leave?' Pele took the piece of beer mat from her and looked at it briefly before putting it into his shirt pocket. At this point, he was strangely oblivious to the girls who were hanging on to his reply. He put his hand over his shirt pocket, pressing against the mat to check it was safe, and said,

'I don't think I've ever wanted anything so much.'

'Awwwwwwwwwwww!' Was the sound that exited the gaping mouths in total unison as Pele extended his hand to Angela, who was smiling coyly at him.

He led her through the crowd and onto the dance floor for the second time. In the background, the drumbeat from '*My Sharona*' started, and Angela moved closer, putting her arms around his neck. He realised that she had probably drank a few glasses of wine, which had loosened her inhibitions. A couple of dances later, her face was inches away from his. 'Will you walk with me to the coach when it's time to go?'

'Yeah, 'course I will,' he replied. 'But in the meantime, we're '*Reunited, and it feels so good...*' he sang into her giggling face as Peaches and Herb played in the background.

Several dances later, Angela reluctantly pulled herself away from him and said that she really had to leave. Karen was calling her from the edge of the dance floor and waving their cloakroom tickets mid-air to get her attention. He saw that the girls had already set off to get their coach, so he took Angela's hand and walked with her to the cloakroom. Retrieving both hers and Karen's coats, she fastened the buttons up, her sleek bob falling across her cheeks as her head bent forward. Pele watched in adoration. He was convinced he could never get tired of looking at her. Karen stood patiently and silently by her side.

One of the bouncers, noticing that he wasn't wearing a coat, told them as they walked towards the exit, 'Sorry mate, but if you go out, you won't get back in; the doors are closing in about ten minutes.' Pele knew that their coach wouldn't be leaving until at least two-thirty. He looked at his watch; it would be at least an hour's wait.

'Look, it's okay, really,' said Angela, as she pushed her arm through her sisters. 'You'll be waiting around for ages if you come outside and it's freezing.'

'No, I want to walk you to your coach and make sure you're safe. I don't mind; wait there a minute.' She rolled her eyes, but he could tell she was secretly pleased. He collected his jacket, and they walked through the double doors linked together as a threesome with Angela in the middle. The cold air made him shiver, which was strange as he could also feel heat pulsing through his veins.

After a few minutes of walking, Angela pointed to the coach parked further up the road. A group of her friends were in front; some had clambered onto the bus to escape the cold air and were making a commotion with shrieks and giggles. 'Karen, you go ahead and find us some seats,' Angela said, speaking gently to her sister. 'I'm just going to talk to Pele for a few minutes, and then I'll join you.' Karen didn't look altogether too pleased with these arrangements, but she obligingly stepped onto the coach without saying anything. Pele knew he wouldn't have long before they had to say goodbye. They walked to the back of the coach, where they were shielded from the streetlights. Pele desperately wanted to kiss her. Angela turned to look at him, grasping both of his hands. 'It's been great to see you again, Pele,' she breathed softly before she reached up and pressed her soft mouth onto his. His hands slipped inside her coat and around her slim waist. He could feel the warm skin of her back, and he desperately wanted the moment to last longer than he knew it would. Her scent was intoxicating and made his head swim. As she pressed against him, her fingers were in his hair and inside the back of his shirt. His heart was pumping like the beat of the drums in *My Sharona*. When she broke away, he thought he would never let her go. Then she lifted her hand and caressed his cheek. 'Worth the wait,' she smiled.

'Oh yes, it was,' he whispered hoarsely. She stepped away, glancing towards the front of the bus. The coach engine revved, and a panicked voice from the front door, which could have only been her sister, shouted,

'Angela! Hurry up, Angelaaaa!!!' The voice yelled with urgency.

'I have to go. Call me tomorrow. Around seven?'

'I will.'

'You still have the number?' she laughed. Pele tapped the shirt pocket.

'It's in here, and Mohammed Ali couldn't take it off me, let alone your dad.' She smiled at this, turned, and waved. He waved back. Then she ran towards the front of the coach, where her sister was hanging wildly out of the door. He watched her being pulled through the door by a frantic arm. As soon as she did, the doors whooshed behind her, and it began to pull away. He lost sight of her until she appeared at the back window and mouthed something he couldn't catch. Then she waved, blew a kiss to him, and pressed her palm against the window. He imagined that she was telling him that she loved him. The bus turned at the next corner, and suddenly, she was gone.

He was left standing in the middle of the road, watching an empty space.

On the way home, Pele looked morosely out of the coach window at the blurred neon amber glow of the M56 while the others spent their time raucously stripping Newtog of all his clothes and dignity.

It had been a long wait in the cold before the coach turned up, and as expected, the bouncer wouldn't let him back into the club. He couldn't afford to pay for a taxi, which left an uncomfortable hour of hanging around in a draughty club doorway. The only relief from the cold was when warm air billowed out whenever someone left the building. Though deliriously happy at the night's events, Pele's thoughts had darkened more than a little since Angela had gone. From the moment he'd returned to the coach, the image of Caroline wouldn't leave him alone. No matter how much he tried to convince himself that kissing Angela wasn't wrong because he wasn't *really* going out with Caroline, and if he were, well, it had only been for one night, the guilt wouldn't go. The problem, as he saw it, was not that he had only been going out with Caroline for one day but that he'd made a promise to her. He'd collected on his end of that promise, but she might not be collecting on hers.

Did that mean he wasn't going to phone Angela? He put a panicked hand in his shirt pocket and reached for the torn beer mat with her number. No, of course, it didn't. He was already formulating a plan. In that plan, he would go out with Caroline for a few weeks, and then he would finish with her. That way, she wouldn't feel used. Then he could go back to living the rest of his life happily ever after with Angela. It would all work out for everyone; everyone that was provided your name wasn't Caroline. Still, though it all sounded easy when he said it to himself, the reality would likely be very different. Caroline really liked him, and before he'd met Angela tonight, he thought he'd really liked her. He did…it was just…just…well… she wasn't Angela. That seemed to be Caroline's only crime in all this mess: not being Angela. Without realising it, he let out a long, loud sigh. 'That sounds like a man with the weight of the world on his shoulders,' said John, sitting down next to him. Pele and John's workmates were now inflicting the last rites on the groom-to-be. The long, established tradition of painting the groom's naked body with lewd words and pictures. 'What's up, mate? Is it that girl tonight? The pretty one?'

'Yeah,' said Pele softly.

'I can see why,' John replied with a wink. 'She's a real beauty. Though I can't see what the problem is. I thought you'd got her number?' Pele looked the older man straight in the eyes.

'Yeah, I did, but I'm, sort of, going out with someone else.'

'Sort of?' John asked in surprise; his eyebrows raised very slightly.

'Well, no. Not, sort of,' Pele sighed. 'I *am* going out with someone else.'

'You sly, old dog,' John muttered in surprise but immediately saw the wounded look in Pele's eyes and backtracked. 'I mean, obviously, that's a problem. You just have to decide which one you like the most and then dump the other. Simple, really.' When John said things like that, they always sounded so simple. He had such an uncomplicated view of the world that it could have been him with the carefree 19-year-old life and Pele with the complicated 29-year-old one.

At this point, shouting from the front of the coach broke Pele's misery, and they both looked up to see what was happening. The driver was harangued into stopping on High Street, where some of the lads from the old town district wanted to get off. This was also where the police station was located, so it made perfect sense that it was here that they were going to handcuff Newtog to a lamppost directly outside of the station. 'I'm not so sure this is a good idea,' John said, getting out of his chair and moving towards the front of the coach, where five lads were carrying the remains of Newtog's semi-unconscious body down to the exit.

When the coach dropped him off at the shops around three-thirty, it had been raining heavily. Thankfully, it was just light drizzle as Pele started the short, ten-minute walk back to his house. The estate was quiet; most of the booze crowd would have been kicked out of the Cherry hours ago. A couple of the remaining lads on the back seat of the coach were jeering at him through the window as the coach veered off. He flicked a friendly V-sign at them before buttoning up his granddad's jacket against the biting cold while sparing a thought for a naked Newtog cuffed to a lamppost in the High Street.

As he turned sharply onto Acacia, he pondered if he shouldn't take the slightly quicker route through Laburnum. It would save him a few minutes and get him out of the rain and cold sooner. He took the right turn down behind the garages and immediately regretted it.

Three figures emerged from the back of number three, the dreaded Cross house. He put his head down, hoping they wouldn't spot him, and if they did, maybe they wouldn't bother with him at this time in the morning. He recognised two of the voices, Slug MacDonald and Sean Cross. 'Well, well! It's puffy Smith,' shouted Cross. 'Look at that clobber he's wearing. What a prat!'

Pele contemplated running. He still had ten yards on them, and though the three were now crossing over and closing rapidly on him, he would almost certainly be able to outrun them. But running wasn't something you did on the estate. It was liable to get you into even more trouble the next time. Seconds later, he felt an arm pulling him sharply round. It was Slug.
'Where've you been, Smith?' Slug slurred cheap cider droplets mixed with spittle that landed on his face.

Pele hadn't seen Slug for a year or so and was surprised to see how much he had filled out. The tall frame had developed thickset shoulders and a broad, bull-like neck. Even though he wore a heavy donkey jacket, it wasn't difficult to see that his arms had acquired muscles comparable to Popeye's. Pele had heard that he was working on a demolition site in the New Town, and the physical labour had transformed his once slim frame. Since the jumper incident, there had been a few run-ins at school, and Pele had occasionally come out on top. He sensed tonight wasn't going to be one of those occasions. 'What's it to do with you, MacDonald?' he asked, standing tall and using a confident tone to show he wasn't afraid. Slug, Cross, and a ginger lad who he'd never seen before but who looked like a weasel had instinctively encircled him. Pele recognised the tactic and knew that a kicking was imminent. It was Cross who spoke next.

'It must be nice. To have mates. They're not here now, though, are they? I mean, when you really need them.' Sean Cross was, and always had been, pure malevolence, and Pele was already working out how he could temper the beating that would inevitably follow these ritualistic opening asides. He wondered if he shouldn't just get one good, hard dig in at Cross as some minor triumph to take out of the battle, but he knew that such an act of defiance would be rewarded with a far greater level of violence in retaliation. So, he tensed and waited, though it wasn't Cross but Slug who spoke next.

'Ah, just leave him, Sean,' said Slug, turning away. 'I need to get to bed. I've got a Sunday shift in a few hours, and I can't be arsed with this.'

'You going soft or something?' Cross snapped, his dark, beady eyes glaring over now at Slug. His shaven head and tattooed neck were in keeping with the pair of knuckle-dusters he removed from his jacket pocket. 'Or do you fancy the punky bum-boy?'

'Give us a break, Sean.'

'Do him them! Show me you don't fancy him.' It was a classic Cross tactic. Pele decided to get this over with.

'Look, if you three muppets are going to do something, just get on with it. I have to get-'

It was the quiet weasel that struck Pele in the mouth from the side. Pele had been hell-bent on watching the other two and hadn't seen it coming. Though the blow's force wasn't that great, and Pele had marked the ginger's card if he ever saw him out on his own, he found himself down on the cobbled floor, in a puddle and getting his best clothes soaked. Without any hesitation, Cross booted him in the back of his thigh with what felt like steel toe-cap boots, causing him to cry out loudly in pain. The weasel gave an elated hyena-sounding laugh at this before joining in and kicking his shoulder and upper arm, which Pele was using to protect his head. He gritted his teeth, crying out and writhing in agony with each blow. A nearby house light flooded the dark alleyway, and a loud, shrill voice, which sounded very much like Mrs Jacobs, cried out in the darkness, 'You lot better clear off! I've already phoned the police, and they're on their way.' Then she banged the door shut, cutting out the light, but not before telling someone inside, 'Those Cross boys are making trouble again.' Cross was well known to the police, and he didn't want any undue attention from the boys in blue.

'What are you playing at Slug? Don't just stand there, kick him!' Slug aimed a half-hearted kick at Pele's midriff, winding him and making him curl up even more. At this, the three lads took off, hoping to avoid unnecessary conversations with the local constabulary.

Pele lay there for a moment, feeling sick and dizzy. He took stock of his pain and realised that as beatings went, this hadn't been the worst one he'd ever had off Cross, who clearly wasn't on his game tonight. He slowly picked himself up, and the world reeled in a sickening, lurching motion. He focused on breathing and stood with his forehead against the cold brick wall until his vision cleared. After a while, his legs stopped shaking enough for him to think he might just be able to make the rest of the walk home without being sick. Even though it was icy cold and he was soaking wet, he was sweating heavily. He reached for a tissue in his back pocket to wipe a trickle of blood that was running from his lips, only to find it was too wet to be of any use.

He hobbled the remaining few hundred yards to his house, occasionally spitting out blood from his mouth. When he finally got to the front door, he took the key from his back pocket. He pushed himself through the door, trying desperately not to drip blood anywhere or, even worse, make any noise and wake his mum up.

Once inside, he got a pint of water from the kitchen and swilled his mouth out, spitting thick red saliva into the sink. Then he grabbed half a bag of peas from the freezer and took it to his bedroom. Pele sneaked into his room very quietly. The last thing he wanted now was his mum on the scene, asking questions and dragging him outside to knock on the Cross's door at four in the morning. He removed his clothes carefully, trying not to make any noise from the pain. He pressed against his ribs to see what damage had been done, but other than emerging bruises, they seemed okay. When he had stripped down, he looked at himself in the mirror to examine the wounds on his body. Thankfully, his clothes would hide most of them, and his mum would only see the split lip and bruised eye. He hoped the bag of peas would reduce the swelling, and his eye might not look so bad by morning. He lifted the sheets, stumbled into bed, and fell into a deep, troubled sleep.

1979 (IV)

The next morning, he was sound asleep when his mum popped her head around his door, and stage whispered, 'Brian, get up!' Pele's eyes tried to open, but only one did. It spied the alarm clock, which told him that it was 11 o'clock. He lifted his head, covered with soggy peas, to look at her. 'God's truth! Will you look at the state of your eye, Brian? Oh, good grief. Just take a look at your lip, too!' She closed the door, muttering under her breath and stepped into the room.

'Mmm, what's going on?' asked Pele, his brain slowly shifting into gear as he moved onto his elbow, causing the remaining squashed peas in the open bag to spill onto his pillow.

'And what did you do to your clothes? They're all muddied and soaking. What on earth did you get up to last night, Brian?' Pele carefully felt the puffed, taught skin around his eye and cheek with his fingers and watched her pick up his wet, soiled clothes off the floor.

'Oh, err... Some lads were causing trouble when we came out of the club. I was just trying to get onto the bus, but I got dragged into it. I'm fine, mum, honest.' He gave out a groan, mainly from the pain but also from tiredness and the effects of alcohol.

'Fine, are ya?' she cried. 'Well, that's because you haven't seen yer face yet!' Her eyes were wide as she took in the scene before her. 'And just look at the state of your bed, Brian! It's covered. What is that? Peas!!' He twisted his head around to see that she was right. His pillow and bed sheets were covered in a soggy, green mush.

'I'm sorry, mum...' he groaned again. 'I'll sort it out. Just give me ten minutes to get up, and I'll change the bed.' Taking Pele totally by surprise, she stepped towards him and leaned over; instead of leaving him to get dressed and strip the bed, she breathed in a voice just above a whisper,

'There's no time for that now, Brian. Just get yerself ready. There's a young lady waiting for you in the front room.' He knew instantly who it was. This was something he really didn't need right now and something he hadn't prepared for. Pele's mum opened the door and flashed a broad smile at him as she left. Despite the bruises and the mushy-pea disaster that was all over the bed, she'd had a distinctly pleased look about her, and he couldn't for the life of him work out why that was.

Falling out of bed, Pele clambered across the room, let the bird out of its cage, and dressed very slowly. His legs and backside were particularly painful and aching from the beating. Pip flew over and perched on the chair where he sat, chirping softly, his head tilting from one side to the other as he followed Pele's movements. If Pele hadn't known any better, he might have thought the bird was commiserating. He could hear his mum downstairs talking to Caroline, and from the odd word he could decipher, she was relaying the state he'd come home in last night. He sighed and pulled on some clothes before going to the bathroom, where he inspected the damage to his face. He splashed cold water over his face, then carefully removed the peas stuck to his cheek and forehead with a wet face cloth. The eye, thankfully, wasn't completely closed, although it was very swollen and sporting a multi-coloured bruise of red, purple, and blue hues.

On the whole, it wasn't as bad as his Mum was making out, and he'd had worse in the past. His lip was slightly split and swollen, but there was nothing to worry about. All the other bruising was to the body, and that wasn't a problem as neither his mum nor Caroline would get to see it.

He quickly brushed his teeth, splitting his lip open and spat out a mouthful of pink, foamy toothpaste. Then, he tentatively descended the stairs, holding firmly onto the handrail. From the front room, he could hear his mum making loud, we-have-exalted-company, gushing sounds.

Pele steeled himself before pushing open the door to the living room. When he entered, Caroline was perched on the edge of the sofa with his mum's 'posh' china teacup in one hand and a plate of Ginger Snaps in the other. Though it was only eleven in the morning, Caroline looked dressed for a night out and had been up for hours. She was immaculate in hair, make-up and demeanour. 'Hiya, love,' she called over to him as if they'd been married for thirty years. 'Oooh! Your eye does look sore. You weren't exaggerating Mrs Smith.' Pele was almost as much out of his depth here as he had been two nights before when she'd asked him what he was doing with his penis. And '*love*'? Where had that come from?

'Well, Brian,' his mum chuckled, leaning over and patting Caroline's knee, who accepted the gesture as if it had been happening for years. 'Why didn't you tell me you were courting such a lovely young lady?' Pele stood by the door, unwilling to fully enter what suddenly seemed to him a very dangerous place. An unholy alliance was taking place here, and it was one that was clearly going to be directed against him.

'We're not courting Mum,' he said peevishly. 'People don't court anymore these days; they go out with each other.'

'Oh, pay no attention to him, Mrs Smith,' Caroline said, putting down the tea and biscuits and getting up to walk over to him. 'Brian, love? What happened to your eye?'

'Err...' he stammered, wondering how he'd suddenly become Brian to Caroline and no longer Pele. 'Oh, it's nothing, honest. No, it's... No, don't touch it.' It was too little too late, as she stroked his swollen eye and cheek, winking at him.

'If this was someone from the estate, Brian, you must tell me who it was. No one gets to hurt my boyfriend.'

'Oh, Brian, you've only gone and got yourself a wonderful girl there,' his mum clucked from behind Caroline's attentions. 'Just wait 'till I tell your Aunt Bricey.' Pele felt Caroline's lips press gently against his, and he knew it was going to be a very, very long day.

Pele somehow managed to convince Caroline that he wasn't about to keel over and die from his injuries, and she left around one o'clock with the promise that he'd get to her house by eight thirty to meet her mum and watch the Professionals. Feeling overwhelmed by events and his inability to deal with them, he returned to his freshly made bed and slept for hours. He was woken from a dream where Angela was shouting something at him from the bus, but he couldn't hear what she was saying because of the distant sound of his mum calling him down for dinner. In his semi-conscious state, an idea began to emerge that became all the more obvious as he came around. He should seek someone's advice as to what he should do about his mounting problems.

And he thought he might just know the right person.

An hour and a half later, Pele stepped into the cold entrance of St Jude's Church and looked around. There were a few of the regulars knocking about. These were older folk on the front benches kneeling in prayer. The evening service didn't start until 6 o'clock, so they were putting in a bit of overtime. Pele figured the older one got, the more pressing the need to square things up with the man upstairs. He looked around at the sculptures of saints and various Virgin Marys lined up in rows along the wall. Their poses were serene, heads meekly tilted, and hands held out in benediction. In some ways, he missed going to church; he'd always found it a peaceful place to sit and let his mind rest. The stained-glass windows reflected the soft lighting and candles the faithful church members lit.

He unbuttoned his jacket and sat down on a pew to wait. He winced as his backside made contact with the hard, wooden seat, a sharp reminder of last night's encounter with Slug and Co. Beyond the alter rail and table, a large cross was suspended from the ceiling. From it, Jesus looked down from the cross, his mutilated body barely covered by a small cloth around his hips. Pele didn't find that image quite as tranquil as the others and shifted uncomfortably on the hard bench. He glanced around on hearing Father O'Malley's booming, deep voice. He was over by the confessional booth talking to two of his alter boys and ruffling their hair. Pele bet a pound to a penny that the conversation was centred on yesterday's football matches. The Father was a keen Manchester United fan and always ready to engage in football banter with the boys or his congregation. Pele looked at the shaggy mop of grey hair and the portly figure, who was rumoured to be fond of the odd glass of Guinness. He stayed where he was, watching the priest banter with the boys. It was reminiscent of his time here many years ago as a young altar boy.

After a moment or two of observing the scene, he caught the father's kind eye, and he was rewarded with a broad smile of recognition and a small wave. The priest continued talking to the young boys for a little longer before eventually patting them both on the head and walking over to Pele. 'Well, hello Pele. It's very good to see you, even if it isn't as often as I'd like.' Pele took the dig in the good-natured way it was intended.

'Oh, you know how it is, father? Busy, busy.'

'Like your back four yesterday,' laughed O'Malley. This was a reference to Pele's favourite team, Everton, and their shocking defeat the day before. Pele shook his head in good humour.

'Could I have a word, Father? I'd like your advice on something. Do you have the time?' The kindly priest looked at Pele with twinkling eyes and gave a wry smile.

'It seems that's why I was put on this earth for, young man. It's in my job description, you know. Why don't we go to my office and have some tea?'

Ten minutes later, Pele carefully sipped on a strong Irish brew and recounted the previous day's events to O'Malley. When he'd finished, he sat back in an armchair and exhaled like someone who'd gotten something momentous off his chest. The priest sat opposite him. He wore suede loafers and a pair of black trousers that were visible underneath his robes. His legs were outstretched, and a mug of tea rested on his stout gut, one large hand wrapped around it. He lifted the mug to his mouth and listened without interrupting. Finally, he drained the contents with a long gulp and satisfied gasp and raised his eyes at Pele, which were now solemn. 'Tell me, Pele, if you can. How much does it weigh?'

'Eh?' Pele replied, narrowing his brow to show the priest his confusion.

'Why, the weight of the world? You've been carrying it around on your shoulders for years. Certainly, as long as I've known you and I've known you nearly all your life. Why, I never did meet a child who worried about things like you do.'

'Yeah, I know, Father,' Pele agreed, putting his hands up to his temples and rubbing them fiercely. 'But even you have to admit, I'm in a bit of trouble with this.' The priest set his mug on the table and took his glasses off. He began to polish them with his sleeve. He lifted them to the light before putting them back on and gave Pele a stare without saying anything. He sat back with a soft sigh, folding his shovel-like hands on his large midriff.

'And you want to know what I think you should do?' Pele flexed uncomfortably in the chair, and it wasn't entirely down to his bruises.

'Well, yeah. I wanted your advice, as it's a sort of, well, a sort of… moral problem. The sort of area I thought… the church… well you… might be able to help me with.' The priest's eyes glinted at this, and he scratched his head as if considering something of great importance.

'Pele, can I ask you something?'

'Sure,' said Pele, a little apprehensively. Pele knew from years of experience that the priest only asked pertinent questions and was highly skilled at making you face up to your problems, even when they were usually the very last thing you wanted to face up to.

'How long have you been coming to St Jude's?' Pele hesitated before replying.

'Sixteen years or so, I guess. On and off.'

'And if I had to ask you, how many sermons have you sat through in that time?' Pele didn't have to think long; he shrugged his shoulders.

'I don't know – hundreds?'

'Hundreds,' said the priest, nodding in agreement. 'And, apart from being bored most of the time, what's the one thing you took away from them on the few times you listened? The one thing we try to impress on you here at St Jude's?' Pele suddenly felt six years old again, like he did that Sunday when he was in trouble for dropping communion wafers into the sacramental wine. He looked away from the priest's gaze and down at the floor.

'That we all have free will, but we should always try to do the right thing with it. The thing that Jesus would want us to do.'

'Ah! Pele. Always the clever one. Always sat there, looking like you weren't listening but nevertheless always taking everything in. And such a good little soul. Sure, you did the boy's pranks with the rest of them, and we had to reprimand you, but we all knew that God was working in you.' Pele listened but wasn't sure that God had been anywhere near him, never mind any working.

'Well, can I ask you this then?' Pele said while the priest nodded slowly back at him. 'Why would God let you fall in love with someone and then let you know it was wrong to be with them? It doesn't make any sense to me.' On hearing the question, the Father put the soles of both feet down on the floor, got up slowly, and meandered over to the narrow, wooden window where he gazed out into the night and upwards to the heavens.

'An excellent question that young Pele, and one that deserves a better answer than you'll get from me. Nevertheless, it still deserves the best answer I can give it. That is to say, I myself have long ago abandoned questioning as to *why* God does anything at all. He has *His* ways, and I only know that the more you try to figure them out, the less sense they seem to make. But I'll tell you this one thing, the one thing that I have learned in all my years of living on His earth, and that's the more I stopped trying to understand why and accept that it's all under His control, the more sense everything seemed to make. Now, I'll leave you to mull that over and make your own decision as to what to do about your predicament. But I want you to know that I have every confidence in you making the right one, Pele, and I'm sure God does, too.' Pele got up from the chair, sighed, and began to fasten up his coat. The Priest didn't move from the window but merely continued to look out to the heavens.

'Thanks, Father,' he said on reaching the door and turning the large wooden knob. 'You've helped me.'

'Have I?' the priest asked, turning to him. 'Sure, if there isn't a first time for everything, just like they say. So, if you don't mind me asking, what is it that you're going to do?'

'I don't know,' Pele sighed again. 'I'm going to see if I can figure out *His* plan and go from there.'

'God bless you, my son. I hope it doesn't take you too many years.' The sound of Father O'Malley's jolly laughter followed Pele as he closed the door behind him and headed out into the night.

When Pele returned home, it was just after six-thirty, and the house was empty. It made him realise how little he saw of his mum these days. When he was a child, she seemingly never left the house, but now that he was older, she would often be out visiting friends or doing charity work. Not that he could have broached his problem with her. He knew only too well what her response would be. Katy Smith's morals were cast in the sort of rigid Catholic stone that even the Pope might have deemed a little too theologically rigid. She would have told him immediately to phone Angela and tell her he couldn't possibly see her again, but then his mum didn't feel the overwhelming pangs of longing that manifested in his chest whenever he thought of her.

As Pele closed the door behind him, he switched the light on in the hall and stopped to stare at the grey trimphone on the small, wooden table in front of him. He thought about Angela and wondered if she was sitting by the phone at home, waiting for his call. He was supposed to phone at seven. He figured she probably was, and he should at least call her. He wondered what he would say. Should he tell her all about Caroline? Maybe he should tell Caroline all about Angela? Somehow, though, that didn't seem like the smartest of ideas.

He trudged wearily up the stairs to his room and found the shirt he wore last night on the back of the chair. Was it only 24 hours since he'd worn it and been in her arms? He slipped his fingers into the top pocket to where the phone number was.

He pulled out the beer mat. It was soaking. He frantically flipped it over to read the number. Staring down at it, he saw that the ink was smudged. Now, there was nothing but a black splodge where she'd written the number down. All he could remember was that Angela's number was a 051-42-something number, which left him in a position similar to that of Captain Hook, namely, five digits short. He lifted his head, looked skywards, and let out a long sigh. 'Well, don't you just work in mysterious ways?' he said aloud before slumping back on his bed and lying there silently for the next hour.

A little later, he walked to Caroline's just as she'd planned. She met him at the door dressed in the usual tight-fitting skirt and even tighter top. As she let him in, she couldn't help but be a little disappointed at the lack of response to her earlier efforts, as it was clear his mind was elsewhere. He seemed to be so distant, like a walking ghost. 'Is everything all right, Brian?' she asked, taking his coat from him and hooking it over the coat hook. Pele stood quietly before her; his dark eyes seemed momentarily to expose his very soul.

'I'm fine, Caroline,' he mumbled. 'I'm just a little nervous about meeting your Mum.' Caroline felt relief flood through her body. For a moment there, she was sure he was going to…but she decided it was best not to think about that. She leant forward on her tiptoes and kissed him on the cheek, which wasn't bruised.

'Don't worry,' she said, looking intently into his eyes. 'She's going to love you. Just like I do.' She saw a small smile emerge at the corner of his mouth. Satisfied, she took his hand and led him into the living room. If she hadn't been so excited about everything, she might have noticed that it wasn't a smile of happiness but one of resignation.

1987

*The Great Storm; Fatal Attraction; The Joshua Tree
Talking Alf; Smiley faces; Never Gonna Give
You Up; Strangeways Here We Come.*

Pele was late. He dragged a wooden kitchen chair from under the table and sat down to eat a bowl of Weetabix. His mum's uninvited voice snuck into his head, 'Always behind Brian, like the cow's tail.' He wondered, and not for the first time if his internal clock would ever regulate itself. The central heating began to rumble. It sounded like a second-hand boiler installed by Del Boy and Rodney. He cast his eyes over the small kitchen; the bright electric strip light only seemed to magnify its shortcomings. He was slurping loudly on his tea when Caroline strode through the kitchen door in search of something or other. 'Brian! You're like a four-year-old,' she lightly scolded him whilst scanning the surfaces for something elusive. 'Have you seen my keys? I can't remember where I've put them.' Pele smiled to himself. He was always late, and she was always losing things. He thought for a moment.

'On the living room table, under the mags,' he replied.

'Oh, great. Thanks, love.' Caroline did an about-turn and exited the kitchen as quickly as she'd entered. He could hear her chuntering under her breath and fumbling around in the living room. A quick look at his watch confirmed that he was going to be very late if he didn't get a move on. He took his bowl over to the sink as Caroline reappeared, 'I'm off now, Brian.'

'Okay then. See you tonight,' Pele replied, offering his cheek where she planted a brief kiss.

'*Brian.*' Even after all this time, she still insisted on calling him Brian. 'We're adults, Brian, and I'm going to call you by an adult name. Not a childish nickname that your mates called you when you were ten years old.'

Pele's mum had predicted that Caroline would be good for him, and it had turned out she was right about that, too. Whilst working for Cousins, she'd had several promotions and was now an area manager. As she'd advanced in her own career, she began to badger Pele to leave his safe office job and go back into education to get a degree. 'You need to make the most of yourself, Brian, because you're too clever to be wasting your life in an office. You should be using your brains to teach.'

Pele finally took a leap of faith and went to night school before taking an even bigger leap of faith, leaving his job to attend Liverpool University. Caroline's increased salary, an ever-diminishing grant, and a series of crap summer jobs enabled them to survive, if not thrive, financially. Her determination and his hard work paid off a year ago when he was taken on as an English teacher at a local comprehensive high school.

As Pele heard Caroline's car starting up, he thought about how it was almost a certainty that she'd be working late this evening. She was late most evenings. Pele lived a somewhat solitary existence during the week, but all things considered, they had a lot to be thankful for. He didn't know many people from his estate who had escaped the inevitability of their fate, but somehow, he and Caroline had done it.

So, things were good.

But...

But...he couldn't shake the feeling that something was missing. It was like an itch that he couldn't scratch. No matter how much he analysed his life or his relationship with Caroline, he couldn't find a logical explanation for the empty space he felt inside. Inner peace, joy, happiness, whatever you wanted to call it, there was a void that couldn't be filled.

It wasn't as though he was unhappy, and he recognised that he had much to be thankful for. He had a great job, a wonderful partner, their own home, a car, and no debt. It was a long tick list if you thought about it. What more could any man ask for? He didn't know the answer to that particular question, but whatever it was, it nagged away at his head like Pip used to when he wouldn't get up in the morning.

Tired of thinking, he washed the cereal bowl and spoon and went off to work.

When he got home later that evening, he was pleasantly surprised to see Caroline's Vectra was already on the small drive. Opening the front door, he shouted through to the kitchen at the back of the house, 'Hey Caroline. You're home early.' As he did so, he slipped off his coat and walked through to find her sitting at the kitchen table reading the local newspaper.

'Yeah, I am, Brian. Hiya, love,' she said, yawning and rubbing her eyes as he entered. 'The Warrington shop manager cancelled the meeting 'cos she had to collect her kid early from school. So, I beat the rush hour traffic for a change.' He placed his hands on both of her shoulders and bent down to kiss her on the top of her head. She smelled of freshly baked bread. Tilting her head back to look at him, her eyes found his, and they smiled at each other.

'Do you want me to make some dinner?' he asked, giving her shoulders a squeeze before turning to fill the kettle at the sink. She put her head back down to the paper.

'No thanks, Brian. You've had a longer day than me for once. I'll have a cup of tea, though.' Glancing up at him, she asked, 'Why don't I drive out to The Dragon in a bit and get us both a Chinese for a change? It's been ages since we had a take-out.'

'You're spoiling me,' he told her, dropping teabags into two cups. But her head was now so immersed in whatever story she was reading that she ignored his comment. Pele poured hot water into the cups and went to fetch the milk from the fridge. A few moments later, Caroline's eyes peered over the newspaper that she was holding.

'Carol Johnson got married at the weekend,' she stated, with a touch of frost in her voice. When her proclamation failed to elicit any response from Pele, she lowered the paper further and continued. 'Do you remember Carol from our year? Tall, sporty girl? Everyone called her Big Jonno 'cos she liked wrestling with some of the lads in the sports field after school?' Pele nearly spat his tea out. He very much did recall 'Big Jonno,' having wrestled with her himself in the aforementioned field many years ago. He'd surrendered quite quickly to her advances from what he could remember, something that he was not about to divulge to Caroline, especially as he recognised that this conversation was inevitably heading into the dreaded 'how come we're not married yet' territory.

'Vaguely,' Pele replied as nonchalantly as he could muster. 'Who'd she marry? Anyone we know?' Caroline made a big deal of closing the newspaper as if it had personally offended her. She tossed it across the table with a scowl to reinforce her objection. The tone of her voice when she replied was in perfect harmony with the pout on her face.

'No, no one we know. Some lad she met from Manchester. Wonder how long they were together before he proposed to her?' Her eyes were fixed on his. Pele grimaced. They'd trodden this well-worn path more than a few times over the years, and it appeared they were going to have another wander down it yet again. He put the two cups of tea on the table and sat opposite.

'Caroline. Why is this such a big thing?'

'Why's what such a big thing?' Caroline echoed disingenuously.

'Stop it,' he said tersely. 'You know exactly what I'm talking about, Caroline. Marriage.' Pele could feel the exasperation rising in his chest, and he tried to quell it. 'Honestly...I really don't understand Caroline. I just don't get it.' Pele knew that Caroline had been exhausted lately from the long hours and late nights, so he was not totally surprised when her pent-up frustration caused an uncharacteristic outburst.

'Oh, I can see that, Brian! And it's patently clear that *you* don't get it. Because if *you* did get it, then maybe, just maybe, I'd have a ring on my finger.' She waved the back of her hand at him, demonstrating her ringless finger. 'And then, maybe, just maybe, I could stop my mum and your mum asking me when we're getting married all the time.' Her voice had escalated past the pitch it usually did whenever this topic of conversation cropped up. Despite knowing Caroline was tetchier than she would usually be, Pele still found the whole thing grated. This time, he made no attempt to control his temper.

'Well,' he barked back, 'it's got absolutely nothing to do with my mother or yours, Caroline. Whenever we get married, or even *if* we get married, it will be our decision and ours alone.' He regretted saying this instantly. He knew what Caroline's response was going to be before she spoke. This was, after all, a road well-travelled.

'Oh, it's '*if*' now, is it, Brian? IF!!' she spat at him. 'Is that what our relationship comes down to? You still won't commit to me after everything we've done together?' She sniffed loudly, and her mouth began to quiver at the corner. As her eyes began to water, Pele's resolve melted. He hated to see her cry. He realised that he would have to backtrack a little and give her a peace offering. However, it wouldn't be the one that solved anything because that could only come from an actual proposal. He just needed something to put it off until another day, something to put things right for a little while so he could get some breathing space.

In other words, more words.

'How can you say I'm not committed to you, Caroline?' he asked in a conciliatory tone. 'I've lived with you for the last eight years. I never go anywhere. When I'm not at work, I'm with you. I spend virtually all of my free time with you. We're saving for a new house. Isn't that a commitment? I just don't understand why you think a ring would make any difference. How many lads do you know from around here who got married and aren't half as committed to their wives as I am to you? We're together, aren't we? I don't know why that's not enough.' He realised that it was all a variation of words he'd spoken before. Caroline wouldn't ever be happy until he finished with words and started with some action. It was just…

'And I'm soooo very grateful for your commitment, Brian,' she said sarcastically. But by now, she was spent and seemed as tired with it all as he was. 'I'm going out to clear my head and to get us some dinner,' she said wearily and got up from the table. She reached over to the hook on the wall near the fridge and pulled off her car key. Pele stood up, put his hands on her waist and spun her around to face him.

'We've both got a lot going on with our jobs right now, Caroline, especially you, with the long hours you're working. Let's give it, give me a bit of time. Caroline, please look at me?' She looked up, and he could see that her face had already softened. Her tired eyes were searching his. She reached up with both of her hands and cradled his head.

'Promise?' she implored.

'I promise we will seriously revisit this once we've bought a new house and I've got my feet under the table at work,' he assured her. 'We've both got enough to think about with our jobs and saving for a new place to live. Let's get that out of the way, and then we can really think about it.'

Her arms circled his waist as he held her chin and kissed her on the mouth. Her lips pressed back, which was a good sign. Historically, this particular 'discussion' had led to painful exchanges that would take days for them to recover from. All in all, this was a much better outcome than he could have hoped for. He'd made a promise of future commitment, which was further than he'd gone on previous occasions. Would he regret his promise when time eventually caught up with him? He couldn't be sure if all he was doing was putting off the inevitable.

The next morning, everything seemed, on the surface at least, to be back to normal. Caroline had left, but not before giving him instructions as she unlocked the front door with one hand and hooked a bag over her shoulder with the other. 'Will you pick up a pizza for later? I'm probably going to be late, but I'll phone if I am. And Brian, please don't go to the pub with Newtog!'

'He's gone to visit his mother. So don't worry, and don't drive too fast.'

But Pele's reply was addressed to an empty room and the sound of a door slamming shut.

It was 4:00 pm, and Pele was driving towards Sainsbury's in the retail park. Once inside the superstore, he took the shortest route to the fridges to track down Caroline's favourite pizza: spicy pepperoni on a thin and crispy base. The only other thing on the list was a couple of bottles of wine, and then he could go home. He was standing aimlessly in the checkout queue, observing the overly make-upped, gum-chewing girl at the till. She was fiddling with the till roll and doing it with all the enthusiasm of someone walking to the gallows. A task that was seemingly beyond her skill set. So, she pressed the call buzzer without offering any explanation to the queue of people. Pele noticed a faint smell of Paco Rabanne coming from the guy who was standing in front of him. His jacket and shirt sleeves were rolled up, and his arms were tanned in the style prevalent amongst the new 'yuppies.' He looked at Pele and gave him the depressed smile of a man who had also been cajoled to go to the supermarket by his other half. Pele smiled amicably back. They both looked into each other's baskets and laughed. The guy had eight cans of Stella, a bottle of red, and a thin and crispy Margherita. Pele glanced around to see if it might be quicker to move to another checkout, as there seemed to be a shortage of supervisors.

And then he saw her.

She was standing side-on, emptying the contents of her basket onto the conveyor, whilst chatting animatedly with the checkout lady only four tills away from where he stood. It had been eight years since he'd last seen her at the nightclub. She was wearing very little makeup, dressed in a pair of acid-wash, slim-fit jeans and an unzipped, brown leather aviator jacket that was worn over a cream, knitted sweater.

He didn't know how long he'd been staring at her, but the girl at the checkout was suddenly all-systems-go. The Paco Rabanne guy in front of him picked up his carrier bags loaded with beer and pizza and made towards the exit. Pele continued to stare while Angela packed her shopping, blissfully unaware that he was ten yards behind her. The unenthusiastic gum chewer serving Pele beeped his items through and said in a bored voice to the back of his head, 'Nine pounds fifty, please.' Groans emanated from the people in the queue behind him as Pele slapped at his suit pockets for his wallet, and someone irritably whispered the supermarket mantra, 'I always pick the wrong queue.' He pulled out a ten-pound note and scooped up his bag.

'Thanks,' he mumbled as he pocketed the change. He could feel his heart thumping wildly in his chest as he started walking towards Angela. She was putting her card and till receipt into her inside jacket pocket. As she looked up, she did a double take.

'Pele?' she exclaimed. 'Pele Smith? Is that really you!'

'Hey Angela! How are you? Long time no see,' he said in a voice he didn't recognise as his own. They stood and looked at each other for a second, and then Angela's shocked countenance was replaced by a wide grin.

'What are you-'

'It's been-' They both spoke over each other and laughed.

Angela finally said, 'I can't believe it's you! I hate to say this again, but you never called me!'

He pulled a face as he told her, 'Yeah, I know. I'm really sorry. And if I told you what happened, you wouldn't believe me anyway.'

'Oh? You should try me,' she replied with a wide grin and one hand on her hip. He glanced at his watch.

'Well, actually. Erm... Do you have time for a quick coffee or a drink somewhere quieter? It would be so good to catch up with you. Only if you have time?' She surveyed the crowds in the store and nodded her head in agreement.

'Yeah, okay,' she agreed, checking her watch as she did. 'I've only got an hour, but that would be great.'

Ten minutes later, Pele was driving into the car park of the

Jolly Roger, which was down towards the river. He couldn't help but feel an element of shame, having suggested a pub where he felt it was unlikely that anyone would recognise him. He sat uneasily in the car, waiting for Angela to arrive in hers. His eyes scanned the dark car park to confirm there wasn't anyone around that he might know.

Now that he'd arrived, he didn't know what he was doing there. Common sense told him he ought to be heading home by now, but common sense had been drowned out by the louder voice of longing. He looked at the time on the dashboard. It was five o'clock. Caroline wouldn't be home until at least seven, but she would have phoned and left a message. The fact he hadn't answered would make her think that he'd ignored her previous instructions and had gone for a drink with Newtog.

He decided that whilst he'd never lied to Caroline about his whereabouts in the past, he'd have to tell her that's where he'd been when she got home. After all, she was bound to ask, and he would simply have to lie. He jumped at the sound of tapping on his window. It was Angela. Her long, dark hair whipped furiously around her face in the wind. He immediately pulled the key out of the ignition and turned off the voice of another angry listener on Radio 4. He seemed to be holding Michael Fish personally responsible for the hurricane last week that had killed eighteen people. Pele stepped out of the car into gales that nearly took his breath away, and together, they ran towards the pub entrance.

Once inside, Pele ordered drinks at the bar. They sat down facing each other in an empty booth. Angela pushed her fingertips like a comb through her windblown hair. She took a sip of Appletise and placed the glass back on the table. Her cheeks were ever-so-slightly flushed, and her eyes glinted back at him. Pele discreetly looked at her ring finger, and there were no signs of any significant commitment. Given his own relationship status, he wasn't sure why he was checking. But just sitting in proximity to Angela was scrambling his brains to the point that caution wasn't exactly being thrown to the wind.

It was more like being hurled at great velocity into the teeth of a hurricane. He took a sip of lager and smiled at her. Pele wondered if she had any idea of the inner turmoil her presence stirred in him. 'So, go on then,' she prompted eagerly, putting her elbows on the table and leaning in towards him. 'What's your excuse this time?'

'This time?'

'For not calling?' she pressed. As she leant forward, a subtle, light, musk scent filled his nostrils. Her face was uncomfortably too close for comfort, so he leant back against his seat.

'Ahhh... Well, I'm not sure that I shouldn't take the fifth. You're not going to believe me...' he laughed as she began to make slow circular motions with her hand, signalling for him to get on with it. 'Yeah, okay,' he said, smiling in defeat. He began to recall the events of that fateful night to his increasingly sceptical audience of one. '...And then when I went to get the phone number out of my shirt the next day...' He ended with a sigh, 'Well, it had gotten soaked and wasn't legible. All I could make out was 051-42 something.' Her raised eyebrows told him all he needed to know, but she pressed her lips together in case he was in any doubt.

'You were right about that. You should have taken the fifth.'

'I know how implausible it all sounds,' he shrugged. 'If it hadn't happened to me, I probably wouldn't believe it either.' Pushing his hand through his hair, he suddenly remembered something. 'You know... I even went to your cousin's house to try and get your number -'

'But they'd moved?' she interjected.

'Yes! So, do you believe me now?' he grinned triumphantly.

'Hmmmm! I suppose I could give you the benefit of the doubt,' she replied while squinting at him through narrowed eyes. Pele wondered if she did or if she was just saying she did. Either way, he decided that changing the subject was a good idea.

'So, how's your sister? Karen, right? How's she doing?'

'Oh, she's doing great, actually,' replied Angela. 'She did some voluntary work with Oxfam for years, and now she's on their payroll.'

'Hey, that's great. I'm really pleased to hear that,' he replied, genuinely happy for Karen.

'Yeah, it took a while for her to find her feet. But, well, Dad was so overprotective, you know? To the point that he almost crushed her. She wasn't quite as headstrong as I was,' she chortled mischievously.

'Yeah, I do seem to recall you being a bit of a force of nature,' he replied wryly. Her eyes locked onto his, hinting at something he couldn't decipher.

'I still am,' she said with an exaggerated wink. A little flummoxed, Pele switched to safe ground.

'Where are you working these days?'

'Oh, gosh. I keep forgetting. It's been such a long time since we last saw each other.' She slipped off her jacket and tossed it onto the seat next to her. The cream jumper she was wearing was cropped and tight-fitting, revealing a slim waist. Her long legs brushed against his as she moved them underneath the table. The contact sent a fresh flood of desire to surge through his veins. 'Well, I'm a freelance designer. I've got a couple of projects with an up-and-coming brand. It keeps me busy, probably too busy, in all honesty,' she said, stirring the ice slowly in her glass with a plastic straw. She watched him as he nodded with understanding. Pele knew all too well how difficult a work/life balance was with a demanding job, and he was trying hard to focus on what she was saying rather than the effect she was having on him. 'It's so great to see you again, Pele,' she smiled. 'What have you been up to since we last met? Are you still playing table tennis badly?'

'If I played badly, it was only because you kept cheating,' he replied. His leg touched hers again accidentally under the table. She tipped her head back and laughed, but the undercurrent between them was growing. She lightly bit her lip and stared into his eyes. Pele felt as though she was looking into the very depths of his soul, a part of him that no one had ever looked into before. He felt utterly powerless under her gaze.

Later on, when he thought back to what took place, he didn't know if it was the barely concealed desire in her eyes that tipped him over or if he just couldn't wait any longer to find out, but he suddenly blurted, 'So, are you seeing anyone at the moment?'

'Erm… No, actually.' She looked away briefly as if gathering her thoughts. 'Not anyone for a few months anyway. I've seen a few people on and off over the years,' she stalled, and her eyes scanned the air above him as she searched for the words. Fixing her gaze on his face, she carried on, 'I suppose what it comes down to is that I don't have the time or the energy to work at relationships.' She opened her hands palm up to indicate it was all a bit pointless. 'I mean, they're not easy, right?' she said, raising her eyebrows. Pele felt a strange sense of relief flood through him. 'Not that I'm complaining. It's just a matter of timing, and I'll meet the right guy. I'm just not in any hurry.' She cupped her chin in a delicate hand and looked back at him with enquiring eyes. The ghost of a smile played on her lips as she asked Pele softly, 'And what about you?' He said the first thing that came into his head.

'Well…erm… It's complicated.'

'Oh?' she replied softly, her eyes narrowing for the second time that night. The first light of understanding began to dawn on her. She leant back against her seat, removing any proximity of her legs to his, and tilted her head slightly to one side. With a wry smile, she said, 'Whenever a guy says that to a girl, it usually means they're in a relationship?' She searched his face, looking for some signs that would either deny or confirm her statement, but none were immediately forthcoming. She said, 'Not that it's really any of my business, Pele, but you began this line of conversation.' She folded her arms. 'And you've been flirting with me, so I'm kinda getting mixed signals?'

'Well, I'm not married,' he began somewhat defensively. He swallowed, and her blue eyes held his. 'But yeah. I'm living with somebody…' Her face registered a flicker of disappointment, and her smile stiffened. She had the look of someone who'd just been to the dentist and had a mouthful of novocaine injections. To make matters worse, her already folded arms seemed to tighten closer to her chest defensively, and they were now joined by folded legs. There was also something else that seemed to flash in her eyes at his answer. He might have recognised that flash as a stop warning sign, but instead, he bumbled on. 'Look. This, well…This is all coming out all wrong.'

'Is it?' she asked, her eyebrows raised. 'It sounds to me like it's all coming out just fine.' Pele was acutely aware that the conversation was spiralling down into depths where he wouldn't be able to swim. But he couldn't pull it back. He didn't know how to pull it back. It was all going wrong because, well, it was wrong. He shouldn't be here, and neither should Angela, but he'd not been able to stop himself. Feeling hopeless and on the back foot, what came out next would be replayed on a loop in his head for weeks to come.

'Is it just me? Don't you feel like the universe has conspired against us since we were kids? I mean, is it such a bad thing to wish it could be our time now?' he asked, fixing his eyes onto hers. If Angela seemed somewhat surprised by this impromptu outburst, she didn't show it. She sat quiet, still, and pan-faced as he continued. 'Full disclosure? I've been in a relationship for the last eight years. And what makes it all worse is that she's a great person. She encouraged me to pursue my education. I wouldn't be where I am if it wasn't for Caroline. I've never been unfaithful, but the thing is, I've never really loved her in the way that she deserves. There's a limit to what I can give her because I'm not *in love* with her. The truth is: I'm in love with you. I always have been.' He stopped and looked at her face, trying to gauge her reaction. His heart was thumping in his chest, and he felt like the rest of his life was about to turn on the following sentence that came out of her mouth.

Angela didn't stir. She had been sitting quietly, observing him and biting her lower lip as she listened. He watched nervously as she slowly unfolded her arms and extended them out in front of her on the table. She laced her fingers together as if she was about to read the evening news on BBC1, and in a firm tone, one he recognised quite well being a teacher, she began calmly, 'Pele, I'm not sure how you think I should respond to what you've just told me? I mean, whatever decisions you need to make for your future are yours to make. And frankly, I'm a bit confused about our little 'catch-up' and what you hoped would come from it. From what you've just told me about your partner, she sounds like a really nice person. One who deserves everything that you can give her and, dare I say, more.'

'I-' She shook her head at him to let him know she hadn't finished.

'I won't be an excuse for any future decisions that you decide to take.'

'But-' She raised her hand to him.

'Look, there could never be a right time for us while you're in a relationship, and the very last thing I'd ever want you to do is end yours because of me. Do you really think I could be with you knowing that I was responsible for ruining someone else's happiness? You really don't know anything about me if you think I could.' Pele kept his head down.

'I get it,' he told her. 'I was just laying my cards on the table. I think it was your dad who said we can only play with the hand that we're dealt?' He hoped that might raise a smile from her, but she didn't respond. So, he dug his hole a little deeper. 'I was simply explaining that she's a great person, and, in many ways, she's been really good for me. For one thing, I'm doing a job that I love because of her. But what I never said, and I hope this makes some sense, is that she pursued me to the point where I never felt I was given any real option. She somehow pulled me into a relationship that I always knew wasn't the one I really wanted.' Angela's eyes flashed at this. Her mouth opened slightly as though she wanted to say something, but the words were stuck in her throat. When she forced them out, they weren't words that Pele wanted to hear.

'Did you really just say all of that?' she spluttered. 'Because you honestly managed to sound like you're some kind of a victim.

For heaven's sake, Pele! You never felt like you had an option? She pulled you into it. How old are you, ten!?!' Pele felt the full force of her attack. It hit him hard, so he immediately hit back.

'Of course, I'm not saying I'm a victim! And I'm certainly not trying to portray myself as one. You're twisting my words there, Angela.'

'Am I? Well, I know what you said, and I know what I heard. Of course, it would have to be me that's 'twisting' your words. It seems to me you need to do a bit of growing up, Pele, and work out what you want to do with the rest of your life and who you want to do it with. For your partner's sake as much as anyone's.' Pele felt angry and confused. He'd never considered himself a victim. He'd only been trying to explain how he'd found himself in his relationship. It wasn't loveless, but in his heart, it wasn't where he wanted to be either. How could she have not understood that?

'That's a bit below the belt,' Pele gasped. 'I'd hoped-'

'Hoped for what? That I'd tell you that I loved you too and that I was sorry you were in a relationship that isn't perfect? But as you don't love her, and you do love me, then we can be together and live happily ever after. Was that the scenario you had in mind?' Angela stared at him steely-eyed again. 'I think it's time I went, Pele, but I'll tell you something before I go. Every date I've been on since I saw you at the club has never felt right. Everyone who asked me out, wined, and dined me got as far as a second date and occasionally another one after that. Every single one: well, they weren't you,' her voice sounded gravelly. 'Maybe the universe has conspired against us, but we make our own choices in life, Pele, with what we're given, and you've made yours. This childhood, teenage thing, whatever it is, whatever it was, it just isn't meant to be. All that's left is for us to move on now. And I strongly advise that you think carefully about what it is you want in life.'

Pele knew that he didn't have anything left to say that wouldn't make things worse, if that were even possible. He watched dejectedly as she stood and pulled up the zip of her coat.

He could see her eyes were glassy, but she wasn't going to let him see she was upset. Instead, she pressed her lips together, turned away with a brief, 'Goodbye, Pele,' and headed out into the dark stormy night.

When Pele got home at 6:30 pm, the house was completely dark, and Caroline's car wasn't on the drive. Juggling a bunch of keys to locate the front door lock wasn't easy whilst holding a grocery bag and his briefcase in the storm. He thrust the key in the lock and rammed his shoulder so hard against the door that it made the wine bottles bang together in the carrier bag. He hoped they weren't broken. There was no way he was driving back out in that weather to buy more. Once inside, he saw the answering machine glowing ominously in the dark. He closed the door behind him with his foot, dropped his briefcase onto the floor, and walked over to the phone, where he pressed the play button. Caroline's was the only message: 'Come on Brian, pick up.... Hmmm! I guess you decided to go for a pint with Newtog after all. I'll be in around eight. Just got to pop into the Widnes shop on the way back. Hope you didn't forget the Pizza...Love you.'

When he heard Caroline's key turn in the door at ten past eight, he put his empty Stella can on a mat and went into the hall where she was attempting to pull her wet coat off. She turned towards him as he approached. 'Oh! Hiya, love. You okay? What a night. I could barely see the road, and the police had a detour on the dual carriageway because a tree was on the road. I thought I was never getting home.' She was slightly breathless and looked exhausted from the long working days she'd been putting in.

'Well, you're home now,' he replied, stepping over the shoes she'd kicked off and holding her coat so that she could pull her arms through more easily. He secured it on the coat hook while she attempted to kiss him enthusiastically on the lips. He pointed towards the front room, which had the gas fire on full blast. 'Right, go and sit down. The fire's on, and Dirty Dancing is in the video, ready to play. I'll go and put the Pizza in the oven and get you a glass of wine.'

'Oh, Brian, you're so masterful,' she giggled. 'Dirty Dancing? You hate that film!' Suspicion crept into her voice, 'What've you done wrong?'

'Nothing,' he protested, his face flushing slightly.

'Oh yes, you have,' she replied. 'Going for a pint with Newtog when I distinctly asked you not to.' Then she winked, but he could only return a half-hearted smile. She made her way into the front room whilst Pele busied himself with the task of removing plastic wrapping from the pizza and pouring her a large glass of wine. He contemplated whether lying by omission was as bad as lying to someone's face. He didn't know, but he wasn't ready to ruin Caroline's life just yet by unloading his guilt on her. It was better to go down the path of omission for now.

Forty minutes later, the crusty remains of the pizza and two half glasses of wine were left on the coffee table. On the screen in front of them, Baby and Johnny were swaying provocatively in each other's arms. Caroline was leaning back with her head on Pele's shoulder. Pele's own head, however, was not in the Catskill Mountains but somewhere altogether less pleasant.

It occurred to him that Angela's harsh words weren't completely without merit. His relationship with Caroline was founded on a lie. And what was worse was that it was a lie of his own making. He'd somehow fallen into their relationship because going with the Caroline flow was so very easy. Living with someone who was the equivalent of a human dynamo for most of the time meant he didn't have to think about anything. She'd taken the reins mainly because he didn't want to. Only now, he was beginning to understand that his passivity had meant he'd short-changed them both.

He had no idea after all this time how to put things right. Caroline would be devastated if he told her that he thought they should end things. But this was warring with the guilt that he didn't love her in the way that she deserved to be loved. Caroline, who seemed oblivious to his inner turmoil, took a sip of wine from her glass, put it back on the table, and asked, 'Are you okay, love? You seem distracted by something.'

'No! No, I'm fine, honestly,' Pele lied. 'I'm just really tired and a bit under the weather. It's been a tough day.' He yawned on cue. 'And I've seen this hundreds of times. I think I know it word for word.' He planted a small kiss on the top of her head to reassure her that there was really nothing to worry about. Caroline lightly bit the corner of her mouth and studied his face. Unable to discern anything tangible in his expression, she started to turn back around towards the video.

Then, lifting her head to look him straight in the eyes, she said, 'It's just that… well… if there was anything the matter, you would talk to me about it, wouldn't you?'

'Of course, I would,' he said. Seemingly satisfied with his answer, she put her head back on his shoulder to watch the rest of the film. Pele looked through the window at the impenetrable darkness that now seemed, somehow, lighter than his mood.

When the video had finished, a tipsy Caroline had smiled a mischievous grin at Pele and promptly went up the stairs to the bedroom. Meanwhile, Pele went about the business of turning off the TV and locking up the house before clearing away the pizza leftovers and wine glasses.

After brushing his teeth, he entered the bedroom, undoing his belt and looking forward to the oblivion of sleep. Exhausted by the day's events, he needed a temporary reprieve from the battle in his head. When he entered, he was bemused to find a very tipsy Caroline lying on top of the bed, wearing only lingerie. Ordinarily, in such regalia, Pele wouldn't have hesitated, but not tonight. Tonight, he'd made a poor excuse, 'I really do feel a bit peaky, love. I'm not sure I'm up to it.' Then he wearily dropped onto his side of the bed, where he proceeded to pull his socks off with his back to her. But Caroline, confident of her ability to arouse Pele despite his 'peakiness,' spent the next few minutes attempting to seduce him by playing all the little tricks that would ordinarily have him doing anything she wanted. Eventually, with a sigh, Caroline gave up trying to cajole him. Exhaustion took over, and she fell into a deep sleep. She was disappointed but understanding, just as she always was. Pele simply lay there with a thumping headache and hating himself. Was it the lingering infatuation he carried for someone else? Or was he just incapable of loving Caroline with the same passion? He couldn't fathom it all out for the life of him.

The way he saw things, he was left with Hobson's choice. There was a nice irony in all this as his year 9s were currently working through this very same text in his lessons. When he broke all this turmoil down into its basic parts, he had two options:

He could leave a wonderful girl who was devoted to him, or he could stay with her and almost feel like he was leading someone else's life.

Just acknowledging those facts put him on a guilt trip to Mars and back. But maybe it would hurt her more in the long run if he stayed. One day, she might come to realise that the man she lived with was, to some extent, going through the motions. If he did leave her now, she would at least have the opportunity to meet someone else while she was still young.

Faced with the impossibility of his own 'Hobson's Choice,' it was four o'clock before he fell into a somewhat fitful sleep.

Pele usually slept in on Saturday mornings, while Caroline rose early to make the most of the day's shopping. She loved window shopping, which, to Pele's mind, had to be one of the surest signs of insanity that there was. This morning was no exception, and Caroline, in a surprisingly good mood, had left an hour ago. Pele was lying in bed, but he wasn't sleeping. The events of the previous night still occupied his mind to the point that he now felt completely dysfunctional.

When he'd woken up, it had been ten o'clock, but despite the time, he was still exhausted. The seconds ticked by and morphed into hours. When he next looked at his watch, he was staggered to find that he'd fallen asleep again, and it was almost midday. Pele realised that as much as he wanted to hide from reality, lying in bed was not going to solve anything.

He forced himself into the shower and got dressed. Although he wasn't very hungry, he had a late breakfast of bacon, eggs, and a huge dollop of HP sauce, accompanied by a pot of strong tea. Then, he sat down with some reluctance to work on his novel.

Pele was attempting to write a historical thriller set in Tudor Britain. So far, he'd managed about twelve thousand words on the typewriter, which he kept in the sideboard cupboard. In Caroline's view, this practically rendered him on a par with Ernest Hemingway. She regularly enquired as to how many words he'd done in total, how the plot was going, when it might be finished, etc. He supposed her fascination stemmed from the fact that she believed it was something beyond her ability. Pele had tried to convince her that running five shops was something he couldn't do in ten lifetimes and that he wasn't sure he would finish the novel anyway. 'Oh, never mind that, Brian,' she'd say, dismissing his pessimism with a wave of her hand. 'You have a chance to do something amazing! Imagine someone from our estate actually writing a real book.'

Today, though, he sat down to writer's block. While his personal life entered a period of turmoil, which he felt more than matched that of the French Revolution, turmoil being something writers were supposed to thrive on, he was capable of writing nada, zilch, and the big fat nothing.

After an hour of staring at the typewriter, managing two sentences, and making three more cups of tea, the phone rang and thankfully broke his concentration. It was Caroline who told him that her purse had been stolen at the market. 'How much?' he asked, with a sinking feeling in his stomach.

'A hundred.'

'A hundred!' he gasped, offloading some of the blame for how he was feeling onto her. 'For God's sake, Caroline!' He knew it was inexcusable, even as it tripped out of his mouth. After all, in the last few years when he'd been at university, she'd earned nearly all the money.

'What the hell, Brian!' she shouted back incredulously. 'I

didn't do it on purpose.'

'I'm sorry Caroline…' he said to a dead phone.

About half an hour later, he'd given up any idea that he would be able to write anything and was sat in front of the TV, attempting but failing to watch the sport. The front doorbell chimed, which only made him groan. To his mind, the day was already going badly, and in his experience, things only went downhill once they got started.

When he opened the door, he was half expecting to find a couple of Mormons or a double-glazing salesman. Instead, a slightly dishevelled John O'Leary was standing there as large as life. It had been six months since they'd last gone out, and in this short time, his friend had gained a little weight. The skin on his unshaven face was blotchy red and purple with tiny spider veins across his cheeks. The whites of his eyes had an unhealthy yellow tinge to them, and his previously immaculate hair had become dishevelled with more than a few grey specks. Pele was shocked and a little taken aback by how quickly his appearance had deteriorated since he'd last seen him. But it was the crumpled suit that gave Pele real cause for concern. What had happened to that impeccable dress sense?

Shocked by John's unexpected arrival and demeanour, Pele stood a little flummoxed at the door. It was John who spoke first, 'Aren't you going to invite me in then, Pele lad?'

'Of course, John. Sorry. Come in,' Pele said, beckoning him in and pointing towards the living room. 'To what do I owe the honour?' John just gave him a pat on the shoulder as he passed by and shuffled down the hall towards the living room without replying. Pele followed uneasily behind, and they both stood awkwardly face-to-face in the middle of the room. 'Can I get you a cup of tea or anything?' he asked, breaking a somewhat uncomfortable silence.

John looked around nervously and coughed, 'Err… no thanks, Pele. Is Caroline in?'

'No,' Pele replied, wondering what was wrong. 'She's out shopping and probably won't be back for half an hour or so.

What's up, mate?'

John seemed pleased at hearing this and appeared to relax a little. He lowered himself onto a sofa using the arm to steady his descent. 'Sorry for turning up unannounced Pele. It's just that I don't really have anyone else I can go to.' Then he leant forward and buried his head in his hands, breathing in what sounded like a muffled cry. When he lifted it again, the stubble on his face rasped against his palms like sandpaper. 'I'll get straight to the point. Janey's left me. She's moved out and gone to her sisters.' He shook his head momentarily, which was followed by a short sniff. 'This time, I'm pretty sure it's final.'

'Oh no, John. That's bad,' Pele exclaimed, getting up. 'I'll go and get a couple of cans, shall I?'

'No, honestly, no. I'm okay.' John waved his hand up and down to indicate he wanted Pele to sit back down. 'Look, I've come to ask a favour.' Pele got a sinking feeling in the pit of his stomach. He had an idea as to what the favour was going to entail, and it fitted neatly with its own beautiful irony into the day he was having so far.

'Oh? Ok. What can I do?' Pele asked evenly. John looked at him with watery-yellow rabbit eyes and then lowered them to stare at his hands that were resting on both knees. The delay was a sure sign of what was coming. He wriggled about in the chair.

'See, last night I went out with our Davey. It was only going to be for a couple of pints, but we bumped into a group of girls from work. Do you remember Mandy?' Pele vaguely recalled a blonde girl in her thirties who wore very short skirts and encouraged male attention of any age between twenty and fifty-five. He nodded while John continued. 'Well, anyway, she was there, and I ended up going back to hers, only for a drink, mind, and then I fell asleep on the sofa. Nothing happened! It's just, well, when I got back home this morning, Janey was livid. She was angrier than I'd ever seen her before. She ranted at me, accused me of all kinds of stuff, and said it was the last straw.' He finished with a huge woe-is-me sigh and pushed the flat of his palms along the creased fabric of his trousers like he was attempting to iron out all of his problems with a simple hand movement.

Pele recognised the game. It was one John had played many times. The only difference was that the stakes were at maximum bet this time. Pele would be expected to lie for John to salvage what might be left of John's marriage. Pele felt the beginnings of anger simmer inside. He loved this man but gone was the eager kid who was willing to please, at any cost, to secure that love. He had his own problems and couldn't even lie competently for himself, let alone anybody else. 'No, sorry. I can't, won't, do it, John, this time,' he said quietly. John looked up with utter surprise, sketched across his face.

'Look, this really is the last time, mate. I can't tell you how much I've learnt my lesson. Even though I haven't done anything wrong, I know I should have just gone home. Please? Just give her a call. She's at her sister's. Here's the number.' He fumbled around in his pockets and pulled out a small black book with telephone numbers in it. He hastily thumbed through it until he reached the page he wanted and then held it out to Pele with an outstretched, trembling hand. 'Just tell her I was here with you all night.'

'No. I've said I can't do it,' Pele reiterated in a firm, steady voice. John looked distraught, like a man who'd bet everything he owned on red, and the wheel had come up black. Pele was his last chance, and he could see it all slipping away.

'Listen, Pele. I don't mean to push this, but you don't seem to understand. I really need you to do this for me! If you don't, she isn't coming back.' John's voice was infused with panic. He was holding both of his arms out to Pele in pleading desperation. Pele's anger escalated like a kettle, from simmer to boil instantly. He didn't often show his temper. In fact, he was generally accused of being too laid back for his own good. But the events of the last twenty-four hours had mentally exhausted him, making him less sympathetic than he might have been. Like lava from a volcano, he erupted, spewing anger and frustration onto an unsuspecting John.

'Don't you dare put that on me! It's on you and no one else.

Do you have any idea what *my* life is like at this minute? Do you have any idea of what *I* might be going through? No! You don't. The only thing that you're interested in is you. I don't even know why you're here because the truth is you don't love Janie. You can't. If you did, you wouldn't have shagged half of the women in this town.' Pele should have stopped there, but he didn't. Instead, he went on way longer than he should. He would regret this outburst in later years, but he didn't know that then. 'And you want me to bail you out for what? The thousandth time? All those chances Janey's given you over the years. And here's me worrying over something I haven't even done yet. I'm sorry, John, but you'd better go before Caroline gets back. The best I can say is that neither Caroline, Janey, nor anyone else will ever hear about this.' John looked bewildered and at least ten years older than his age.

'Yeah, course, Pele. I'm sorry I bothered you with my problems.' It came out as a whisper. He retrieved his small black book from Pele's shaking hand and walked down the hall, closing the front door softly behind him. Pele sank onto the sofa, buried his head in his hands and sobbed. But his tears were not only for John's mess of a life but for his own.

When Caroline came back home, it was 5:30 pm, and Pele was in the kitchen preparing spaghetti Bolognese. He heard the front door shut, and it was closely followed by the sound of light footsteps ascending the stairs. He had little option but to follow her to the bedroom. When he entered, she was lying on her side of the bed in a semi-foetal position, which was ironically reminiscent of his own, only four hours earlier.

She was holding a damp tissue, which she was using to dab at the steady flow of tears under her eyes. His heart sunk that he could have done this to her. Caroline, who always forgave him. Feeling totally disgusted with himself, he sat on the side of the bed and gently brushed damp hair away from her eyes. 'Caroline, love. I'm so sorry. I had no right to talk to you like that. Please don't be upset about it. It's only money.' To Pele's dismay, this only seemed to make the tears flow faster. She was gulping in air, and her mouth contorted as she tried to speak. It came out in jerky, broken sentences.

'I'm sorry… I lost… the money, Brian. I should have been… more careful in the market… There are signs up everywhere warning you about the thieves.'

'Hey, it wasn't your fault, sweetheart,' he said gently, kissing her wet eyes. 'Just forget about it now. Like I said, it's only money. Look, why don't we go down to the Cherry for a drink after we've had dinner?'

'We can't afford it now,' she said, her sobs slowing down. She reached over to the bedside cabinet for another tissue and blew her nose loudly.

'Course we can,' he said, wiping under her eyes with his thumb. 'We can use the pig money.' Pele got the reaction he thought he'd get from suggesting they used the savings. She had her heart set on a semi-detached house near the park, which for her was a 'dream' move.

'No way, Brian. You know what that money's for. It's for our future.'

Pele gave out a small sigh, 'Look, we can put whatever we spend back in on Tuesday when I get paid. And a little extra for good luck.' She looked at him with mascara-streaked eyes and a red nose as he stroked her hair again. He felt terrible that he'd caused her so much pain.

'Promise?' she said.

'Promise,' he whispered.

'Pele,' she asked softly. 'Do you still fancy me?'

'Yeah!' he answered honestly. 'Of course I do.'

'And do you still love me?'

'Yeah, loads.'

And he did love her. He loved her very much. So he hadn't really lied to her. But she hadn't asked: are you *in* love with me?

He guessed there might be a reason for that.

When they got down to the pub, Newtog and his wife, Sheena,

were sitting near the fruit machine. They beckoned at Caroline to come and sit with them. Pele had gone straight to the bar. He caught Newtog's eye and tipped a hand to his mouth. Newtog gave a thumbs-up and pointed to a pint of bitter and to Sheena's usual rum and coke.

While he waited to get served, he looked around to see if John was there. He saw no sign of him and relaxed a little. The last thing he needed right now, with everything swimming through his brain, was another meeting with John. He felt a tap on his shoulder and turned to find Newtog standing behind him. Newtog had filled out dramatically in the last few years. His drinking, which might have been described as 'somewhat excessive' at one time, had now all but dispensed with the 'somewhat.' The burly frame, which he fitted so well in his early twenties, had turned into a huge beer gut. Newtog's face had a permanent ruddy hue to it these days. He still had dimples, bright blue eyes, and the often misleading, easy-going demeanour to those looking for trouble. His brown feather cut had been replaced with a slick back hairstyle. 'I'll take these back to the girls, shall I?' Pele asked, picking up the two rum and cokes and slipping easily enough back through the crowded pub.

Pele glanced over to see Caroline deep in conversation with Sheena and was glad to see she was smiling. He dropped the drinks with the girls, said hello to Sheena, then went back and picked up his own lager, Newtog's pint of bitter, before walking over to the bandit where Newtog was happily ensconced, having put a couple of pound coins into it. Pele took a drink from his pint and then said in a low voice, 'I saw John today.'

'Oh? Where?' replied Newtog, showing little interest in anything except holding his plums.

'He came to the house. He wanted me to cover for him again.'

'And you did, I suppose,' assumed Newtog, as the cascading lights flashed up the £10 win sign, the machine to start chugging out coins into the silver tray below, causing Newtog to bellow a loud, 'Get in!'

'No, actually, I didn't this time,' said Pele, feeling that

attempting to engage in this conversation and hope for a two-way process was, at very best, pointless. Newtog lived up to his role by ignoring this comment for a moment and was now busy sliding the coins out of the tray into his large hands. As usual, once he'd extracted them, they didn't go anywhere near his pocket but straight back into the machine. 'Why don't you keep some of the winnings? They're programmed to make you lose, you know?'

'So, you didn't cover for him?' said Newtog, ignoring the gambling dig.

'No, not this time,' said Pele, swallowing another mouthful of his lager. 'I've had enough of it; besides, I've got my own problems without dealing with everyone else's.'

'He won't have been happy about that,' replied Newtog, who had now begun to slap the machine hard with his palm. 'Such a cheat!'

'Leave it, mate,' said Pele, seeing Caroline and Sheena look anxiously over at him. 'I've told you before you can't do that. You'll get us kicked out.'

'Yeah, sorry,' said Newtog, reaching up for his bitter, chucking it back in one, and nodding down at Pele's glass. 'What do you want?' Pele looked at his, still almost full, glass.

'Just a half, mate.'

'A half, ya big puff. I'm not buying you a half,' he snorted while turning to go in the direction of the bar. Pele realised that the rush to get to the bar was not only to order another drink but also to break a note in order to get some more coins.

'I'll be over with the girls,' said Pele. 'I'm not standing here all night watching you pour hard-earned money into that thing. Newtog shrugged his shoulders and wandered off while Pele went to sit down.

Caroline slid her hand under the table and squeezed his thigh affectionately as he sat down while Sheena continued to tell her about the new tanning salon that had opened in the High Street.

Then Slug MacDonald walked in.

Pele hadn't seen him for a few years. Though his head was

shorn of hair these days, and he wore expensive clothes, he was instantly recognisable. Slug went straight to the bar and started talking to a couple of gorillas. Pele knew from experience that they were likely to be trouble. From where Pele was sitting, Slug had more of a menacing air about him than when they'd had their last encounter. The word was that he spent a lot of time at gyms on the other side of the river, and Pele knew that one or two of those gyms dealt liberally in steroids. As Pele watched him, Slug turned his head and stared directly back. For a moment, their eyes met, and then Slug looked away indifferently and carried on his conversation. Pele scanned the pub to see where Newtog had got to and saw him walking back with a tray of drinks and about to have a head-on collision with MacDonald's group.

Pele sensed the impending threat. Newtog was quick to anger, and although hugely overweight and slower than he was a few years ago, he was more than willing to respond to any trouble that might come his way. But any trouble with the three who'd just entered was not likely to work out in Newtog's favour. If he could pre-empt things, it would be to everyone's advantage.

Leaving Caroline and Sheena obliviously chatting away, he got up and zigzagged in between tables until he reached Newtog. His friend had now stopped in front of the first gorilla. The narrow space necessitated one of them would have to give way if the other was to pass. 'Scuuze, matey,' Pele heard Newtog ask in a less than polite manner.

'Back up, Pal,' the gorilla growled. Then he turned around to ensure that Slug and the other gorilla were directly behind him.

'Or what?' Newtog stood rigid, like a Rottweiler about to attack. He was gripping the sides of the tray as a potential weapon that Pele feared he might use over the gorilla's head if pushing came to shove. Pele was standing on the other side of the confrontation and looking past Newtog's tensed shoulders.

'Or else you'll lose those drinks.' The gorilla's voice was a low rumble and full of menace. Slug had edged forward and pushed himself past the second gorilla.

'Smith,' he said, his eyes narrowing at Pele, 'get your mate out of the way before he hurts himself. There's a good lad.' Pele considered the odds. Three onto two and… Although Newtog might be handy, he'd not be much use against these three. Still, he'd had kickings off Slug in the past and lived to tell the tale.

'Once you and your mates have backed up, we'll be through and on our way,' Pele said in a neutral voice. 'So if you'll just excuse us.' Newtog pressed forward, the edge of the drinks tray touching the first gorilla's chest. The gorilla pressed back, and the drinks began to wobble. A pint of lager spilt some of its contents onto the tray. Pele sensed that Newtog's first move would be for the gorilla and Slug to wear the drinks. He quickly assessed the situation. But far worse than any kicking would be Caroline's lecture on how: 'You can take the boy out of the estate…'

Suddenly, a voice rang out, 'Alright, Big Dan. Don't see you in this neck of the woods often. Come and sit down over here, lad.' Pele recognised the voice instantly. It was John. He must have entered through the car park door. The big gorilla suddenly twisted around to see John pulling a table out of the way and clearing a path.

'Alright, John boy,' the gorilla beamed. Then, directing a hard 'this-isn't-over glare' at Newtog, he turned towards John, who thankfully, once again, was playing his best local football celebrity card to great effect. The absence of Big Dan left a space for Pele and Newtog to push through the gap between the tables. Pele saw the opportunity and pushed a reluctant Newtog in the back and over towards the relative safety of the girls. As they passed Slug, their shoulders brushed, Slug leant into his ear and murmured, 'Do yourself a favour, Smithy: teach yer mate some manners.' Pele held his gaze for a second, smiled, and then, without replying, walked on.

When he reached their table, he saw John had pulled up chairs and was sitting down with the two gorillas on the other side of the pub. John had his arm around the first one, and the other was laughing. Meanwhile, Slug was still standing where he'd left him, staring over at Pele. Caroline immediately asked, 'What was all that about?'

'Something about nothing,' said Pele. 'Just some guys that John knows are being awkward.'

'Some guys that were nearly wearing these drinks,' said Newtog, putting the wet tray down and handing the drinks out.

'Isn't that Slug MacDonald with them?' Caroline asked, craning her neck to see through the crowd. 'I heard his sister's getting married next week.'

Pele picked his pint up and looked over to see Slug's back as he walked over to the gorillas. 'Do you know what? I think it might be.'

Shortly after the last orders, Pele and Sheena managed to jostle a very drunk but thankfully now jolly Newtog into a taxi home. Pele re-entered the pub to find John in a deep conversation with Caroline, who was holding his hand and clearly consoling him. He was sitting side on to Pele, but he must have seen him approach from the corner of his eye. Lifting Caroline's hand, he bent over to kiss it and then stood up to leave. Pele reached out and grasped his arm to restrain him. 'John?' He lifted his face towards him, and Pele felt almost bereft when he saw the deep sadness etched in the older man's face. 'Thanks for stepping in earlier, John. That could have turned nasty. You know what Newtog's like when he's had too much to drink.' He realised he was still holding on to John's arm and let it go. Caroline was observing them both curiously.

'Yeah, no problem,' John replied, avoiding eye contact. His fingers reached for the zip on his jacket, and he pulled it up to his throat. 'That's what mates are for, isn't it? To back one another up.' He left that hanging in the air before winking at Caroline. 'Take care, sweetheart. And take care of this one. He's a diamond.' And with that, John turned away and headed for the exit. Pele stood silently watching him go.

Caroline began buttoning up her coat, muttering, 'Janey's thrown him out, and he's really upset about it. Looks like it's for good this time. Still, he's been playing with fire for a while now. When will men learn it's the one thing that women won't put up with?'

'Eh?' replied Pele, not quite following Caroline's logic.

'Why lies,' she exclaimed, her eyebrows raised at his question. 'We won't stand for lies, Love. Now, come on. Walk me home, Mr Smith.' Pele felt a stab of guilt and a warm flush creep up his face. He was thankful it didn't fall under Caroline's gaze. She was already snuggled into his shoulder, her arm entwined in his. There had been a break in the weather earlier, so they walked home on what was a beautiful still night under a full moon. It was only at that point Pele felt the strain of the day's events begin to disperse.

A week later, Pele rose early on a Sunday morning, something that he was not accustomed to doing. The reason for this unusual occurrence was two-fold. Firstly, he wanted to leave Caroline sleeping in bed. She'd had another stressful week at work and was putting in ridiculously long hours, so she needed the rest.

The second reason was that he wanted to get out for a walk to clear his head. The more time he spent with Caroline, the more he realised just how much he loved her. Was that enough to sustain their relationship for a lifetime? He thought it might be, but he needed some space to think.

Pele dressed quietly in the bathroom. He buttoned up his jeans and slipped a khaki gilet over his grey Fred Perry polo shirt. With his hiking shoes and thick socks in hand, he crept out of the bedroom. Caroline's sleeping habits had altered over the last few years, and she'd become quite a heavy sleeper. In fact, she used two alarm clocks to make sure she didn't oversleep during the week for work. But he wasn't taking any chances; he tiptoed quietly downstairs.

He'd left the bedroom door slightly ajar lest the noise from closing it woke her. He could hear Caroline breathing deeply upstairs, a sure sign that she was still resident in the land of

Nod. Then he blew out a small sigh of relief and quickly laced up his boots. He wrote her a short note to say he'd gone to watch the park football and that he'd be back for dinner at around two. Lifting his coat and scarf off the bannister, he closed the front door and made his way down the narrow, brick path. It was only when he turned out of the cul-de-sac and onto the main road that he felt some relief from escaping the house.

Pele wandered down sleepy Sunday morning streets. There were a few cars on the road, but virtually no one else was around. The early morning sun felt good on his face, and he picked up a brisk pace, cutting across the farmer's field and heading towards the Bellvale Woods, which were located on the far side. It was his favourite walk, and it usually came with the promise of solitude and isolation.

Pele loved days like this; the surroundings and sheer tranquillity were already having a positive effect on his mood. He continued on through a multi-coloured carpet of dry leaves, which scattered into the air like small waves with each step. It was immensely satisfying and brought back nostalgic memories of such walks with his mum when he was little.

After a little while, he sat down on the thick trunk of a fallen oak, one casualty of many from the recent storm. Listening to the branches of the trees creaking softly overhead, he promised himself to do this more often. His breath lingered like ephemeral mist in the crisp, cold morning air. He was so absorbed in the beauty of his surroundings that he lost track of time. It was only when the cold began to seep into his bones that he forced himself up. When he exited the woods on the other side, he was only five minutes away from the town park. The cacophony of loud, distant cheering, interspersed with more than the odd angry shout, could be heard from a distance. As he got closer, he recognised the colours as those of his old *Alma Mata*, St Jude's under 13s.

Pele watched as the boys energetically ran around the field, chasing the ball as one. They seemed to be demonstrating more enthusiasm than they did talent. Parents stood on the sidelines shouting encouragement to the boys and instructions to the referee in equal measure.

On the far side, he was surprised to see the portly figure of Father O'Malley in residence and hollering at the top of his voice for the St Jude's boys to 'Get stuck in.' Normally, at this time of day, O'Malley would be in the pulpit preaching on forgiveness or some other commandment to his ever-diminishing flock. Very much intrigued, Pele walked around the back of the goalpost and over to the other side of the pitch. As he did so, one of the St Jude's boys beat three 'men' and fired off an unstoppable shot that hit the back of the opponent's net. Loud cheers erupted from St Jude's parents as the boys on the field charged around the pitch in excitement.

Pele wandered over to the priest, but O'Malley was so engrossed in the game he didn't see him as he approached. The priest was in the midst of a crowd of supporters punching the air excitedly, waving his scarf around, and evidently having a great time. 'That's the way Brendon, my son,' he shouted. 'What a great goal, young fella, me lad. You'll be on United's books next year for sure, so you will.' Pele found himself laughing as he politely nudged past two onlookers to get to the priest's side.

'Hey, Father! What's the score?' he asked, causing the priest to momentarily turn away from the game. He immediately stretched his hand out to grasp Pele's.

'Why Pele, isn't it grand to see you!' he exclaimed, now shaking his hand firmly up and down. 'Why, it's six-one to them, but what a goal anyway!' Pele lightly clapped the priest on the back and pointed to the young goal scorer, who was still being hugged and jumped on by his excited teammates.

'Is that Robby O'Leary's lad?' he asked. 'He's a bit of a chip off the old block if it is.'

'It is indeed,' the priest replied. 'He's a dedicated altar boy and decent midfielder to boot. Why he reminds me of yourself, so he does.' Pele sucked in a breath of cold air.

'I think the resemblance finishes on the pitch, Father.' The priest held out his right hand and tipped it from side to side.

'Maybe, maybe not.'

With that, the referee blew the final whistle, and the boys on the field started to shake hands and slap each other on the back. The parents who had been watching from the edge of the pitch were dispersing, and the two men eventually found themselves alone. 'So how come you're here watching the match?' Pele inquired as the priest blew into his clasped, reddened hands. 'Aren't you supposed to be saving souls from the pulpit at this time of day?'

'Ah… well now. You see, we have a trainee: Father Callaghan. He's taken a lot off my very considerable load. So, I'll just be doing the evening service tonight. The Lord moves in mysterious ways, doesn't he?' Pele fixed the priest with his eyes.

'Doesn't he just, Father.' The priest gave a loud chortle and pushed his large hands into his jacket pockets.

'The weight of the world, eh Pele?' he asked. Pele's lips pressed together in something resembling a smile, and he simply nodded back at him. 'You should come see us more often in church, Pele. Let us help you take a load off ya.' Pele raised his eyebrows.

'I don't think even He can help me this time.'

'Oh, you'd be surprised at what He can do when He has a mind,' the priest replied, his kind eyes smiling at him.

'Well, maybe. But for now, I think I'll see you around, Father. Take care.' Pele clapped him again on the shoulders and turned away.

And he would see O'Malley again, only it was much sooner than he could ever have imagined.

When Pele got back to the house at around two, Caroline still wasn't back from her mother's. He could smell the aroma of dinner before he went into the kitchen. A leg of lamb with garlic and rosemary was slow roasting in the oven. The veg was neatly prepped and waiting to be heated up. His mouth watered in anticipation.

He put the kettle on and made a strong mug of tea and a

slice of toast smothered with peanut butter, which was still his favourite comfort food. He couldn't wait until dinner was ready, as he was starving after his walk. He carried the tea and toast into the living room, where the next thirty minutes were spent watching Out of Africa on ITV, but instead of passing a pleasant hour, he found the aptness of the doomed love affair playing out in front of him spoilt any enjoyment. So he was glad when he heard Caroline push through the door. He wasn't glad for very long. 'And just where the bloody hell did you get to this morning?' she demanded to know after bursting into the living room and employing the hands-on-hips routine that he figured was written into the female DNA. Pele recognised Caroline was genuinely unhappy with him. Less by the hands-on-hips routine but more by the fact that Caroline only ever swore when really angry or hurt. It sounded like this time, he managed to achieve both.

'I wanted to get out for a walk and think,' he told her truthfully.

'Think!! Think about what?' she snapped, clearly agitated by the evasive reply. She stood rooted to the spot, her brown eyes blazing at him. If his last answer had been truthful, he knew his next could not be.

'You know? Stuff? John last week... work, just stuff.' He shrugged his shoulders as if he didn't know what else to say and looked at her warily, trying to gauge if she could sense anything that might indicate he wasn't being totally forthcoming. If she did, she didn't reveal it. Instead, her charged posture seemed to deflate like a punctured tyre, and she looked as if she might be on the verge of crying.

'Well, you know that we only have the weekends together and that I want to spend them with you. Otherwise, what's the point of it all? I need to tell you that I'm really worried about you, Brian. You don't seem yourself, and you've been like this for a while.' Pele got up and moved over to her.

'Look, I don't want you to worry. I knew you were really tired and needed a lie-in.' He tried to gauge her facial expression and reached out to take her hand in his. 'And I knew that you would want to go to your mother's, but I really didn't want to go. If I'd been in the house, you'd have gone on about it and made me feel guilty. You have a knack for that.' He smiled at her and then could sense her softening. He could always soften her. It was a knack he had, a sort of counter knack. That fact that he could do it so easily, though, didn't always sit well with his conscience.

'But families are important, Brian. You know how I feel about that.'

'I know they are, and I don't want to fall out with you, Caroline. I should have told you yesterday that I didn't want to go. I'm sorry,' he said, now squeezing her hand. 'We don't have to fall out about it, do we?' She shook her head and sighed; returning the hand squeeze, she half-smiled back at him.

'No, we don't, Brian. Okay. I'll try not to nag you about giving up your weekends to go visiting.'

'Right,' said Pele, trying to brighten up the day that he'd seemingly spoiled. 'Here's what we're going to do. Why don't you get yourself a glass of wine and your new book? I'll finish the dinner, and when we're done, we'll go out to the pictures. That film you wanted to watch, that Fatal Attraction thingy, is showing at seven. Let's finish off the weekend doing something together.' She leant in and kissed him.

'Sounds great, but I'm finishing dinner. You can wash up afterwards.'

'Deal,' he said, putting his arms around her waist and drawing her into him. She really was very pretty, and he really was very lucky, he thought as he lightly kissed her lips.

The next day after work, he sat down on the sofa, staring at the muted TV. That new quiz thing that Caroline really liked, Going for Gold, was on. It had to be said that their taste in films, music, and TV were vastly different. He loved sci-fi films, and Caroline couldn't stand them. In the last couple of years, he'd begun to listen to the Smiths a lot. And Caroline hated them too. She thought they were 'miserable' and 'boring.' So, he rarely listened to them in the house, sticking to playing them on cassette in the car when he was driving alone.

After thinking about this, Pele stopped the train of thought in its tracks before he started examining what else they were incompatible with. With all of the recent drama and turmoil, he'd finally come to a decision. He wasn't sure if it was acceptance, resignation, or the film they'd been to see the night before, where he thought that Caroline could just go all bunny-boiler on him if push came to shove. Whatever it was, it was the only resolution that he could find with any kind of a clear conscience and sense of peace.

He reflected on how passive he'd been throughout his life. His inability to take control of his own life over the years was what was making him feel so adrift and lost. If he honestly thought about things, he couldn't remember a single occasion where he'd made a conscious decision about what he actually wanted. It had all just kind of happened. But the irony was that he liked having someone to do the thinking for him. And Caroline had fit that bill to perfection. She'd only ever loved him, only ever encouraged him, and been there for him when no one else had. Could he really have thrown that back in her face?

He knew that he couldn't.

And then there was his mum to consider. She'd have been devastated if he went down what he'd started to think of as the 'other' path. She loved Caroline, and there was no telling how hurt and angry she would be. After all, this was a woman who'd remained faithful to her dead husband for the past twenty-three years. So, it was inconceivable that he could leave Caroline and that his mum would accept it in a million years. Or even longer if he really thought about it.

He sat for a while, mulling everything over. 'The burden of guilt,' as Father O'Malley had referred to it, had been like the weight of the world on his shoulders this past week. His thoughts drifted back to the last sermon he heard O'Malley preach years ago. For some reason, it had always stuck with him. It had been on the theme of forgiveness. He'd said that forgiveness and peace could only ever follow true repentance, and true repentance meant turning around and going in a different direction. Pele reflected that perhaps, in some way, he'd been unfaithful, even if, thus far, it had only been in his heart. He hoped time might remedy that and that he could become the partner that Caroline deserved.

He looked at the clock on top of the gas fire and saw it was gone seven. Caroline hadn't called, but he guessed, as usual, she'd be home in half an hour, which would give him enough time to take the first step as the new changed man that he was envisaging.

He hunted about for a notepad and pen, then began to write. When he finished, he read over it and was satisfied that it conveyed everything he wanted to say. Folding the paper into an envelope, he wrote her name on it and placed it in front of the glass-domed anniversary clock on the fire. The clock had been in his family for years and had been a gift from his proud mum when he and Caroline had bought the house. He felt relieved and, for the first time in a long time, with some much-needed inner peace. A knock on the door startled him. 'Caroline,' he thought. 'What's she done with her door keys?' He opened the door. 'Oh! Hello?'

A man was standing there. A man Pele had seen before but couldn't place. He had a flat and earnest voice and began to talk slowly, asking if there was anyone at home with him. As the man spoke, the creeping sense of dread that was growing inside Pele's stomach became a full-blown explosion in his head. The man followed him into the living room and helped to sit him down, but Pele reached a point at which he was no longer listening; he gazed at the man in shock until the man's mouth stopped moving, and Pele asked him to leave.

He closed the door behind the man and wandered back into the living room, where he fell down onto the sofa. Glancing over at the clock to try and get back into the here and now, he saw the marriage proposal letter he'd written and began to sob. It was a noise that came from the depths of his soul, and it sounded more like a wounded animal than anything human. He gripped the sides of his head as he sat on the sofa. His eyes were so bleary from the tears streaming down his face that he could no longer see anything.

He'd never felt so alone and bereft in all of his life.

Sometime later, when he'd regained enough control to speak, he picked up the phone and began to make some of the worst phone calls of his life.

1999

IE5; American Pie; S Club 7; Game Boy Colour;
Six billion people; Sex and the City; M&M.

Pele pulled out his briefcase from the boot and locked the door on his Audi. Navigating his way around small pockets of rowdy pupils, a couple of the older and slightly bolder kids called out to him as he made his way towards the lower school classrooms, 'Morning, Sir!' and 'Are you going to be my new English teacher this year, Sir?'

This produced stifled giggles from some of the younger girls. He would no doubt get to meet some of these youngsters in his lessons over the coming week. As he walked past, he maintained a relaxed smile and firm eye contact with a few of the more precocious boys. Pele had learnt quickly in his early years of teaching that first impressions were everything. If you displayed any sign of weakness, some pupils could be merciless in the classroom. Meanwhile, most of the new intake pupils, the year 7s, were huddled together near the entrance and clearly anxious about their first day in the 'big school.'

Pele had secured the position of head of English some five years earlier. During the summer break, he'd been in several meetings with his new staff members and the Senior Management Team. The time and effort preparing for a new year had left him with very few opportunities to relax. If nothing else, he was prepared, he supposed. Burying himself in work was a comfort blanket and gave him a much-needed focus. Keeping busy wasn't enough to outrun the sense of existential pointlessness that hovered around the edges of his life, though, but it was enough to help keep it at bay.

Pele stepped into his classroom, holding his briefcase in one hand and a cup of strong, black coffee in the other. He deftly flicked the worn, metal light switch into the up position with his elbow. Three ceiling strip lights momentarily buzzed in synchrony before flickering reluctantly to life, illuminating the dark room with a pale, yellow haze. The building had been constructed in the 1930s, and the architects had curiously designed narrow slits for windows, so there wasn't very much in the way of natural lighting.

He sat down at an ancient oak desk, covered with enough graffiti and etchings to suggest it had probably been there since the school first opened. He spent the next ten minutes putting some finishing touches to his preparation for the coming day. He picked up a computer printout sheet of his new form, year 7. It was listed in alphabetical order. He scanned through the meaningless names before one caught his attention halfway down. His eyes stopped, hovered over the name for a second, and then continued slowly down the list. He put the folded paper into his top pocket and got up to walk the short journey to the upper school. He had a staff meeting to attend, and by the time he'd closed his door, he had forgotten all about the name on the list.

A quarter of an hour later, Pele returned to his classroom to find his brand-new form lined up in the corridor and chaperoned by two of the more sensible year 11 girls. The young pupils were fairly quiet except for a couple of larger boys hanging with minor ill intent at the back of the line. Seeing Pele's arrival, most of the group was silenced by the authority that a teacher in a suit still engendered. The only exception to this silence were the two boys at the back, who continued to talk and jostle each other despite being directly under Pele's gaze. For the moment, Pele ignored them and nodded towards the year 11 girls, saying, 'Thank you, ladies. You can head off to your class now.' The two girls smiled politely and scampered off in the direction of the upper school.

The orderly queue of pupils had fastened their eyes onto their new form teacher as he slowly walked along the line until he reached the two oblivious boys at the back. His solemn presence was enough to stop the jostling; they dropped their hands and went quiet. 'And you are?' Pele challenged, falling into the established teacher routine.

'Badger, Sir,' said the first boy, grinning. He was tall for his age with a mop of unruly black curls. He could see there had been a nominal attempt to imitate the school uniform, but his black trousers were about the only thing that Pele recognised as being part of the authorised uniform. Pele knew instantly it was the Cullen boy whose special needs file he'd read extensively just the night before.

'Hmmm, Badger?' said Pele, feigning as if he didn't understand. 'Badger? Is that your real name?' The boy held Pele's gaze, not out of insolence but more out of curiosity, as if he was trying to figure out where Pele was going with this. While this was going on, the rest of the group held its collective breath.

'No, Sir,' said the boy eventually. 'It's Danny, Sir. Danny Cullen.'

'Ah!' said Pele, unable to help himself. 'When you said Badger, I wondered if you were trying to bait me.' He'd no sooner uttered the words when a small giggle escaped from someone towards the front of the queue, causing the group to turn as one towards it. Pele also turned in sheer surprise that anyone from this young form group had understood the joke.

One of the things that he did to amuse himself in teaching was to make small, private jokes that he knew most of the pupils wouldn't understand. In its own small way, the laugh from the front intruded on that privacy, and Pele was intrigued to see who it was that made it. He walked back down the line to the front, where three fresh-faced girls stood wide-eyed at his approach. Two of the faces were apprehensive and seemed pale with the sort of mortification teachers sometimes produced in a new intake.

However, Pele was captivated by the third face, which showed no fear whatsoever and was regarding him with a frank, open-faced look that might have been worn by somebody twice her age. Pele smiled inside as he thought that you did not have to be Sherlock Holmes to trace the provenance of the laugh. She had sharp, clear eyes that betrayed a keen intelligence. 'Hmmm, you found that funny?' he asked, stopping directly in front of her.

'Yes, Sir,' the girl replied, her face beaming in a way he found mildly disconcerting.

'And would you mind explaining to the rest of the group here what you found funny about my comment?' he replied, expanding his arm into an arc to include the line of children.

'You made a pun on Danny's nickname with the word bait, and it has a double meaning, Sir.' When she'd finished, she smiled brightly, and Pele could feel a grin breaking out that he was finding impossible to suppress.

'Well, young lady,' he said, 'it appears you've caught me making a very bad joke. And all this before we've even got into the classroom. Could I have your name, please?'

The young girl nodded and spoke, 'It's Caitlin, Sir. Caitlin MacDonald.'

Pele's mind was still reeling an hour after he'd registered the pupils, handed out their timetables, and packed them off to get set upon for the purposes of 'initiation' by the older kids in the yard.

Caitlin MacDonald!

Slug had even named her after his sister.

Slug? How could that wondrous little thing out there be related to him in any way? Let alone be his daughter! And yet, his daughter she certainly was.

Earlier in the form session, she'd finished copying the timetable into her diary and was adding it to the pile on Pele's desk. Before she turned to go back to her chair, Pele couldn't resist asking her, 'Caitlin. Just as a matter of interest: what's your dad's first name?'

'Stephen,' she replied. 'Why, do you know him, Sir?'

'Erm, I don't think so,' Pele replied dishonestly, hoping his facial expression didn't reveal the truth. 'There were a lot of

MacDonald's where I grew up. I thought I might have known him or someone from the family.'

'I wouldn't be surprised,' the girl said before turning away. 'I've got hundreds of aunts and uncles.' Pele smiled at the exaggerated size of her family, but then again, knowing the family she was talking about, she probably wasn't that far off the mark.

At break time, he watched Caitlin through the narrow window. She was chattering with her friends in the playground. He mulled over the ethics, if there indeed were any, of continuing in the role of her form teacher. He decided it simply boiled down to one thing: he had known her father, and they hadn't liked each other very much. It was hardly ethical grounds for moving her into another form. Still, he wondered how pleased Slug would be to hear that he was teaching his daughter. Slug MacDonald hadn't crossed Pele's path for years, but he'd heard that he owned a large demolition company somewhere on this side of the river. In Pele's mind, this confirmed what he'd long suspected, that Slug's talents as a wrecker of objects and people were very much innate. It was a temperament that Pele had been both subjected to and observant of many times in the past. Yet it now seemed he'd move on to being a married man and a father. And it appeared he'd made a very good father. That's if his daughter was anything to go by. Pele couldn't help but wonder if perhaps most of the child's natural grace and intelligence hadn't been bestowed to her through her mother. In all the years he'd been teaching, he could count on the fingers of one hand the number of pupils who carried Caitlin's natural bearing and poise. It wasn't just her intelligence that made her stand out from the other pupils; it was the way in which she was so comfortable with that intelligence. He'd seen many bright pupils who were precociously aware of their gifts and used them to gain attention. Yet some could be overcome with the embarrassment of them and tried to hide their intelligence, but there was no evidence of either with Caitlin. It was a rare breed of pupil who had a calm acceptance of their unique abilities that always made such pupils stand out.

Pele reached for the mug of coffee on his desk and put it to his lips. Taking a cold, bitter swig, he grimaced and turned away from the window. He looked down again at the register: Caitlin MacDonald. The more he thought about it, the more convinced he was that there was no conflict of interest to worry about on his part. The problem was that he couldn't confidently predict that Slug's feelings would be reciprocated. Pele didn't want to cause any more distress to Caitlin than was necessary, which meant he would have to make a tough judgement call.

The next day before form, Pele headed down to see the new head of year 7, Dominic Price. Pele had got to know him over the previous terms, and last year, a friendship of sorts had developed. They discovered a shared love of running, The Smiths and Kubrick films over cups of coffee in the staff room. He'd initially struck Pele as an intelligent, upwardly mobile twenty-something who often frequented the ranks of junior management positions. He was a smartly dressed, tall, dark-haired PE teacher who was popular with staff and pupils alike. But Pele discovered he was much more than a career teacher. He actually cared a lot about the kids and was very suited to the job. The move into pastoral care was, in some ways, a calculated one, meant to increase his opportunities for promotion to middle management in the not-too-distant future. But it was also a role that Pele knew he would be absolutely committed to and one in which he would unfailingly look after his pupil's interests.

Pele reached his open door on the noisy upper-school corridor. He could hear Dominic conversing on the phone. Presumably, the restrained tone he could hear in his voice meant he was taking a tough call from an anxious parent. He knew only too well that Dominic would earn his extra £2,000 a year with a lot of hard work, sweat, and more than a few tears. 'I will, Mrs Johnson. I'll watch him for any signs; you have my word on it. Yes, certainly. I'll be in touch. Yeah, sure, okay then... Bye.' With that, he dropped the phone handset into its cradle and closed the folder before him. Pele rapped lightly on the cheap, wooden door and pushed his head into the pokey space that senior management called an office. Dominic's face instantly changed into a cheerful beam. He rocked back on a plastic-cast chair and placed his laced fingers behind his head. 'Welcome to my new office. Sit down, comrade!' Pele went in and took a seat on the chair opposite, craning his neck as he looked around the claustrophobic space.

'Yeah. Nice cupboard, Dominic.'

'That's harsh but true, Smith,' he said, rocking forwards. They both laughed. 'So, did you drop by just to hurl abuse, or was there something you needed?'

'I'm after a favour, actually,' Pele told him, opening up his satchel and taking out his form list. 'It's about my form.'

'That's what I'm here for. If I can help in any way, I will.'

'Well, it's a bit tricky,' Pele confided as he glanced up at Dominic, who had settled back into his seat. His face was still open and warm, but his expression had turned quizzical. 'I'll get to the point. I'd like you to move someone in my form. If that's at all possible.'

'Ahhh! Comprendo, amigo. Is it Danny Cullen by any chance?' Dominic asked, the side of his mouth slipping into a knowing smile as he reached to open a drawer on his filing cabinet.

'Err...no,' said Pele. 'It's Caitlin MacDonald.'

'Caitlin MacDonald!' he burst out, his face creasing with bewilderment. 'You want to move Caitlin MacDonald? Why on earth would you want to do that? Her SATs say that she's probably the brightest girl in the year. I'm laughing here. Come on! I do not get that at all, Smith?' Pele knew there was little sense in not telling the truth. He was rolling a pen back and forth across the desk absentmindedly; he raised his eyes and said,

'I know her father. We go back a bit, and there's some history.'

'Oh! Erm... Right. I see,' said Dominic, not seeing at all. 'Some history. Okay then.' At this point, he was pretending to flick through his filing cabinet in the absence of knowing what to say. 'Erm...well, I can tell you one thing: the other tutors will be queuing up to take her, so it won't be a problem.' He stopped riffling through his folders and turned to look at him. 'Are you absolutely sure about this?' Pele sighed and dropped the pen he'd been rolling into a wooden pen holder on the desk.

'I wish there was another way around it, but there isn't. I've given the situation a lot of thought, and it just seems to be the best option, all things considered.' He leant forward with his elbows on his knees, tipped his head to look up at Dominic, and said, 'I can see she's a great kid, but I'm flagging stuff here. Being ultra-careful, probably, on balance. I just don't think it's a good idea that she's with me.'

'Well, I'll trust your judgement as only you know what you're dealing with here. As far as I'm concerned, there's going to be no problem moving her,' the young teacher mused, slightly perplexed. Pele stood up and reached the door before Dominic had his last word. 'If I move her and the parents want to know why, will that be a problem?' Pele stopped.

'I honestly don't know. It's been years since I've even seen the guy. Maybe he's changed. He might well have if Caitlin's anything to go by. It could be I'm overreacting and being too cautious, but parent's evenings could be a strain. Most definitely for me and very likely for him, and then any future parental contact. So, for the kid's sake, I'm just thinking it's for the best.' Dominic nodded.

'Okay, consider it done. I'll catch you at lunch and let you know where she's going.'

'Thanks, mate. Appreciate it.' Pele pulled the door open, nodded at him, and left.

Five minutes were remaining before the morning buzzer went. Pele turned into his corridor, and as fate would have it, the only person standing outside his room was Caitlin MacDonald. 'Good morning, Mr Smith,' she said brightly as he walked towards her.

'Morning, Caitlin,' he replied, somewhat uneasily. He busied himself with the catch on his satchel and searched for his keys. He was unable to hold eye contact with her for long, even though what he'd just done in his own mind was entirely for her benefit.

Meanwhile, Caitlin had reached into her bag and pulled out a crumpled, white form.

'Mr Smith, would you like to sponsor me? I'm raising money for Water Aid by doing a sponsored swim. I'm quite a good swimmer, and I'm hoping to swim at least ten lengths.' Pele smiled.

'That's a really great cause, Caitlin. I'd be more than happy to sponsor you.' He took the form from her and removed a pen from his inside pocket. On the line provided, he wrote an amount and added his name to the list. Then, he handed the form back to Caitlin and unlocked the door to his room.

'Mr Smith?'

'Yes, Caitlin,' he replied, turning around to face her. Her head bobbed up from the form she held in her hand to his face and then back again.

'Did you mean to put that much on the sheet, Mr Smith? Most people only put a pound or two?'

'Yes, I did, Caitlin. I think it's a very good cause,' he said, pushing against the door, forcing his way in, and hoping she wasn't yet old enough to recognise a guilt-ridden face.

Seven hours later, Pele was packing up at the end of what had been a difficult day. Besides having had a couple of difficult groups in the afternoon lessons, Pele also knew Dominic would have caught up with Caitlin MacDonald by now. He would have broken the news to her that she was no longer in his form. He wondered how she might have taken it.

He didn't have to wonder for long.

Not long after his group had disappeared out of the classroom, making a din in the corridor as they went, Caitlin appeared at his door with a look that could only be described as '*Thatcheresque.*' Though she knew he'd seen her, she still politely knocked and stood in the doorway, indicating she wasn't going anywhere soon.

In truth, Pele wasn't particularly surprised to see her. He hadn't imagined that someone with Caitlin's character could be moved so easily and without putting up a fight. 'Come in, Caitlin,' he gestured whilst locking the drawer on his filing cabinet and putting the key in his pocket. He sat on the edge of his desk and looked directly at her. 'I take it you've come to see me about the move?'

'Yes, I have, Mr Smith,' she said, moving decisively into the room and standing at an appropriate distance in front of him. 'I don't understand why it's me that has to move. Mr Price said that there were too many pupils in your form. But there are more people in the form I'm going to. So, I don't think Mr Price is telling me the whole truth.' Pele winced as he realised Dominic's inability to be more than economical with the truth had fallen foul of Caitlin's intellect. It seemed that Pele was, quite rightly, going to have to clean his own mess up.

'You're right, Caitlin. It's not totally down to numbers,' he agreed, shifting his position on the corner of his desk to face her and hopefully reassure her with his body language. 'It's just that this is a bit of a difficult group. We must look at the group as a whole and determine what's best for everyone. On doing that, I felt it needed to be a bit smaller, and that's why I wanted you to move. You're very bright, Caitlin, and I think you would benefit from being in a group where there are fewer distractions.' Pele knew it wasn't exactly the best excuse, but it was all he could come up with, considering there wasn't a great deal of room to manoeuvre into. Caitlin saw through it quickly enough, though, drew out her logic cannons, and blew Pele's ship of obfuscation clean out of the water without any real difficulty.

'So why not move someone who doesn't listen that much, Mr Smith? Why move me?' Pele raised his eyebrows and puffed out his cheeks in response. He didn't really have an answer.

'Well, it's just that...'

'Can I tell you what I think, Mr Smith?' By now, her face was a picture. She wore the tiniest of pouts on the corner of her lips while her small nostrils flared out ever so slightly with indignation. Pele could do little but pay attention to what she had to say and inwardly smile. Her exact phrase and posture reminded him of what Caroline or his mother would do in similar circumstances. The fairer sex often reacted like this when they knew intrinsically that they were in the presence of male BS. He also knew from historical experience that Caitlin's inquiry wasn't a real question and that perhaps only the presence of a large policeman on horseback could ever stop them from telling you what they were actually thinking.

'Please do, Caitlin,' he said, gesturing with his hand for her to continue, a forlorn attempt to convince himself he had any real choice in the matter.

'I think this has something to do with my father,' she stated matter-of-factly. Her eyes studied his face carefully for a reaction. He gave off none he could sense but felt that might not be enough to dissuade this young firebrand.

'Oh, you do. And why would you think that?' he asked, already a little fearful that the game might well be up.

'Because you didn't ask anybody else about their dad, but you did ask me about mine. And then, all of a sudden, I'm the one being moved.' Pele groaned inwardly and didn't see the point in continuing to be evasive.

'Okay, Caitlin, here's the truth. I asked Mr Price if he could move you because, yes, you're right, I do know your dad, and I'm not sure that he would be very happy if he knew I was your form teacher.' Caitlin rolled her eyes, crossed her arms, and exhaled loudly as if what he'd just said was simply the most ridiculous thing that she'd ever heard in all of the eleven years she'd lived so far on God's green earth.

'Mr Smith, my dad's a brilliant dad!' she exclaimed. 'Why would he be bothered if you were my teacher? But anyway, you don't need to worry about what he might think because he works all the time. My mum does all of the stuff to do with school. He never comes to any of the parent's evenings because he's so busy. How would he even know? Pleeeeeeaase, Mr Smith? I really don't want to move. I like being in this form, and all of my friends from primary are in it.' Caitlin had uncrossed her arms and was imploring with her eyes, which were beginning to well up with tears. It had taken a lot of courage for her to make the speech, and Pele could see that although she was fighting the tears back with no small aplomb, they were threatening to spill over at any moment. Pele himself was a sucker for any female tears, but the fact that Caitlin was upset because of him made him feel terrible. Pele rose from the desk and handed her a tissue from a box.

'Well then, Caitlin, let's backtrack a little,' he said. 'I'm really sorry I've caused you any distress. It wasn't my intention. I only wanted to do what I thought was the best for you. If you want to stay so badly, I will tell Mr Price you can stay with me.' Her teary face broke out in a bright smile that warmed his soul.

'Thanks, Mr Smith. Thanks a lot.'

'You don't have to thank me, Caitlin. I shouldn't have tried to move you in the first place. I want you to promise me that you won't lie to your dad. If he finds out who your form teacher is and he's not happy, then I'll talk with you both. Do we have a deal?'

She picked up her bag, slung it over her shoulder, and gave him another grin. 'I won't, Sir. But he won't really care. He's nearly always at work, except on Sundays when he takes me swimming, and then we go to the pictures afterwards.' With that, she positively skipped out of the room, leaving Pele with the distinct impression that he'd been no intellectual or emotional match for a determined 11-year-old girl.

A few months later, on a cold, wet November night, Pele entered the upper school gym clutching his appointment sheet, unmarked exercise books, and a mug of coffee. Paddy, the caretaker, a huge bear of a man, had set tables for the staff around the perimeter of the room. Rows of plastic chairs were placed down the centre for the soon-to-be waiting parents. Though it was only 5:15 pm, a few of his colleagues were already well ensconced in their early appointments, and the quiet hum of their chat filled the gymnasium air. Pele's first appointment wasn't until 5:30 pm, and looking at his list, he saw he had six before the big one: Caitlin MacDonald's.

Earlier in the day, he asked Caitlin if her parents were coming, and she shrugged her shoulders and told him what he wanted to hear: 'My mum's coming, not my dad. He's working.'

He walked over to the desk that had his plastic nametag on it and put a pile of unmarked books down. They would act as a crutch for the empty moments between talking to a parent and sitting like you'd been stood up on a date. Pushing his right hand into the inside of his suit pocket, he checked for the tenth time that his pens were there. He then placed his appointment sheet down on the desk and cast a glance around the small gym. To his left, he saw Alison Janners from the Art department, sitting twiddling her thumbs while waiting for her first parents to arrive. Alison was a pretty, intelligent divorcee and mother to two children. Whenever Pele saw her, she always looked like she'd never had a stressful day in her life. She seemed to exist in a stratosphere of calmness that pervaded her classroom. Her cutting humour and challenging teaching techniques meant her pupils genuinely loved her. She'd told him over coffee in the staff room that she put it down to a lot of exercise. That and the fact that looks were deceptive because she ran around like a headless chicken for most of the time at home. As far as he could tell, she was about the same age as Pele and had been single for a couple of years. A few weeks ago, she'd hinted at a staff course that she was interested in more than a professional relationship with Pele. But so far, he'd kept things strictly platonic, and he liked that she hadn't pushed anything.

As he looked over, Alison caught his eyes and smiled. He grinned back and gave her a wave. She mouthed something, tipping her hand towards her mouth, which he figured was an invite to go for a drink in the pub afterwards. He shook his head at her, pointing as he did so at his watch. She pulled a face at him whilst giving him the thumbs down. Pele laughed and shrugged his shoulders just as a parent came and sat down. They shook hands, and he went straight into his long-established spiel about how nice their child was and what a pleasure it was to teach them.

The next hour went by in a haze just like every other parent evening he'd ever done, and, after more than ten years, he'd done quite a few. The only difficulty so far was trying hard not to point out to Danny Cullen's painfully young and single mother that she might want to say no to him, just occasionally.

Thankfully, it all sped by quickly, and he barely had time to get nervous about the upcoming appointment of Caitlin MacDonald. No sooner had Danny Cullen's mother stood up and thanked him vociferously for his patience when he turned an even whiter shade of pale than Procol Harem's lead singer could ever have imagined. Approaching the waiting seats in front of him was a very poised and unmistakable Angela. It took perhaps a second for Pele's brain to compute. Angela was with Caitlin. Caitlin was with Angela; ergo, Angela was only Caitlin's mum!

Pele could see them both engaged in what looked like an animated discussion. He put his head into a marking book and pretended to read it as he tried to get a grip of himself. He was dumbstruck. His mind reeled with the possibility that something like this could have happened. He quickly realised that he had to compose himself and deal with it. He was shaken, yes, but he was still Caitlin's teacher, and he had to be professional, however awkward that this might feel. He looked up briefly again. Angela was dressed in a long dark coat, Matrix-style, with black jeans, a figure-hugging crew neck, in bright saffron, and signature flat, lace-up boots. Her hair was pulled back into a claw clip with wispy strands framing her face, accentuating a long, slim neck and those ever-so-high cheekbones. Even though she was dressed down, she looked every inch like the well-to-do wife of a successful local businessman that she now was.

Finally, Caitlin and Angela finished their discussion, with Caitlin pointing over in Pele's direction. Angela started to walk over and then faltered when she recognised Pele. Her composure wavered, but she fixed a faint smile on him as she approached the table. Pele could see over her shoulder that Caitlin was now engaged in a conversation with another girl from her year. He stared transfixed at Angela, who was trying hard not to show the same signs of shock and disbelief that he was clearly feeling, but it was obvious that she, too, was floundering as much as he was, which in some comforting way made him feel a little less anxious. He noticed she was gripping her Aspinal leather handbag as she stared with wide eyes at him like a rabbit in headlights. After what seemed like hours but was in reality only seconds, she eventually raised a slightly trembling hand out to him and said, 'Pel...Mr Smith. I'm Angela MacDonald. Caitlin's mum.' Pele ached at the stilted formality, but the awkward situation compelled him to follow her lead. So, he shook her hand all too briefly.

'Thank you for coming, Mrs MacDonald,' he said, looking down into his mark book and trying hard not to stare at her face. 'Please sit down. Can I start by saying Caitlin is a remarkable young lady? I'm sure you are very proud of her. We're all very pleased with her progress, and she's settled into secondary school exceptionally well.' His blustering didn't seem to help settle Angela in any way. She sat stiffly with her legs crossed and hands folded across the handbag in her lap. Then, after a quick look around and seeing nearly everyone in the surrounding area was in deep discussions, she suddenly leant forward across the desk, putting her head close to his. Pointing a finger at Pele's mark book.

'I really didn't know. Know that you were Caitlin's 'Mr Smith, I mean,' she told him. 'I just didn't connect the dots. I probably wouldn't have come if I'd known. I don't think I should have come.' Pele's senses were spinning towards 'red for danger' on the emotional scale. His head was swimming with the painful memories of their last meeting in the pub, and now Angela's scent was slowly filling his head. To make things worse, her delicate hand had inadvertently brushed against his on the table. Her troubled eyes, set in a pale face, were looking deep into his, only inches away, and it was only by sheer force of will that he stopped his hand from reaching out and touching her. He leant back a little to create some space, and as he looked up, he noticed Alison staring over at them with a peculiar expression on her face. He forced a smile, but he could see from her expression that she saw right through it. He turned back to Angela and the notebook as though there was something of extreme importance in it.

'I'm glad you did come,' he said in a low voice. 'As hard as this is for me, let me tell you I'm glad it's you and not your husband sitting here.' Angela looked startled as she thought about what he'd said. Pele scanned the room to see if anyone else was watching, and he could see that Caitlin was observing them with interest. He sat back in his chair, conveying what he hoped would be cool indifference, and Angela followed. 'Yes, she's very talented at English,' he said in a louder voice. 'Always does her homework; always completes the classwork she's set. Caitlin is an absolute star. She's a real pleasure to teach and a credit to you and your husband.'

'I'm very pleased to hear that, Mr Smith,' she replied while fiddling nervously with her scarf. 'My husband and I are both very proud of her. Well, I won't take up any more of your time.' With this, she stood up and hooked her bag over her shoulder whilst extending her other in one easy movement. Pele lifted himself to his feet rather abruptly, pushing his chair backwards and scrapping it loudly across the wooden floor, where it almost toppled over with the force of the movement. She smiled nervously at the attention the noise drew while her eyes darted around the room. After a second or so, he placed his hand in hers, and even though it was only a brief handshake, he found it almost impossible to release again.

'It's been a pleasure, Mrs Macdonald,' Pele said, dropping his hand by his side after she removed hers first. As she turned to leave, he blurted out, 'Mrs MacDonald?' She spun around to look at him. 'If there's anything you ever need to talk to me about, anything at all, please contact me. I mean, let me know?' Her face seemed to go even paler at this.

'Thank you,' she replied before speeding off towards the now bemused-looking Caitlin.

Pele didn't get through the rest of his appointments until 8:45 pm. The rest of the evening was far less traumatic. Still, the residue of his meeting with Angela hung heavy like static from lightning on a stormy night, exciting and scary simultaneously. Most of the tables were now empty. A couple of parents and teachers were milling about, but most had gone home. It was only as he'd finished packing away that he turned to find Alison Janners behind him, leaning up against the wall with her arms folded and a mischievous grin playing on her lips. 'You sure you don't want to come for that drink?' she teased. 'You look like you could really use one.'

'Is it that obvious?' he laughed and felt some of the tension leave his body just being in her orbit. He grinned as she nodded her blonde shaggy bob at him in an exaggerated up-and-down motion.

Twenty minutes later, he was on his way back from the bar at the Griffin pub, a small, cosy, old man's pub just across the road from the school. He placed two halves of lager on the small, round table where Alison had taken a seat. She was waiting for him with her enthusiastic, wide smile. 'Cheers,' she said, lifting her drink to take a small gulp. 'Mmm... Oh, I needed this.'

'Cheers,' said Pele, sitting opposite on a small, red leather stool he'd pulled under him.

'So, was it a bad night?' Alison asked, reaching down into her bag and pulling out a packet of cigarettes and a lighter.

'Yeah. You could say that,' Pele said glumly. 'I saw someone I used to know, which was a bit difficult.'

'Ah, really?' said Alison. 'A parent?'

'Yeah,' he sighed. 'It's all a bit complicated.'

'Intriguing,' she replied, leaving the comment hanging in the air. It indicated that she was interested in the details but wouldn't press him. Her eyes flashed at him impishly, and she smiled a dazzling, full-on beam. Then, opening her cigarette packet and taking one out, she asked, 'You don't mind if I do, do you?' He shook his head, and she lit up. Her green eyes squinted a little as the smoke wound a lazy spiral into them. 'Parents can be a bit tricky. I had a year 10 boy in my form a couple of years ago, and let's just say his dad was a little bit too keen.'

Pele laughed, 'I imagine you get quite a bit of that.'

'Not as much as I'd like!' she chuckled with a knowing grin before she brought the cigarette back to her mouth and inhaled deeply. Her head was slightly tilted, and he could almost see the wheels turning in her brain as she studied him. He had a sense of where she wanted the conversation to go, but she was treading oh-so carefully. After a small silent pause, she ventured to say, 'I've been single for ages and not really seeing anyone serious. What about you?' she asked, stubbing out more than half of her cigarette. 'Are you seeing anyone?'

'Me? No,' Pele spluttered. 'I was seeing someone a while back, a girl who teaches at another school, who I met on a training course. But it petered out. There's been a lot of petering out where my relationships are concerned.' Her eyes were locked onto his with thoughtful interest. Everyone at work knew what had happened, even though he rarely talked about it, and it had now been over twelve years. But something like that had a habit of following you around, perhaps even defining you in other people's eyes. He'd spent many of the intervening years painfully avoiding conversations about it. He supposed bringing it out into the open might be simpler. Alison seemed to sense his discomfiture and, to her immense credit, tried to ease the situation.

'Hey, we can talk about something else if it makes you uncomfortable?' She held his gaze with her soft, green eyes. They were warm, and she stared at him with kindness and understanding without even a hint of unease. Very few people had managed to convey that kind of empathy in the past twelve years. In the end, it was just easier not to bring it up. But this felt different, somehow.

'No, it's fine. I just haven't talked about it really with anyone for a while. I'm a bit rusty,' he told her.

'I'm okay with rusty,' she said, leaning forward. When he

nodded and smiled, she took the lead and gently asked, 'I heard it was a heart attack?' Pele's thoughts went back in time, back to that day: the worst day of his life. The moment that his world got turned inside out.

'Sort of,' he replied. 'She had an undiagnosed blood clot, which caused a pulmonary embolism. It brought on a cardiac arrest.' Alison didn't say anything, but her face somehow reflected the pain she saw in his. Retelling the story he'd told many times before, but one he'd not spoken of for several years, Pele felt the surrealness hit him all over again. He dropped his eyes and stared into his drink. 'She was on her way home from work and collapsed in the car park. And that was it. They said she died instantly and, thankfully, painlessly.'

'I'm so sorry that happened to her. And to you,' Alison said, reaching out and putting her hand on his arm for the briefest of moments. 'It must have been hard for you to lose her so young. How long had you been together?'

'Eight years,' Pele said, rubbing his hand across his neck. 'I found it difficult to move on. At least, I did for more than a few years. There was just a lot of guilt about stuff that I found almost too difficult to work through. And honestly, I almost didn't get through it all, except for willpower,' he spoke wryly as he looked at her. 'Mostly my mother's willpower.'

'Mothers, eh? Where would we be without them?' Alison said, looking straight at him. Pele told her about the daily phone calls for weeks and how she'd gently chivvied him along to get through every one of the dark days that followed. She understood only too well the pain he was in and miraculously had kept him from sinking into depths he thought he'd never get out of.

'I still carry a fair bit of guilt about it, I suppose. Too much guilt if you ask my mother. But I think I'm loads better than I was.'

'Well, it's hardly surprising you'd feel like that, though,' Alison said cautiously. She had put her hands back onto her lap, but her eyes never left him. 'My best mate lost her husband a few years back. He was only 32. He fell off a roof he was fixing on a work site. He went to work that day as usual, dropped the kids off at school, and the next thing she's getting a visit telling her she's a widow.'

'Father O'Malley used to say our lives are a vapour, just a breath, and then we're gone,' Pele said solemnly.

'I didn't have you down as a holy roller?' she grinned at him.

'An altar boy, no less,' he laughed loudly, but he was keen to change the subject. 'So, what about you? Divorce, wasn't it?'

'Yeah, I was lucky; it wasn't anything tragic. We just drifted slowly apart. An age-old story, which I suppose is its own tragedy. It was especially hard for the boys, though. They both worship their dad, rightly so, as he's really good with them, but they were only young. To be honest, I was glad to get out of it, and I think he was too. We made the mistake of having kids because we couldn't think of anything to say to each other. We share the child-care, which has worked out quite well, to be honest.' She shrugged, then reached down and pulled out another cigarette.

'Are you gonna smoke that one, or just stub it out after you light it?' Pele asked with a glint in his eye.

'The latter,' she said in a low voice. 'Always the latter.' Then she lit up again, and they started to laugh.

When Pele got into his car an hour later, he was in much-improved spirits. Alison had been really good company, and she'd managed to distract him from the trauma of the night's events. He had felt a little awkward when she'd suggested a nightcap back at hers. He'd declined, saying he was exhausted, but Alison had taken it all in her stride and didn't appear to be put out in the slightest by his rejection. What he'd really liked about her was that she'd managed to skate down the fine line of letting him know that she was interested but without coming over as either pushy or needy. He'd taken the number she'd offered him and added it to the list of contacts in his new Samsung flip phone.

But he hadn't committed to calling her.

As he drove over the bridge, his thoughts turned back, as he knew they would, to Angela and why he'd said what he had before she'd left. He cursed himself; she was a married woman. Married to someone he'd never liked, but that didn't make it okay. His temples began to throb with a familiar ache brought on by the day's events. As he turned the car into his close and up the driveway, he parked before the dark, empty house and thought about how it had tragically become some kind of metaphor for his life.

The next evening, Pele arrived at his mother's house at the usual time. Friday night dinner had become a ritual since Caroline's death. His mother had insisted that he came over as a way of getting him out of the house at least one night a week during those bleak, post-Caroline days. He wondered if she'd had any idea she'd be letting herself in for a twelve-year-long slog. Pele no longer knew if he went weekly for his mother's sake or his own. He figured it was probably a bit of both. He pushed the key into the door lock and shouted out, 'It's me, Mum!'

'I'm in the back.' She was always in the back. 'It's nearly ready. Steak pie, chips and peas.' Pele had long given up telling his mother that he tried to eat a tad more healthily these days. It wasn't a concept she was able to grasp, preferring to serve up 'Good, solid, British food and not any of that foreign rubbish you eat.'

He went through to the kitchen, where she was engaged in shaking a basket of chips over an ancient, deep-fat fryer. She lifted the metal sieve out and tipped a pile of steaming chips onto a heap of paper towels before scrunching them half to death. Pele winced at the size of the chips and the amount of oil that would be on them. He'd made some small progress over time as she used vegetable oil instead of lard and bought paper towels to absorb the excess. Still, despite his misgivings, he'd guzzle them down all the same. Given the miles he was racking up each week, he didn't have to be overly concerned about the calories.

He placed a kiss on her smooth, upturned cheek as she dabbed at the chips. Then he removed his coat, which he hung on the back door hook. Her face still maintained a youthfulness that defied her age. 'Hiya, love. Will you take the bread and butter through to the dining room, Brian? I'll only be a minute. And pour the tea, will you?' He followed his mother's orders and lifted a wooden tray carrying a plate stacked with white bread, a butter dish, and a pot of hot tea into the dining room. The wooden floor that lay beneath the antiquated carpet creaked underneath his weight as he walked across it. His mother's 'posh' china dinner set rattled in the dresser with each step he took. The room seemed to amplify every little noise, whether it was a footstep or the ticking clock, as though they were an intrusion upon its silence. There was a sense of time standing still in this room, as though life was happening everywhere else but here. The Damask curtains were nearly as old as he was, and the cream and gold drapes were in remarkable condition considering. The last glow of the setting sunlight spilt into the room, and happy memories from his childhood flooded in. Apart from a lick of paint every now and then, the house hadn't changed since he'd been a small boy. It was furnished in exactly the same way as it had been all those years ago. It all seemed like a lifetime ago to him now.

And he supposed it was.

From the set table, he looked out of the window and into the back garden. The rhododendrons needed cutting back, and the grass was overgrown. He'd been so busy with his own life that he'd not done as much as he ought to for his mother. She would never complain, and gardening was her passion, but she struggled with the heavier maintenance side of it these days. He made a mental note to get around to it before the weather got too cold.

A few minutes later, she burst through the door carrying two china plates in her liver-speckled hands and placed one down before him. 'Steak pie and chips,' she announced as if she was serving up a Lobster Thermidor.

'Thanks, Mum. That looks great,' Pele said, shaking the salt pot over his chips. 'I'll be coming over in a few days to tackle that back garden. It needs sorting before the winter sets in.' They both sat eating in silence. The only sounds emanating from the dining room were forks and knives scraping against the plates and the ticking of the clock on the wall.

'You know,' said his mother after a little while, pointing her fork in his general direction. 'I don't think you should come around to do the garden or even next Friday for dinner, to be honest.' He paused eating, holding his cutlery just above the side of his plate.

'Oh? You don't?' he replied, knowing exactly where this was going. 'And why's that then?'

He watched her resolute face, which was set like granite, as she completely ignored him. She began to butter a slice of bread with all the concentration of a micro surgeon. Her frail features belied the strength and determination she was capable of. When she'd smothered every inch of the bread with a coating of butter, she put her knife down and looked at him. 'Because Brian, you need to get out a bit more. A single man your age coming to his mother's house for dinner every Friday night just isn't healthy. Is this what you think Caroline would have wanted for you? For you to just throw your life away. You should be going out and meeting people your own age, not sitting here with me.' It was all the same stuff she'd said the last time, and he didn't want to hear it then, either. And even though she probably had a point, he felt more than a little irritated. How did she know what Caroline would have wanted? How could anyone know?

'What? Do you mean like you did after Dad died?' He immediately regretted the impulsive reply.

'That might be a fair comment, Brian, but you're forgetting that I had you to look after,' she said quietly. 'And apart from that, I was quite happy on my own. You need a woman, Brian. You're not like me because I actually like being alone.' She pressed her lips together and breathed in through her nose. Reaching to gently pat his cheek, she said softly, 'It's time, son.

You're not getting any younger, and you need to move on.'

'Well, here's something that might cheer you up: I was having a drink with someone last night. A colleague from work. And an attractive one my own age, too. So, if it's all the same with you, I will still be coming around to do the garden this week. The two aren't mutually exclusive, you know?'

Her mouth dropped open in surprise, and her tired eyes lifted in shock and obvious delight. 'Well, good!' she exclaimed enthusiastically and returned to her meal, which she finished in silence. The happiness etched on her face didn't fade the whole time she was eating.

After a little while, Pele sat back, bloated; the remains of a few chips lay uneaten on his plate. He was more unable than unwilling to finish them. He picked up the teapot with a multi-coloured, homemade warmer covering it. He remembered his mother knitting it when he was a child more than two decades ago and thinking how cool and quirky it looked. He poured the dark amber liquid into his cup. 'Do you want another?' he asked, holding it over his mother's cup.

'Yes, Brian. That would be lovely, thanks,' she beamed at him.

A couple of hours later, he was sitting in his front room, attempting to mark books and finding it impossible to concentrate. His mother had unwittingly stirred up emotions in him that he'd been trying to keep in check all week. He was irritated that she could press buttons he didn't even know he had. She had never abandoned the premise that she knew what was best for him because she could 'Read him like a book,' despite the fact he was now an adult. And while this might have been true to some extent, why did she have to make him analyse things he'd prefer not to think about? He massaged his temples and looked at the clock despondently.

After finishing the last book in the set, he dropped his pen onto the table and stood up, groaning. His lower back ached from sitting in the same position for too long. He stretched and bent backwards a few times to relieve the tension and then went off to the fridge to pour a glass of orange juice from a carton. He sat down on the sofa and took a long swallow, freezing his tonsils as he did and sending a shooting pain up into his head. It reminded him to adjust the temperature of the fridge. He put the empty glass on top of the coffee table and reached into his pocket to pull out his mobile phone. He idly scrolled through the numbers and found Alison's. It had a 01925 dialling code as she lived out in east Warrington. He stared at it and thought about Caroline, Angela, and his mess of a life. What had Father O'Malley told him a while ago? Something along the lines of: 'If you keep doing the same old thing and expect a different outcome, it's a sure sign of madness.'

He brought his thoughts back to the present; he liked Alison, and they were both unattached, so why not go for it? His heart had begun to beat a little faster. At the same time, doubt began to edge its way into his thoughts. Was he doing the right thing? Meanwhile, his thumb seemed to operate independently of his will and was already pressing on the phone number. He wondered if he should put the phone down, but it was already ringing. 'Hello?' said a chirpy voice.

'Oh! Erm...Hello Alison. It's me, Brian...err...Pele. I was just... well, I wondered if you were doing anything tonight?'

Ten minutes later, he was in his car driving towards east Warrington.

On Monday morning, Pele tried to avoid being lured by Alison's flirtatious smile in the staff room. But he found himself drawn to her smiling, green eyes and easy-going banter. Even when she was being serious, she wore an expression bordering on mischief. He found her cheerfulness and exuberance for life very attractive. The warm glow that a new relationship often brings flowed through his veins, and it made him feel alive for the first time in years. The excitement was further enhanced by the fact that they'd agreed to keep it secret for the moment. He was aware that in any school, inter-staff relationships didn't stay secret for long. But for now, at least, only they knew.

Pele's thoughts drifted back to Friday night as the Head talked relentlessly about standards and consistency. When he arrived at Alison's, he discovered that her boys were at their dad's house for the weekend. A couple of glasses of wine and some great blather about music and films turned into a late night and an impromptu sleepover in one of the boys' beds.

When he woke up on Saturday morning, it took him a few seconds to figure out why he was lying in a single bed underneath a Thomas the Tank Engine duvet cover. The walls were adorned with large posters of Rugrats and SpongeBob SquarePants characters. He could hear Alison pottering about downstairs in the kitchen. The radio was on low in the background, and she was humming softly.

He got dressed and padded down the stairs in his socks, where he found her preparing breakfast. The aroma of oven-baked croissants and a large pot of fresh coffee made his stomach grumble in anticipation. She wore a cute pair of pink checked pyjamas and fluffy lilac slippers. Her shaggy hair hadn't been brushed yet, giving her a slightly wild and unkempt look. He liked that she was comfortable about not looking perfect. 'Hmm! This is nice,' he said, leaning against the doorway and making her spin around.

'Hey, morning sleepyhead,' she smiled, lifting the pot of coffee from the percolator to pour him a cup. 'Did you sleep okay? You probably only just fit in that bed!' she said, laughing as she passed it into his outstretched hand.

'Yeah. I actually had a great sleep, thanks,' Pele replied, yawning. He sat down at a large mahogany table, which held a small vase of cut flowers. 'And anyway, I had the Rugrats to keep me company all night.' He smiled, cradling the hot mug of coffee with one hand and the side of his head with his other. The microwave beeped twice, and she took out two warm plates on which she scrapped creamy scrambled eggs from a pan, along with smoked salmon and warm croissants.

'Bon appetite,' she said, passing him one and sitting across from him. She twisted the pepper pot over her eggs, gulped a mouthful of black coffee, and tucked in enthusiastically. 'What are your plans for the rest of the day?' asked Alison, licking her fingers after eating.

'I don't really have anything planned, to be honest. Maybe I'll take a run at some point. What about you? Don't you go to your aerobics class at the weekend?' he asked, pushing his empty plate to one side.

'Mmmm… sometimes. But if you want, we could just hang out together and do nothing in particular. It's nice to have an adult around the house to talk to,' she said, picking up the dishes and rinsing them before stacking them in the dishwasher. 'It's weird, but when we got divorced, the thing that hit me the most was how isolated I felt after he left. I mean, we weren't close towards the end, and it was what we both wanted, but when he'd gone, even though I had the boys, I just felt so alone. It was one of the reasons I joined the gym. I'm a people person, and, believe me, too much of my own company isn't a good thing.' She crossed her eyes and pulled a funny face at him. He laughed at her antics and thought about how easy she was to be around and how nice it would be to spend the day with her.

'Yeah. Sounds great to me.'

He helped to clear up the kitchen and then went to get a shower. She'd given him a new Thomas the Tank Engine toothbrush the night before and a tube of matching toothpaste, and she had chuckled with delight when he took them from her hand without a word and proceeded to brush his teeth.

The lazy morning stretched on into the afternoon. Before they both knew it, early evening was approaching. They were reading the Guardian weekend supplement magazines when Pele looked over and said, 'Hey, that Tom Hanks film is on at the cinema, Saving Private Ryan. Do you fancy going to see it?'

'Ohhh! I love Tom Hanks!' Alison replied, looking up from her reclining position on the sofa. 'I've got a local paper somewhere with cinema listing times.' She removed her bare feet from a pile of cushions they were resting on and went to hunt down the newspaper. Pele couldn't remember the last time he felt so relaxed and without the usual accompanying anxiety.

Everything seemed so easy around her.

After scrolling through the listings, she announced, 'It's showing at six at the Odeon. We could pick up a change of clothes for you before we go and then head to the Chinese takeout afterwards and a bottle of wine?'

This was clearly an invitation to stay another night, and he didn't need to think twice about his answer.

When the Head eventually got to the end of his normal Monday morning staff admonishment, he grunted, bade the bored-looking faces a 'good day,' and walked off, having given the week its usual dreadful start. The staff broke up into pairs and small groups, chatting about the weekend or grumbling about even more government initiatives to come as they headed towards the pigeonholes to collect their post. As Pele put his assorted notes and letters into a bundle to sift through, a cheery voice behind him said, 'Morning, Mr Smith. Did you have a nice weekend?' Pele smiled at the game that lay behind the comment and played happily along.

'Yes, I had a wonderful weekend, Ms. Janners. Yourself?' She leant forward towards her pigeonhole and, in doing so, brushed her body lightly against his.

'Oh, you know? Same old,' she said, pulling the contents from her box and putting them in her bag. 'A film, a Chinese takeout with a glass of wine, and then early to bed on Saturday night.' She was right, he thought. It had been relatively early when they'd gone up, but it was late when they finally fell asleep in each other's arms.

'Seems like you need to get out a bit more,' he said as she turned away and headed for the door.

'I intend to Mr Smith,' she called after him. 'I intend to.' As Pele watched her go, she turned back to wink at him before she exited the door with no small panache. A smile emerged at the corner of his mouth, and he whistled a tune as he picked up his bag and made his way to the classroom.

It was an unusually warm October evening, and Pele was driving towards the bridge that he crossed each day for work. It was a notorious traffic hotspot. He had to leave immediately after school finished or stay until after 6:00 pm to avoid it. As the clocks had just changed, he wanted to leave as early as he could and grab the extra daylight minutes to drive home.

He turned the Audi left to take the slip road to the bridge, and he was dismayed to see a sign indicating a closed lane. Even though it was approaching 4:30 pm, a steady queue of traffic was already backed up as he joined the slow crawl to the bridge.

The dismay he felt at that point paled in comparison to ten minutes later when the car lost power and rolled to a stop. A couple of burly guys from the car behind got out and helped push Pele's Audi into the closed lane. Pele thanked them for helping him out before they jumped back into their car, which was holding up an increasingly growing lane of traffic.

Pele pulled out his mobile phone only to discover that it had gone flat. Could the day possibly get any worse, he wondered? He flicked the hood open and peered hopelessly into the engine. He had no real idea why he did this, as you could write on the back of a postage stamp what he knew about the mechanics of the modern car. If you wanted a Shakespeare Sonnet analysing, he was your man, but if you wanted to know where the petrol cap on a car was, ask someone else. All he could glean was that there was no steam escaping, and all of the wires seemed intact. This was about as far as his expertise stretched. Feeling despondent, he lowered the hood and sighed. The traffic was speeding a little faster past him now that he was out of the way. He looked at his watch. He would have to walk back to find a phone box to call the RAC, and by the time he found one, it would be pitch black.

Great.

He opened the passenger door and slipped on his jacket. As he did so, he noticed that a pickup truck had passed and was pulling in just ahead. Pele was a little alarmed to see the driver of the truck had knocked several cones out of the way without seemingly a care in the world. The truck ground to a screeching halt and then began to reverse towards his car. Pele was finding it difficult to believe his luck. The truck stopped abruptly, and the driver's door flew open almost simultaneously. A man hopped out and came bounding around to the truck's rear. It was Slug MacDonald.

'I thought it was you, Smith,' he laughed, clearly enjoying Pele's predicament.

'If you thought it was me, then why didn't you drive on?' Pele retorted, to which Slug shrugged.

'Aye. Well, I didn't. Even though I maybe should have.' He took his baseball cap off and scratched his head. 'Open her up then, and let's have a look inside.' Pele was more than a little perplexed but also more than a little grateful.

'Thanks, Erm... I didn't see anything obvious,' he mumbled, lifting the bonnet. Wearing black steel toecap boots and a navy blue boiler suit, Slug stuck his head under and looked around. Less than a minute later, he closed it and looked at Pele with a wry smile.

'Right, well, the bad news is it could be your timing belt's gone. This don't look like a simple fix. Get yerself in the truck, and I'll load the car on the back.' Pele had a moment of panic.

'I'm not sure that's a good idea. I mean, I have breakdown cover with the RAC, and it's probably going to be a lot cheaper, no offense, than you doing it.' Slug pulled a big, burly hand out of his overall pocket and slowly rubbed his chin.

'Is it? Might not be, as you don't know what I'm going to charge you, and the RAC won't fix it: they'll only take it to a garage. It's getting dark, and the traffic's building,' he shrugged. 'But here, use my mobile and phone it in, if you want? Or I'll take it back to my yard and get one of the lads to look at it. I'm heading back there anyway. It's your choice. You'll be home with me in half an hour or later tonight if you want to call them out. Either way, your call?' Pele looked forlornly at the crawling traffic with their headlights lighting up the early evening and then back towards Slug, who was holding his mobile phone out and fixing him with an ambiguous stare.

Seeing he had few options, he said, 'Yeah, I think you're right, Stephen. Cheers, I appreciate your help.' And with that, he tossed Slug his car keys.

About twenty minutes later, they'd re-joined the traffic and were heading in the direction of Pele's home. He sat with his briefcase between his feet while the truck's heater pumped out a powerful breeze of warm air into his face. He glanced around the cab, which smelled of engine oil and had a large portion of Slug's 'office' scattered over the floor and dashboard. From the little he'd heard about Slug in the intervening years since he'd last seen him, he was quite a wealthy guy. He owned several businesses, including one in construction, a garage repair, and an MOT place. To look at him, Pele thought, you would think he still lived up on the old council estate. Proof, if ever it was needed, that you couldn't judge a book by the cover. 'So, what are you doing out over this way? I thought you had a big house on the other side of the bridge?' Pele asked, breaking the silence.

'I do,' replied Slug, glancing over, 'but I also have a couple of houses on this side of the bridge, and one or two of my tenants are late with their rent. So, I thought I'd pop over for a little chat. See if I can't work out a payment plan for them.'

'You drove this big truck to do a couple of house visits?' Pele asked incredulously.

'As I said, I was offering to work out a payment plan for their arrears,' he said, in a crafty tone and a smirk that tugged at the corner of his mouth. 'Fortunately for them, they managed to find some money that they'd forgotten about. It must have fallen down the back of a sofa. So, I didn't need to take anyone's car as payment in the end.' The smirk developed into a chuckle, which in turn triggered a coughing fit. He pulled out a tissue from his pocket and coughed into it. 'I'm alright, it's not contagious,' he winked, glancing at Pele's face. 'I think it's an allergy or something,' he said, pushing the tissue back into his pocket. Pele recognised the street kid mentality in Slug that he would probably never shake off. As Caroline frequently told him, 'You can take the man out of the street, but you can't take the street out of the man.' Pele couldn't help feeling a bit sorry for the 'payment plan' tenants, but he said nothing. Slug was silent for a minute before he asked, 'Are you still living off Morval?'

'Yeah,' said Pele, 'I never moved. Not even after...' Slug turned to look at him in the dim light before speaking.

'I was really sorry to hear that, you know. I liked Caroline a lot. And she always had the good sense to keep away from me.' He chuckled to himself at this.

Pele found himself smiling and reassessing his deep-seated ideas about Slug. On the one hand, Slug went the extra mile to help him out. He seemed self-aware, was clearly a successful businessman, and, to top it all off, his daughter was an incredible child. They were commendable characteristics, but the cruel streak he remembered from their youth was still evident. His late-paying tenants were taught a 'Slug' lesson in that he wouldn't let anyone 'get one over' on him. He couldn't help thinking that Slug was as complex a character as anyone he had ever encountered.

Eventually, Pele replied, 'Yeah, everyone liked Caroline, to be honest. She was just that sort of person. Warm, funny...' he tailed off, not really wanting to go any further down memory lane. Instead, he switched tack. 'Anyway, you've done alright for yourself, haven't you? Business, houses, and your daughter Caitlin's a delight to teach. She's quite exceptional, you know?'

'Yeah, thanks. She is that all right, but you can put it all down to her mother,' Slug said, with a slight change in his tone. Pele didn't bite. He turned his face towards the window in silence and held his fingers against the air outlet. 'You know something?' Slug broke through Pele's reverie. 'I met Angela at my sister's wedding. I remembered her from all those years ago when O'Malley ran that youth club thing. Couldn't believe it when she agreed to go out with me, even more so when she turned up and laughed at some of my terrible jokes. I was smitten from the off. I asked her to marry me four times before she said yes. Strangely enough, it was the same year that your

Caroline died.' Pele brought his hand back down as Slug's words hit home. She must have said yes only a short time after their fateful meeting in the pub. He remembered that Slug's sister Niamh was married the week after. Caroline had always kept him informed of the local weddings, hoping he'd eventually take the hint one day.

He turned to look at Slug, whose eyes were fixed on the road ahead, but Slug continued to speak. 'Yeah, four times I asked. The first three times, she flatly said no.' He looked at Pele. 'Do you know why she said no?' Pele didn't answer, hoping that his wild guess was wrong but knowing that he would soon find out. When he didn't reply, Slug told him anyway. 'She said no because of you.'

'Me?' Pele replied in a surprised voice that bordered on a squeak. He couldn't work out why Slug was telling him this. But for some reason that he couldn't fathom, Slug wanted him to know.

'Now, now! You needn't come that game,' Slug said evenly; both of his hands gripped the top of the steering wheel, and he stared straight ahead. 'I'm over all of that business. She said yes, eventually. That's all that matters. But not before she told me about you and her.' Pele was searching for an appropriate response, but the best he could come up with was,

'Me and her? There is no me and her. There never was. Not really.'

'Hmmphh… yeah…Whatever,' Slug snorted and proceeded to change gear while accelerating. 'She told me she'd always had strong feelings for you. That was why she kept saying no to me. Said it wouldn't be fair on me.'

'So, are you taking me home?' Pele asked. 'Or are you taking me to one of your scrapyards to get rid of me?' Slug tossed his head back and gave a loud belly laugh at this, which was followed by another cough.

'No, Pele lad. I'm taking you home. Believe it or not, I'm a changed man these days. She married me in the end. That's all that really matters, well, to me anyway. I've given her everything she could ever want. She has the best that money can buy, and we're still together. Yeah, it's not all been plain sailing, but the old me? Well, that all stopped the day Caitlin was born. I wanted to become a better man from that point. I wanted to be a dad she'd grow up to be proud of. The sort of dad I never had.' Pele's head was reeling, and he really didn't know what to say. He watched the shadows slide on a loop from the front of the cab to the back as they passed below the orange streetlights. In the end, Slug spoke again.

'And then, if things weren't bad enough, the kid sings your praises constantly! Huh! Now there's irony for you: not only my wife but my daughter as well.' He half smiled to himself as though the irony was something that genuinely amused him.

Slug turned the truck into Maple, and Pele realised that they were almost at his house. He felt awkward and a little confused. 'I don't know what to tell you, Stephen. Except I honestly didn't know about any of that, and it doesn't bring me any happiness to hear it. However, I do know that Angela can't take all of the credit for Caitlin. My observations of her are that she's your daughter through and through. You should be proud of what you've done with her.'

'Yeah? Well maybe. And what's done is done. I haven't got any hard feelings about it these days. We get the hand we're given, and I've been dealt a pretty good one compared to most, I reckon.' Pele recognised this philosophy was something he'd clearly adopted from Angela, and it made him smile.

'Do you know what became of the Cross lads?' Pele asked, partly out of curiosity and partly to change the subject. Slug smoothly, moved down through the gears and started to indicate left. He rotated the large steering wheel effortlessly and turned into Pele's street.

'Sean died of a heart attack getting off the Liverpool train a couple of years ago; drugs related probably. The other two are both in the nick. Jimmy did some work for me a few years back, but he couldn't keep on the straight and narrow. You can only do so much to help someone out, and I had to let him go in the end.'

Slug expertly pulled into the side of the kerb and parked right outside Pele's house. Pele was a little shocked that he knew exactly where he lived, but then, when he thought about it, he wasn't shocked at all. 'Right then. This is you. Write your phone number down on that,' he said, handing Pele a notepad and a pen. 'You'll have to get a lift into work tomorrow. One of the lads in the garage will look it over and get in touch with you.' Pele wrote down his number and handed the notepad back to Slug, who gave it a cursory glance before tossing it back onto a pile of paperwork on the dashboard.

Opening the truck door, he said, 'Thanks for helping me out tonight, Stephen. How much will I owe you? Ballpark figure, so I can get it out of the bank tomorrow?'

'No idea until one of the lads tells me. I won't rip you off if that's what yer thinking?' Pele smiled.

'No, that's not what I'm thinking. After all, you know where I live.'

'Yeah, I do,' laughed Slug. 'Now get lost. I'm busy. Someone will be in touch.' Pele got down from the truck and slammed the door. Slug didn't look back but raised his arm out of the window as he pulled away, leaving Pele alone on his drive.

Pele managed to get a lift off Dominic into work the next morning, and when he returned home, his car was already parked on the driveway. On the passenger seat was an envelope. In very bad handwriting, someone had scribbled 'Pele.' He guessed who had written it, and when he pulled the note out, it was only just legible: *'Sorted. No charge. Who knows? One day, I might need you to do something for me.'* Pele put the note back into the envelope and, feeling a little bewildered, headed inside.

He had no idea that one day, he would indeed be asked to make good on his debt.

A month later, on a fine and bright Saturday afternoon, Pele found himself on one of the chilled food aisles at his local M&S store. He wondered at what point in his life he'd begun to enjoy meandering through the food department so much. His general aversion to shopping was very much intact, but he found guilty pleasure whenever he browsed in the M&S food hall. A vivid memory flashed through his mind of Caroline's passion for shopping. He smiled to himself as he recalled her limitless enthusiasm for 'retail therapy,' as she called it. One time, he'd trailed behind her through what must have been ten different shops to get him kitted out for a friend's wedding. He'd started with the mindset of a four-year-old who became increasingly irritable with every shop that she made him go inside.

As his mind wandered over the events of that day, it suddenly occurred to him that he wasn't engulfed in a cloud of sadness from the memory. It was a strange sensation, being able to think about her without the accompanying gloom. Breezing over to the cheese counter, he reined in the impulse to buy all of his favourites and was trying to decide if buying the Manchego, a strong blue and some rather tasty-looking Brie, was too much for lunch. Aware that his mouth was watering and his stomach was making some alarming noises, he made a swift decision and placed all three on top of his basket full of savouries.

The next stop was the Wine Aisle, and then he planned to head back and have lunch. He picked up a bottle of Chablis and was reading the label when he heard a voice say his name.

'Pele?' He looked up and there was Angela. She was elegantly attired in a fitted khaki dress that was just above her knees with opaque tights and flat boots. Pele wondered if she ever had an off day.

'Angela! Hey. It's nice to see you,' he said, unsure of the greeting protocol as her daughter's teacher. He stood with his arms semi-open in a form of greeting. One hand held the bottle of wine, and the other an overflowing shopping basket. 'How are you doing?'

'Yeah, I'm great,' she replied, sounding a little awkward. 'You know? Busy with work. Same-old otherwise. You?'

'Same,' he informed her, trying to find some space in the basket to put the wine in. 'Always too much to do at work and no time to do it.' He felt uncomfortable, but Angela seemed even more on edge than he did. He wondered if Slug had told her about their conversation in his truck. Deciding that neutral territory was a safe bet, he went for some. 'Caitlin's doing very well, you know. She really is a delight to teach.'

'Thanks, Pele. She's a bit of a one-off, that's for sure,' she smiled a little uncertainly and then glanced around somewhat nervously. 'Listen, I just wanted to say that since parent's evening, well, I've wanted to talk to you. Seeing you was such a shock, and I wasn't sure if I should contact you. The thing is, I wanted to tell you how sorry I am about the last time we met and how it ended. It's been on my mind ever since, and I wanted to...' At that moment, Angela froze as Pele felt a hand slip under his arm and hold onto his. There by his side was Alison.

'Hey, Pele,' she said, glancing between him and Angela while she said it. 'Did you get everything we need?'

'Err...yes, I think so,' said Pele, flushing slightly. 'Erm... this is. Do you know Caitlin MacDonald from my form?'

'Yes. I do,' replied Alison, smiling sweetly. 'She's such a lovely girl.'

'Isn't she?' Pele bumbled. 'Well, this is her mum. We met the other week at parent's evening.'

'Lovely to meet you,' said Alison, releasing Pele's hand to extend her own out to Angela.

'You too,' Angela said. Her face had flushed ever so slightly, but otherwise, she managed to compose herself, all things considered. 'Yes, well... I won't take up any more of your time, Mr Smith. It was very kind of you to let me know about Caitlin, and I'll be sure to mention that essay to her. I'm sure she'll have it in on time.' With that, she turned to Alison. 'And very nice to meet you too...err...?'

'Alison. Alison Janners. Art.'

'Yes. You too, Miss Janners. Have a lovely afternoon.' And with that, she turned and headed quickly towards the exit. Alison slipped her hand through Pele's arm, winked, and then pulled him in the direction of the tills. 'Come on. Let's get you back to mine. I'm dying to hear all about the lovely Mrs MacDonald.'

Pele sighed and followed her pull.

He was half expecting to be grilled in the car, but Alison kept her counsel, which made Pele wonder when and how she would start the discussion. If he'd learnt anything about women over the years, there was absolutely no way on God's green earth that she wasn't going to bring it up.

Pele drove whilst Alison played around with the car music. She soon had The Smiths blasting out. He turned his head to look at her, and as their eyes met, she smiled brightly and squeezed his hand. Perhaps he'd gotten it all wrong.

After a short ten-minute drive, they picked up the food bags and headed inside Alison's house, where she went into full-on organising mode. 'I'll put the food away. Will you get a bottle of wine out of the fridge? I fancy a drink with lunch. And you will find the bread knife for the baguettes over there in the knife block. We can have a picnic with some of that cheese and continental meat you bought. There's olives and salad in the fridge, too.' She prattled off the orders without drawing breath or waiting for him to reply. So, he busied himself around her kitchen, wondering when they were going to face what was bothering her. 'There's a Bette Davis film on Channel 4 later, shall we watch it? I'm going upstairs to get out of this dress so I can enjoy my dinner without thinking I'm a heifer.'

'A heifer! Alison, what are you talking about? You're far from a heifer!'

'I am compared to some women; Mrs MacDonald, for example...'

And there it was.

'Alison,' Pele groaned. 'Where's all this come from? Can't we just have a nice evening watching La Davis, listen to a bit more of the Smiths or anything else you feel like doing?'

'We can,' she replied while walking out of the kitchen. 'I promise not to say another word... until I do.'

She returned in a sombre mood, wearing a pair of pale blue lounge pants and a white crew neck sweater. Pele had set the table and was pouring her a glass of wine. He put the bottle back in the fridge, and as he handed it to her, he attempted to draw a smile. 'Is the Smurf look meant to detract from the heifer look?' With hindsight, it probably wasn't the wisest thing he could have said. She plonked herself into a chair facing him across the dining table.

'You might think this is a joke, Pele,' she replied. 'But I'm too old to be played for a fool.' Pele immediately went into defence mode.

'And what exactly do you think is going on, Alison? Before Parent's evening, I hadn't even seen her in ten years. So, this does feel like a bit of an overreaction? I never had you pegged for the jealous type.' Alison's eyes hardened at this. Without raising her voice, she spoke deliberately and precisely. There wasn't any hint of the friendly banter he was accustomed to.

'Okay, Pele, let's lay our cards on the table, shall we? For starters, no, I'm not the jealous type. But I do know when somebody I'm seeing has an infatuation with another woman.'

'I don't know on what basis you've made that judgement?' Pele choked.

'I'm saying it simply on the basis that it's true.' Alison's face softened at this point, but she carried on. 'I saw the way you both reacted to each other at the parent's evening. I dismissed it, but today, I confirmed something that I already knew but maybe didn't want to believe.'

'But it's not…' Pele started to speak and found he couldn't finish. He stared forlornly into Alison's face and knew that he couldn't lie to her. His past had haunted him for long enough, and if he had any hope for his future, it couldn't be based on half-truths. She tilted her head, waiting for him to continue. So Pele began, and she listened without interrupting while he told her it all. They drank wine. Occasionally, but not that often, Alison interjected with a question, to which Pele answered honestly. When he'd finished the whole sorry story, she leant forward on both of her elbows and stared at him.

'Thank you for your honesty. I can't imagine any of that was easy.' She then leant back into her chair; her fingers reached up to slide her hair behind her ears. Her green eyes darted around the room as if the words she sought were hiding in plain sight.

'Pele, I want you to know that I really like you. I mean, I really like you. But I won't; that is to say, I can't put myself in a position where we could get closer, always knowing at the back of my mind that you were really in love with someone else. And I mean, let's face it, she's every woman's nightmare in terms of competition.' She stood up to retrieve another bottle of wine from the fridge. 'One more for the road?'

Pele was back in the Thomas the Tank Engine bed that night, and sleep didn't come easily. Pele knew that Alison was right. How could he promise to stop an emotion that surfaced every time he saw Angela? Who wants to live a fantasy life instead of a real one? He figured one relationship lie was enough to last a person a lifetime. He wasn't going to travel down the same road again with yet another woman who deserved better.

The next morning, he went down to the kitchen to find Alison sitting at the table reading a book and sipping coffee. Pele walked over and sat down. 'Friends?' Pele asked, sliding his open hand over towards her.

'Always.' Alison replied huskily, placing hers in his and squeezing. He got up from the table and collected his things. Picking up his car keys, he leant over and kissed her gently on her forehead before leaving through the front door.

At the end of May, Pele was walking back to his classroom after a particularly difficult last lesson. He turned the corner into the lower school block and was surprised to find Caitlin McDonald leaning against the wall outside of his door. As he approached, he gave her his warmest smile and said, 'Hey, Caitlin. This is a nice surprise. What can I do for you?'

'Oh, hi, Mr Smith. Can I come in? I was hoping that you might be able to help me with a book I'm reading.' Hearing her response, which was a muted one, he couldn't help but notice that the usually indomitable Caitlin MacDonald seemed a little subdued to him, and he hoped there was nothing wrong. Pele put his key into the door and pushed through, beckoning for Caitlin to follow.

'Of course, I'll try to help you in any way I can, Caitlin. Please, come on in.'

Once inside, Pele dropped his admin and schoolbooks onto the desk and turned to face Caitlin, who was definitely not her usual bubbly self. He knew this as she hadn't spoken for at least a minute, which was practically unheard of. Standing perfectly still, she waited until she had Pele's undivided attention before sitting down. 'Okay, Caitlin. How can I help you?' She delved into a small satchel she was carrying and pulled out a small paperback book.

Holding it up in front of Pele so that he could see it clearly.

'I know we don't study this book until year 10,' she said. 'But I wanted to read it now. Firstly, because I really like whales, but also because I like to get ahead of things. But I have to say that I don't understand it at all.' Pele looked at the book she was holding up and raised his eyebrows before smiling and nodding that he'd registered the title. She said, 'I've read it, but, well, it just doesn't make any sense to me, and I was hoping you might be able to explain it, Mr Smith?' Pele reached over and took the abridged version of Melville's Moby Dick from her outstretched hand, flipping it over between his fingers before placing it down on his desk.

'I imagine you found it pretty heavy going. It's not an easy read for many adults, let alone someone your age. Although you are a very intelligent young lady,' he added as an afterthought, not wanting to offend her. Caitlin seemed to ignore his comment. With her brow furrowed and head tilted a little, she stared at his face as though the world depended on it.

'Can I ask you, Mr Smith, do you like the book?' At this, Pele breathed deeply through his nose and scratched the back of his head as he considered his response.

'Do I like the book? Well, let me just say this. I think the opening page and a half is the greatest piece of writing I've ever read, and then the rest of it's not that far behind. So, I guess I can confidently say: yes, I like the book. I like it a lot. What was your overall impression?' On hearing this, Caitlin's facial expression bore a mixture of puzzlement and frustration at his answer. There was only a brief pause.

'Well, I have a problem with Captain Ahab, Mr Smith. And it was him that I wanted to ask you about.' Pele grinned at her passionate reply.

'Well, Caitlin. You wouldn't be the first person to feel that way about the old Captain. Explain to me what your problem with him is if you can.' Caitlin's brow furrowed tighter as she attempted to put into words what she was feeling.

'Well, to my mind, Ahab makes no sense. He's just crazy and a bit mad. And then, in the end, he sort of kills himself. And for no reason! Some novels have bad endings, but they at least make sense. Nothing makes any sense to me about this story, and yet it's supposed to be a brilliant book. I just don't get it.' She stopped there with a pained expression. Pele was transported back to his own childhood literary stumbles when reading the book. After a moment's silence and composing his thoughts, he answered her.

'I think Melville wrote the book to make us wonder about who and what we are. What does it actually mean to be human? What are our limitations? How far will our passions drive us? It could be to our death if we really want something badly enough. Yes, Ahab is someone we could think of as being mad. But isn't he also very alive? It may be that he knows, really knows, that he could die chasing the whale. But that passion, that desire, means he's not going to ever give up, and he's going to keep fighting!' Caitlin studied Pele's animated face.

'Even to the point that he might die, though?' she said, struggling to understand. Pele picked up the book and handed it back to Caitlin.

'I guess Melville's telling us that some things in life are worth fighting for, no matter what it is you might lose.'

'So, are you saying that Ahab is a hero and not the stupid man that I thought he was?' she asked, looking at the book being held out to her and back at Pele's face. Pele shrugged.

'I think he could be both.' Caitlin reached out, took the novel from his outstretched hand, and placed it back into her bag.

'Thank you, Mr Smith. I suppose it makes a bit more sense to me now. I'll read it over again and try to understand the book with what you've told me in mind.'

Despite the fact Pele appeared to have helped, he still couldn't help feeling that there was something more than the book that was troubling her, and so felt compelled to ask, 'Is that all, Caitlin? You seem a little bit, erm…out of sorts?' Caitlin fumbled about with the satchel's fastening and looked down. After a few seconds, she glanced up at him.

'My mum's been sad lately. She doesn't want to come to the end-of-year presentations, even though I really want her to come.' Pele shuffled uneasily in his chair whilst simultaneously hoping Caitlin wouldn't notice.

'Well, I'm sorry to hear that. I really am. Perhaps she's got a lot on? I don't really know what to say, Caitlin.' Caitlin turned away and gave a small sigh.

'I'm sure that's what it must be. I can't think of any other reason why she wouldn't come. Anyway, thank you for all your help with the book, Mr Smith.'

As she left, Pele couldn't help but wonder if there wasn't more to it while deep down knowing that there was.

2010

Downton Abbey; Trapped Miners; Avatar;
Stig Larsson books; Taylor Swift.

It was Friday evening. Pele arrived at his mother's and let himself in with the key. He was going to announce his arrival when he heard a familiar voice coming from the dining room. He pulled off his coat and, since the coat hook was full, he hung it over the bannister and walked down the hallway. The booming, cheerful voice was unmistakeable. Pele pushed against the slightly ajar door and entered, the beginnings of a smile already forming on his mouth. His mother glanced up from pouring O'Malley a cup of tea from the multi-coloured teapot. She beamed a warm smile at Pele.

'Hello love,' she said, whilst offering her cheek for him to place a kiss, which he duly did. The priest was reclining at the table in his ever-so-characteristic posture. Pele figured he had to be well into his eighties now, but he looked ten years younger. His long legs stretched before him, and his giant bear hands interlocked over an even more enormous belly. He looked at his analogue watch with exaggerated mock surprise.

'Ahh! There you are, Brian. I was just telling your mother it wouldn't be like you to be late now, would it?' Pele grinned and pulled out a chair. Furnishing a quick reply.

'Oh, it was touch and go with all the traffic, Father.' He couldn't help but feel amused when the priest called him Brian, which he had only ever done in the presence of his mother. 'Anyway, didn't you know? Punctuality is the virtue of the bored,' Pele teased, taking his place at the table whilst undoing his tie and top button.

'Ah, so yer quoting Waugh at me now, are ya?' Pele shook his head in surprise at the old priest and laughed.

'I am, and I have to confess I'm very impressed at your literary knowledge, Father. You'd have done alright down at the Cherry Tree on quiz night back in the day.'

'Brian!! Father O'Malley doesn't frequent those kinds of places,' retorted his mother with a shocked look on her face. A tinge of colour spread across her cheeks, and her eyes were wide at the mere suggestion of the Father going into a pub. O'Malley bowed his head towards his chest, ruefully nodding as if agreeing with his mother.

'No, indeed. It wouldn't be proper now, Katy, for sure.' He briefly looked up from under his bushy eyebrows, winked at Pele whilst chortling to himself and said, 'But I think I could have won given a chance, all the same.' Katy huffed a little before excusing herself to go and get the dinner ready. She gave Pele a hard stare before leaving the room. It was a stare that was meant to say: behave yourself in front of the Father.

Pele decided to change the direction of the conversation to avoid further disapproval from his mother, even though O'Malley seemed to be quite relishing the banter. 'Hey, Father, did you see any of the midweek United game?' In truth, Pele was really glad to see O'Malley there. The conversation would be easier with the priest around as topics were less likely to focus on him and whether he was seeing anyone.

Katy returned with two plates of large, battered cod fillets balancing on top of a pile of chips and placed them on the table in front of them. 'Don't wait for me. I'll bring some bread and butter through in a minute.' O'Malley proceeded to eat everything on his plate, followed by two more cups of tea and several chocolate biscuits. He then took his leave on account of having more parishioners to see on his rounds. He bade Katy farewell at the front door.

'Well, I'll see you on Sunday morning then, Katy, and thanks again for dinner. It was grand.'

Pele wasn't sure just exactly when his mother had started to go back to church, and he didn't want to pry either. But he was pleased that she was going again after all this time. She'd seemed more at peace lately, and Pele thought that returning to her faith had clearly had a positive effect on her. When she came back into the room, Pele was finishing the last of his tea. She sat down opposite him, fixed him firmly with her gaze, and said, 'Well?' For a moment, Pele thought it was the: 'Are you seeing anyone yet?' conversation, but then he remembered that he'd told her on the phone he had some news for her.

'Oh, right. Erm…yeah. I'm moving house. I'm thinking of buying a place up by the park. I put mine on the market a few days ago and thought it would take ages to sell. But it sold today.' Pele took a large bite out of a chocolate biscuit he didn't want while waiting for this revelation to upset his mother. This was not because he thought she didn't want him to sell the house but because he hadn't told her that he'd already put it on the market. But Pele's mum's face was glowing.

'Oh, Brian. I'm so pleased to hear that. How long have I been telling you to sell and move on? There are too many painful memories in that house.' Pele had lost count of how many times that conversation had arisen, the: 'You need to move out of that house' one. He'd never been able to make her understand that, despite the sad memories, the house had suited him. This was mostly because he was so busy with work and couldn't be bothered with the hassle of finding something else.

'Well, it's all going through,' he interrupted quickly to prevent a full-blown lecture pertaining to all of the advice that he'd not listened to over the years. 'And I should be out in a couple of months.'

'Do you need any help packing?'

'That would be great, Mum, thanks.' She nodded seriously, no doubt already planning how many boxes he'd need and when to start. There was little more that Caitlin Smith enjoyed in her advanced years than being useful.

A few weeks later, the last thing on Pele's mind was moving

house. The weather was the only thing he could think about as he pulled the porch door behind him, instantly dimming the rush hour traffic noise. The wind and rain were hammering so hard at the windows that it sounded like gravel hitting the glass. He shivered from the damp night air and wiped away the trickles of water running into his eyes. He thought of the long, hot bath he would take as soon as he could get out of his clothes. Hopefully, his mother hadn't boxed up his towels when she'd started the packing. She had a key to the house and had been over that morning to make a start on it. 'Because left to you, the removal van will be here before you even think about starting,' she'd chided.

The branches of a silver birch tree cast their shadows across the wall, creating a scene reminiscent of a Hitchcock film. Once inside, Pele's attention was drawn to two letters lying on the mat. He bent down to pick them up. As he straightened, a needle-like pain shot through his right knee. He considered how a simple task like bending down was taken for granted. That was until you reached 50, and then age decided to give you a good kicking every so often. He'd damaged his knee running a few months ago, and the physio said it could be a year before it fully healed.

Pele was a little perplexed as he rose with the two letters in his hand. He rarely received anything of a personal nature; household bills and supermarket flyers were the only things to drop through his letterbox these days. The first one was hand-written in barely legible black ink. It seemed vaguely familiar, though he couldn't think for the life of him why.

The radiator made soft, gurgling noises in his narrow hallway as the central heating kicked in. He shrugged out of his damp overcoat, dropping his bulging, heavy briefcase with a thud onto the worn, paisley carpet. He was tired and looking forward to a cup of tea. A loud, sharp crack followed by low-rolling thunder filled the air. The already heavy rain became a deluge, hammering with ferocious intensity against the living room windows. He pulled the curtains across just as a streak of lightning twisted brilliantly across a black, empty sky.

The central heating was beginning to warm the house, and the gas fire was at its highest setting. Smiling to himself, he thought his mother would probably not have approved. Still, he took comfort in holding his hands as close to the flame as pain would permit. He raised himself up, being careful not to put too much weight on his knee this time and placed the letters unopened on the mantelpiece next to the glass anniversary clock. Then he went into the kitchen to make a cup of tea and saw that his mother had made significant inroads into boxing up his possessions.

Standing in front of the fire, holding a 'Happy Birthday, Son' mug of steaming tea, a sense of foreboding enveloped him, and he couldn't shake it. The clock's pendulum of four rotating balls glided smoothly to the left, then over to the right and back again. He sighed, realising that he could stand here all night and watch the clock idly tick away the minutes as he procrastinated. Picking up the envelopes, he sat down on the worn but still very comfortable Laura Ashley sofa. It was the same sofa that Caroline had bought in 1985 when they'd first moved in. He'd never had the inclination to change the décor much, so consequently, the house looked like a dilapidated cenotaph in Caroline's memory. He was aware of how it might look to an outsider as if it were some Catholic penance, a sort of assuaging of the burden of guilt that he'd carried through the years. But the simple truth was that he just hated shopping.

He reached for a small, steel letter opener that lay on the coffee table and opened the first envelope. Even at arms-length, he knew he wouldn't be able to read the text, so he foraged around in his inside jacket pocket to locate his reading glasses. Pele placed them on his nose and read the letter with growing sadness and some astonishment, so much so that he read it again just to be sure that it said what he thought it had said. Finally, he removed his glasses and wiped his thumb under his eyes, which were a little glassy, then he placed the letter down on the table while he sat staring into the glowing fire as the news slowly sank in.

Eventually, he turned his attention to the second letter. He forced the sharp, steel blade into the edge of the envelope and prised it open with just enough effort. He pulled out two folded sheets of white notepaper with jagged handwriting on all four sides and read their contents. If the first letter surprised him, he had almost forgotten about it as he read the second. The handwriting scrawl on the envelope that had initially puzzled him was no longer a mystery as a distant memory came flooding back to him.

When he'd finished, he put the letter on the table on top of the previous one and removed his glasses again. Pinching the bridge of his nose where they'd rested, he dropped his head. Then, he began to massage both sides of his temples with the pads of his fingers. A headache was beginning to develop, and he suddenly felt bone weary. After a minute or so, he went to the drinks cabinet, poured himself a large Macallan and drank it while standing. Then he poured another and carried it back to the sofa, where he was compelled to read the letter again. The whisky was beginning to take effect, and he could feel the smooth, amber liquid radiating warmth to his stomach. He considered the strange request in the letter and wondered how he ought to respond.

Should he acquiesce, or should he simply ignore it?

In the end, curiosity killed the cat.

Afternoon visiting time at the hospital was between 2:00 pm and 4:00 pm. Though Pele had arrived at a quarter-to, the staff nurse had told him there wasn't any chance of an early admittance, so he'd waited patiently in the foyer. He wandered over to the vending machine to buy a coffee, but it tasted like dishwater. Unable to concentrate on anything, he folded up his newspaper and watched the steady flow of busy medical staff as they went about their business. Shifting about in the uncomfortable chair, he caught his reflection in the window opposite. Whenever he saw himself in a mirror these days, he

184

wondered at the stranger staring back at him. It never failed to amaze him how quickly he'd gone from the flush of youth to quinquagenarian. His mother's genes, though, were evident. His clear complexion, with just the odd line around his eyes and mouth, made him look much younger than his years. His hair had a few traces of grey running through it, but he was physically fit despite the knee. Also, apart from Friday evenings, he ate a fairly good diet, though, like most teachers, he probably drank more than he should.

The letter had requested that Pele visit on a Saturday afternoon, as this would avoid any complications if he tried to take time off work during a weekday. He'd also been assured that there wouldn't be any other visitors and that no one would ever know that he had been.

A nurse appeared at the entrance of the ward and beckoned the waiting ensemble through the opened door. Pele rose from his chair, holding the newspaper under his arm, and followed the small group of visitors into the ward.

The ward had six beds, each containing a male patient, but none were immediately recognisable to Pele. He stood uncertainly, watching as friends and relatives dispersed around the room. With a jolt of shock, he suddenly recognised the face, the ghost of a face, in the last bay. The pale, sickly figure propped up in the bed nodded at Pele and beckoned to him with an unsteady hand to come over and sit down. 'I wasn't sure if you'd come,' wheezed Slug through an oxygen mask strapped to his gaunt, pallid face.

'Neither was I, if I'm honest,' Pele replied, hoping the shock he felt at seeing his old adversary wasn't imprinted all over his face. He pulled out a plastic chair, sat down on it, and looked steadily at Slug. 'I'm still not sure why you asked me?'

'Well, relax. It's not so we can finally be best mates. I think we'll find that time's ran out on that one,' Slug rasped with a laugh, which was followed by a harsh coughing fit. He bent over with the effort, then lifted his mask and, without saying anything, pointed with a shaking finger to a box of tissues next to Pele on a freestanding cabinet. Pele grasped a handful and then pressed them into his open palm. Slug coughed up what looked like, to Pele at least, a small chunk of his lung into the tissue. As he brought it down from his mouth, Pele held out a disposable waste container made of cardboard that contained a small pile of similar bloodied tissues. Slug dropped it in with a trembling hand and nodded what Pele presumed to be thanks. Then, seemingly exhausted from the effort of coughing, he pushed the mask back into place over his nose and mouth and leant back against a mountain of pillows, his chest straining painfully from the act of simply breathing.

'Can't say you're looking your Sunday best,' said Pele. This elicited a small smile from Slug under his mask.

'Well, I won't be feeling terrible for much longer; that much is for certain.'

'Is it…lung cancer?' Pele tentatively asked. 'You didn't exactly say what it was in the letter. You just said that it was-'

'Terminal,' Slug interjected. His voice had a slight muffled sound due to the mask. 'Not saying it doesn't make it go away. I've told the girls that, too.' Pele watched the rise and fall of his chest as he waited for Slug to elaborate. After a moment, Slug gestured to the side of Pele and towards a glass of water. Pele picked it up and passed it to him. He watched with interest as Slug inserted the end of a straw through one of the holes in the plastic facemask. Then he sipped at the water very slowly. As he did so, his gaunt, pale face contorted; swallowing the water looked as painful as drinking acid. 'Mesothelioma,' Slug finally wheezed. Pele's blank look prompted him to continue. 'Basically, it's lung cancer brought on by asbestosis.'

'That's terrible news,' said Pele, unconsciously lowering his eyes towards the floor. Then he looked at Slug and said cautiously, 'If it means anything, I am really sorry to hear that.'

'Yeah, well, don't be,' Slug half-growled. 'Occupational hazard of the '70s and early '80s demolition industry. I was knocking down all kinds of dodgy stuff back then, and no questions asked, for large amounts of cash.' He paused and sucked in some more air. It was like watching a man breathing through a tiny straw after running a marathon. 'See, it was all cash-in-hand back then. That's what you get when you don't have enough brains to get a cushy job like yours. And when it's cash, no one asks any questions about health and safety.' His frail body contorted in another coughing fit. Pele watched helplessly as he lay gasping through dry, parted lips.

'I don't know anyone who's run a successful business without having brains, and you've got three businesses,' Pele said, searching for something kind to say. 'I mean, you've been the very definition of success, haven't you? A nice house, expensive cars, and you've got a lovely family...' his voice tapering off. Slug's eyes fixed on his and then narrowed.

'Aye, a family. Angela and my girl. I've looked after them and loved them as best as I could. But I won't be around to look after them for much longer.' Pele didn't know what to say, nor did he know where Slug was going with all of this. Was it one more chance to get back at him? Or maybe it was a chance to gloat that he'd married Angela? He didn't think so, but Slug still hadn't gotten to the point.

'So, how long have they given you?' Pele asked, eager to change the subject, even if it was to Slug's impending death.

'Weeks. But it might be only days,' Slug croaked hoarsely. He struggled to lean forward on his elbow. His blue, steely eyes glistened hard and bright, contrasting with his grey, skeletal face. 'I can see in your face; you're wondering why I asked you here?' Pele crossed his legs and sat back in the chair, putting some distance between them.

'I came because you asked me to. Honestly, did you get me here so you could finally apologise for wrecking that jumper?' Slug looked at him blankly for a minute and then began to laugh. A rasping, spluttering fit ensued, and for the first time since he'd arrived, Pele saw something that looked like enjoyment under his pained expression.

'I'd forgotten all about that,' he cackled. 'Got a crack and a half off the old fella as well for it. Bigger one than usual.' The jumper story seemed to have animated Slug a little, and the old spark briefly returned to his eyes. Pele smiled, too.

'I remember my mum marching me down to your house, and the whole street was watching. I was terrified. But you know what she was like.'

'Aye, she was fierce, your mam. Not to be crossed. Even my old fella had a healthy respect for her. Is she still around?'

'She is. And doing well. She's probably doing a lot better than me,' Pele said with a wry smile. He felt somewhat guilty telling him how well his mum was and that she was still going to be alive when he wouldn't be. But, if anything, the news seemed to brighten Slug's mood, albeit briefly.

'Anyway, all this chat about the old estate days, that's not why I've asked you here.' Pele raised his eyebrows.

'I can't imagine it was,' he said, resisting the urge to smile as he looked kindly back into the dying man's eyes and held them. Slug fiddled with the green, elastic strap on his facemask and moved it around his ears as he considered what to say. His trembling square-shaped fingers smoothed non-existent hair, and then he said it.

It was the very last thing Pele had expected to hear.

'I want you to look after Angela when I'm gone. I don't mean anything financially. She'll be well looked after in that department,' he said, waving his hand to one side. 'But I want you to start seeing her, you know? Some company for her after I've gone?'

'What???' Pele blurted out in alarm. He sat forward and gasped at Slug, 'You really can't be serious?' Slug reached out and clutched Pele's forearm with a grip so forceful he wouldn't have believed he could still be capable of it. For the briefest moment, Slug seemed to recover his old bearing and became more than the shadow that Pele had witnessed since entering the ward.

'Oh yes! I'm being perfectly serious,' he spat back at him, the force of his exertions causing him once again to cough, and his whole body shook with the effort. He released Pele's arm, and it took several minutes for him to recover. As he regained his breath, he wheezed out again, 'Do I have to spell it out to you? I thought you were the smart one with the big degree in English. I feel like I've lived my whole life being second best to you. Second best in school; second best with the girls on the estate, and the final insult, second best with her.' He flopped back against the stack of pillows behind him. His voice held a tremor, and it wasn't just from the strain of breathing. 'The only woman I've ever loved in my whole miserable life, and, as luck would have it, she loves you!' His head turned towards Pele; his eyes were tearful and accusatory. 'I lie here knowing that I'm going to die any day now, and I have to ask *you* for a favour! And worse, you make me spell it out to you. Don't you get it? The only way she's ever going to be happy is if she's with you. There, you've won.' The tears were glinting in Slug's eyes now. One slipped reluctantly onto his cheek, and he angrily wiped it away. They were the first Pele had seen since that day so long ago when his father had hit him in the living room. The expression on his face was sorrowful but defiant as he looked hard at Pele. His pride was wounded, but he still managed to retain his dignity. Pele's own tears came quickly, and his voice caught in his throat.

'How have I won anything, Stephen? If you think I'm a winner, all I can say is that you have a strange idea as to what the game is. I've lived in a house for more than twenty years with the ghost of a woman looking over my shoulder every day, a woman I never loved in the way she deserved loving. I've paid deeply for my past mistakes. I've been estranged from the only woman that I ever really loved and who married a man who's hated me since I was a child.' Pele tried to regain some self-control. 'Look. I am truly sorry for Angela and Caitlin and the fact that you're dying, Stephen. I will take absolutely no solace in your death or their loss, but what you don't realise is that I'm already dead inside. I have been for years.' With that, he started to get up. Looking around, he could see a few of the other visitors were glancing over, a sure sign that voices had been more than slightly raised. Slug was aware of it, too. He raised his hand and lowered his voice as he did so.

'Sit down...please. Just hear me out, and then you can go. Do whatever you want. Just sit down for two more minutes, will you?' Pele sucked in a deep breath and then turned back and sat back down on the edge of the seat. Slug's nostrils flared as he inhaled. 'It's Caitlin too. I always knew I could never really have Angela. She's always been yours in a way. But Caitlin's special, and I really love her. In a way that I never thought I could love anyone.' Pele saw his tears well up for a second time. He saw the suffering in the eyes, heard the pain in the voice and felt for the boy, who was now the dying man.

'Look, I get all of that. You've had an unhappy life, and I'm to blame for some of it. I'm just not sure what I can do? I can't turn the clock back, wave a magic wand, and make it all right. Nobody can. It's never going to be all right.' Slug's eyes never left Pele's. They watched him until he'd finished, and then a tiny, hard glint returned briefly.

'No one's asking you to put the clock back. I'm just asking you to try and put the future right. Look after Angela, and you'll be looking after Caitlin in a way, too.' Pele felt exasperation well up inside of him. He knew he needed to keep a lid on it and that the circumstances dictated that he did so. He rose slowly to his feet, reached out, and put his hand gently on Slug's shoulder.

'It's not right,' he said, 'and I can't make it right...and neither can you.'

Pele stood by the grave as the pallbearers slowly lowered the body into the ground. Considering who the deceased was, there was only a small gathering. Looking around, he could count perhaps thirty people; of those, he recognised maybe four or five.

The widow, dressed in obligatory black, pressed a small, white tissue against her eyes. Two mourners comforted her on either side, whispering words of consolation and gently rubbing her back as she cried. Once the coffin was in the ground, the pallbearers stepped back. The mourners came forward in a respectful line, and each one threw a handful of dirt over the coffin. Pele was glad he'd come. It had given him some; what did the Americans call it?

Closure.

The priest's earlier sermon had followed the usual funeral format for a deceased person that the priest had never actually set eyes on. The widow's speech was an eloquent, if tearful, summary of their life together. It was only at that point Pele felt the sadness wash over him. He had never been able to patch things up, to set wrongs right, but that seemed to be the story of his life.

When the service had concluded, he waited quietly on one side until he could speak to the widow alone. He offered his sincere condolences and apologised for not being able to attend the small wake that was taking place at a local pub. Then he made his excuses to leave.

Only as he was walking back to his car did he see Janey. She was a short distance away under the shadow of a large oak tree, its low-hanging branches partially hiding her from the group of mourners. She looked like a ghost staring into the distance. 'Janey,' he called out. She turned her head towards him and, for a moment, seemed puzzled. Slowly, her confused look passed, her mouth spoke his name in recognition, and she walked quickly across the grass towards his car. When she got to the path, she placed her hand on his arm and gripped it. 'Oh, Pele! I'm so glad you're here.' Pele could see she was distraught, and her once pretty face was now barely recognisable with the pain and ravages of a life not so much lived but endured.

'Hey Janey. What are you doing over there? Why weren't you in the church service? Or up by the grave?' he asked, putting his hand on top of hers. It was colder than he could have imagined.

'She invited me, you know? Aileen. His new wife. I just didn't think it would be right, you know? I thought it would be better to keep out of the way and not be a distraction for her. But I wanted to come. I never stopped loving him.' She sobbed loudly, and he felt her pain, her loss. Putting his arms around her, they stood together for a long while, comforting each other.

'I know you didn't, Janey,' he eventually whispered into her grey hair. 'And he loved you. He didn't always make it easy for you to do it, though, did he?' She hugged him with a fierce embrace and broke away.

'You were always such a good friend to him, Pele. And he loved you. You did know that?' Pele felt unable to hold her gaze as if unworthy of it.

'I'm not sure that he did in the end. In his mind, I'd let him down. Do you remember Caroline's funeral and how uncomfortable he was around me? We were never the same after you guys split up. I know he blamed me for not covering for him.'

'No! He never blamed you,' she insisted, clasping hold of his hands. 'He always knew it was his own fault. It was guilt and shame that you saw that day. He was ashamed of himself, ashamed of trying to implicate you in his mistakes.'

They held each other tightly before they went their separate ways.

It was another cold winter's day. Pele slipped quietly into an ancient wooden pew at the back of the church. Despite the occasion, sitting there in familiar surroundings that hadn't changed in decades felt strangely comforting. The smell of incense and hushed voices added to the sense of peacefulness. He considered that nearly all of the significant events of his life could be traced back to here in one way or another. From as far back as his baptism to Caroline's death and everything in between, his life seemed to be inextricably linked to this place.

There were six long rows of mourners at the front, obscuring his view of the widow and the deceased's daughter, which was how Pele preferred it. He sat far away from everybody, but occasionally, a head would turn around to look at him, obviously wondering who he was and why he was there. These weren't questions Pele thought he could easily answer.

He unbuttoned his coat as he waited. Loud organ music began to play, removing any sense of peace he'd been enjoying. It was a sorrowful, vibrating drone that entered through his ears and somehow filled his head. An old, shambling figure pushed his way into the pew from the other side. 'Well, well! If it isn't the estate's finest young man that was ever named after a Brazilian footballer.' O'Malley looked like he had put on a few more pounds since Pele had last seen him. His kindly red face was covered in a soft grey beard, and his bright eyes glinted under his large, bushy eyebrows.

'Not so young these days, Father,' Pele smiled softly, extending his hand, which the old man took in both of his and held for a moment.

'I never realised that you and Stephen had finally become friends. There was no sign of that when you were younger,' the priest told him, giving out a small chuckle as he did so.

'Well, we weren't ever that friendly, really. I'm here because of a promise I made,' Pele whispered.

'You were always an honourable lad, Pele. The weight of the world was always on your shoulders, right enough. Carried it around like it was all yours to bear.' The old man stared at him from beneath his eyebrows. Pele gave him a lopsided smile but said nothing. This was the priest's usual lead into a conversation that was about to go somewhere. He would only have to wait a moment to find out where that was. The priest absently picked up a small, red hymnbook balancing on the pew in front of him. 'You know, I took his last confession. He wouldn't let Callaghan do it, and he insisted that it had to be me.' Pele looked down towards the front of the church at the coffin, which had been placed before the altar, flowers and photographs arranged along the top.

'I suppose he had a lot to get off his chest,' he interjected when the priest failed to continue. O'Malley sat preoccupied with whatever thoughts were rolling around in his head.

'Aye, to be fair, that he did. He did indeed.' He shifted his body to face Pele, placed his arm across the back of the pew, and said wistfully. 'You know, there's one thing I'm certain of: he loved his family. He loved his girl there more than life, and he wanted his wife to be happy when he was gone.' O'Malley left the comment hanging in the air like warm breath on a cold winter morning. Pele turned to him, and the two men momentarily held each other's gaze. It was Pele who finally broke the silence.

'I sometimes think that God has a very strange sense of humour, Father, when it comes to me.'

'And just how's that?' asked O'Malley. Pele breathed in deeply through his nose.

'How's that?' he replied. 'Because he gave me a glimpse of true love and then made sure I spent the rest of my life showing me that I could never actually obtain it.' At this, Pele bowed his head and blinked away the tears stinging his eyes. He felt the old man's hand rest on his shoulders and squeeze softly. He finally caught a glimpse of the widow through the mass of heads towards the front of the church.

'Pele, my son. God never curses us with love. It's his blessing. To quote a wiser man than me: 'To love someone is to look upon the face of God.' If that seems like a curse to you, it's because you've not yet understood what that means. Your life, unlike poor Stephen's up there, is not yet over. You don't know what God has in store for you.' With that, the priest removed his arm, and they sat quietly. The organ music thankfully ground to a halt, and the mourners at the front became silent. Then Father Callaghan, Father O'Malley's successor, stood in the pulpit, and the service began.

The rain fell ever so lightly, like a mist. Pele pressed the button on the key and locked the car. An icy wind had blown in from the east, and the Met Centre reckoned there'd be snow later that week. He turned his collar to the cold and walked across the grass verge to the cemetery path for the second time in a week.

He followed it down the hill to where he could see a large group of mourners that, for the most part, had their backs to him as he approached. He was glad of the large numbers, partly because it meant he could hide in plain sight, that was if you didn't count O'Malley. But also, the comfort and love of being surrounded by so many relatives and friends at a time like this would have meant a lot to the family.

Staying out of sight, he watched while the priest said a few more words and family members spoke briefly. He glanced around and recognised a few faces from the old days, some older and some looking much wearier than others. He wondered, with some humour, if they thought the same thing about him.

When the small ceremony at the graveside was over, he made his way over to Slug's sisters, all of whom had grown into striking women, possessing red hair, pale skin, and piercing blue eyes, which were unnervingly reminiscent of Slug's. He passed amongst them, gave his condolences, and they exchanged minor pleasantries.

It was a few minutes before his eyes connected with Angela's. She was still standing at the head of the grave with a tissue gripped in her left hand and holding Caitlin's hand tightly with her right. The solemnness of the occasion was weighing heavily, as they both appeared worn out and fragile. Caitlin's pale face was a little puffy from crying, and her cheeks were red from the bite of the wind.

Angela's eyes locked onto his briefly, and he nodded at her before turning away to slip behind a group of men who were reminiscing about the old days on the estate. He turned around to look back and was a little disconcerted to see that Caitlin had left her mother's arm and was walking directly towards him. He was forced to remain somewhat uncomfortably rooted to the spot. Caitlin extended her hand to meet his, and she spoke before he could articulate anything. 'Hello, Mr Smith. Thank you so much for coming. My father would have been really grateful.' Pele found himself shaking her hand lightly and warming once again to this self-confident young woman. Her hair had darkened a little since her school days, and the tall, gangly frame was now graced with a poise and style that spoke loudly of her mother's genetic influence.

'Thank you, Caitlin. I was glad to come, though I have to confess to the fact that I didn't really know him all that well. We might have grown up on the same estate, but we were never really friends.' Pele realised he was blustering and stopped himself. He then offered his condolences. 'Anyway, I'm so sorry for your loss, Caitlin. I know you loved your father very much. You used to talk about him all the time in form, and from what I've heard, you were the apple of his eye. You must miss him greatly.' She smiled sadly, her tear-strewn face red from all the crying she'd done of late. Her eyes had a lost and confused look to them. One that suggested the idea of a life that no longer contained her father was one that she would find hard to bear. She wiped away a tear.

'Thank you, Mr Smith. He's left a big hole in my life that I don't think can ever be filled. But life goes on, at least that's what he told me before he died,' she said with a contorted smile on her face, which somehow managed to look happy and sad at the same time. Then she took a deep breath to calm herself and said to him, 'You know, he also told me you'd been to see him at the hospital. That was very kind of you, and I think it meant a lot to him.' Pele's head reeled slightly at this news. It seemed that Slug hadn't kept strictly to his word and had kept a few tricks up his sleeve to play even after he'd departed. First O'Malley, and now this revelation. Pele figured it was probably a dying man's prerogative. Yet it made him apprehensive. Caitlin's eyes seemed to be watching him carefully for his response. She appeared to be more in the loop than Pele would have liked her to be, and he was unnerved to think about what else she might know.

'Err…yeah. He asked me to come and visit, so I did. We caught up on old times back at school, and…' he was floundering, but thankfully, Caitlin stepped into the breach.

'I'm really glad he had someone to reminisce with about the old days,' she said softly, pulling her hand away and looking around. And in a pleasant voice, she said, 'I should get my mother. You do remember her, don't you?' It came out of her mouth almost like a statement rather than a question. Pele was alarmed at the turn of events, even more so as Caitlin's eyes were holding his firmly. He wondered again just how much Slug had told her.

'Oh! No. Please don't!' Pele blurted. 'I wouldn't want to intrude on your mother's grief. I mean, she'll most likely be busy with all of the family. Please give her my condolences, but I can't stay. I have to get back to school for a meeting.'

'Well, I seem to have lost her anyway,' she said, twisting her head around as she tried to locate her. 'If you change your mind, there's a buffet and drinks at the Griffin. It'll probably be a long, loud, and rowdy affair, and that's just the priests,' she said, her eyes twinkling mischievously. Pele smiled at that, but he was desperate to leave.

'I'll also have to give that a miss, I'm afraid. Like I said, I've got a meeting and I really can't miss it. It was really lovely to see you again, Caitlin, despite the sad circumstances.' She nodded her head and smiled, and he saw just how much she looked like her mother.

'Thanks, Mr Smith. It was nice to see you again, too. I do hope we'll see each other again soon.'

He smiled, waved and then turned away to walk down the path.

Though he still came to visit his mum every week, he hadn't driven past the old Cherry Tree pub for years, so he decided to take a detour the following Friday afternoon and drive down memory lane. It was boarded up, no doubt going to be sold off to some property developer and turned into an office block or retail shop that would further suck the character out of the old town.

He drove into the derelict car park, which now contained two overflowing skips that someone had attempted to set fire to. Discarded cans of alcohol had been thrown amongst the weeds that were everywhere. Local teenagers clearly used it as a place to hang out and dump their empty cans.

He parked up, and as he got out, the memories from his past came rushing back. The hundreds of different nights he'd spent in that old building, his pool-playing teenage years, his married years, the live music nights, quiz nights, Christmas and office parties, fights, laughter, christenings and funerals.

So many different recollections attached to a single building. The name 'Cherry Tree Lounge' was faded and peeling on an old wooden placard hanging above the door. The entrance and windows were plastered with posters and graffiti. Someone had painted over a David Cameron poster 'Vote Tory if you've had a lobotomy.'

As he stood observing the local artistic talent, he heard a familiar voice behind him. 'The estate's not been the same since they closed it. If I remember rightly, you still owe me a pint from the pool game you lost.' Pele spun around in surprise, recognising the voice instantly. 'Newtog!" he cried. Although the voice was recognisable, the man standing before him had radically changed. Newtog was wearing black jeans, a double-breasted wool coat, and a grin that stretched across a face that looked ten years younger than when he'd last seen him. He'd lost a phenomenal amount of weight, and his once bloated, reddened face was unblemished and lightly tanned. 'Wow! You look great,' Pele exclaimed, stepping across the old chains of the pub car park to give him a bear hug.

'Thanks, Pele,' he grinned self-consciously. 'You don't look too bad yourself for an old man.' Pele laughed, enjoying the familiar teasing from this man he'd lost touch with.

'Seriously though, you look great. How have you managed… all of this?' Pele asked, stepping back and holding out both of his arms at his new shape.

'An ultimatum is the long and short of it, I suppose. When the grandkids started to arrive, Sheena started on at me. She told me straight that I wasn't going to be around to enjoy them, and she didn't want to be a widow in her fifties.' He shrugged lightly and continued, 'I'd lived in self-destruct mode for years; you know better than anyone what I was like. It all catches up with you in the end, but love conquers all, as they say. So, I'm a reformed man; I've not had a drink in five years, and the weight's dropped off. Never felt so good, actually.' The evidence was standing there right in front of him, and Pele felt so pleased to finally hear some good news.

'Well, you look ten years younger than when I last saw you. That ultimatum paid off in more ways than one.' As he said this, his train of thought moved to their mutual friend, who'd passed up countless ultimatums. 'I thought I might have seen you…at John's funeral?' Newtog brushed his hair back and looked down.

'Yeah, I feel really bad about that. We got the news that he'd passed three days before we flew out to Lanzarote. I didn't even know when the funeral was. I heard he died from one of the lads I used to work with in the factory. Never had much contact with John since I stopped going to the pub. Anyway, by the time we got back, they'd already held it.' Pele nodded at him.

'I remember how much John loved his Benidorm holidays with Janey back in the day. I'm sure he would have approved.' Newtog's face lightened at this. He grinned widely, which revealed his dimples, and then placed his hand lightly on Pele's arm.

'And you, mate? How are you doing? You know? After all these years. Still at that school across the water?' Pele smiled.

'Yeah, doing ok. Still at the same school. Still tragically single and still listening to the Smiths.' Newtog chided him.

'God, they're depressing. I remember Caroline agreed with me on that point. Whenever you put them on in the Jukebox in there, she'd roll her eyes.' He nodded towards the old pub.

'Yeah, she did. She was definitely not a fan,' Pele laughed. 'Are you still living in the same house?'

'No, we moved a few years ago out towards the old town. Sheena got a new job, and we had a bit more money, with me not drinking it away anymore. He pulled a face. 'Actually, a lot more money,' he laughed loudly.

'Well, I'm moving up to the Park area. So, I won't be too far away from where you are. Maybe we'll see a bit more of each other? Here's my number.' Pele pulled out a pen and started to write his mobile number on the back of a shopping list he had in his pocket.

'I'd like that, Pele. It's been too long,' said Newtog, looking over Pele's shoulder. 'That's my taxi. I've still never learnt to drive, so it costs me a fortune to visit my mother, but it keeps me in the will,' he chortled. 'Great seeing you again, mate.'

'And you too. It's really great to see you looking so well. My best to Sheena.'

'Will do. Take it easy.' And with that, he opened the passenger door of the taxi and got in. Pele watched him go before heading back to the car.

Pele was finally packing the remnants of his old life away. Like most people, when they move house, he found it both a physical and mental process. The physical side involved finally putting the memories of the house he'd shared with Caroline into boxes. He knew he should have done it years ago as he'd lived so much of his life in the past and had held himself back for so very long.

In the end, guilt had led to the loss of so many opportunities and had cost him dearly. But now he was finally boxing the past off. He'd sold the house and was moving into a semi down by the park. Caroline would have approved, he thought.

He was also boxing off things mentally. It was time to move on, to look forward to whatever lay ahead, instead of constantly looking backwards at the things he could never change. So many years lost in regret, grief, and apathy. All of the: *'what might have beens'* and *'if onlys'* had robbed him of a future. Slug's demise had been a wake-up call if nothing else. Life was for the living, not for the giving up and dying.

Pele began stuffing the ornaments from the mantelpiece into cardboard boxes, wrapping them first in old copies he kept of the Guardian; as he did so, the Smiths rang out in the background 'A Hatful of Hollow' was on the CD player, and Morrissey sang to him about his life like no one else did. He looked up at the clock again. He was due to move in three days if the solicitors got their act together. He was part of a small but seemingly volatile chain and hoped that it wouldn't go wrong. He remembered then he hadn't phoned the removal company to confirm, so he picked up his mobile off the coffee table and scrolled through for the stored number. As he was scrolling, the door chimes went.

Pele couldn't imagine who it could be. As he approached the door, he felt the same nervous feeling he'd felt that day John had appeared all those years ago. He reached for the catch, and with an unsteady hand, he flicked it back and pulled open the door. At first, he didn't recognise the figure standing shivering in the cold due to the hat and scarf. He was more than surprised when he did.

It was Caitlin.

Five minutes later, they were sitting on two dining table chairs in an otherwise Spartan front room. Caitlin was sipping a cup of tea from a cup that Pele had had to locate from an upstairs' box in order to make a pair. 'Looks like you're all set for moving then. I'm really very impressed with your organisational skills,' she said, nodding approvingly at the stacked boxes against a wall. The contents of each were individually labelled, packed and coordinated by room. Pele laughed out loud.

'That's my mother's handiwork. I'm about as organised as a toddler.' He grinned, hooking his thumb over at the box he'd been packing. In it were two half-wrapped ornaments firmly wedged between a sofa cushion, a couple of books, and a bedroom lampshade. Caitlin giggled and took a bite from a chocolate digestive. 'Anyway, as nice as it is to see you, how on earth did you find me?' he enquired.

'Oh, you can find anyone these days. What with the Internet, 192.com, all those sites, etc. It wasn't that difficult, even if you do have a common name.' She grinned at him while brushing crumbs off her lap.

'Ah, technology,' he replied, leaving the sentence hanging as he weighed his next words carefully. He leaned forward on his elbows and asked, 'Now I've ascertained how you've found me. I just need to ask about the 'why' you've found me?'

'Well, that's easy,' she replied without any hesitation. 'I'm here because of my mum.'

'Oh! Right,' said Pele, sitting back quickly. He was startled by the direct and somewhat unexpected answer. Lowering his gaze in an attempt to escape her scrutiny, he began to lightly drum his fingers on the dining room table in the silence that followed. 'I don't know what I was expecting you to say, but… well, it wasn't that.' He sighed, the weight of all the things he suspected she wanted to say suddenly bearing down on him. He knew that she had a right to know the truth, and he was ready to be honest with her. What he wasn't ready for was her response.

'Yes, that,' she said, putting her half-empty cup on the mantelpiece and staring at him. Pele looked into her eyes, eyes which were steady and unwavering, a prelude for the words that were to follow. 'When you grow up in a house like mine, a house where there are frequent arguments and your parents lower their voices whenever you walk into a room, or they whisper if they think you're in the next room, then everyone assumes that you don't notice anything. They assume that you don't hear anything, too. My dad was a great dad, but I'm not so sure he was that great a husband, but that may or may not have been because his wife was in love with somebody else.' Caitlin paused and then shrugged as if she genuinely didn't know the answer to that question and was thinking about it. Pele didn't offer an opinion, so she continued. 'I knew from an early age that something was wrong with my parent's marriage. I eventually worked out that what was wrong was mostly my mum. Yes, my dad was overly loud, and he could be very difficult when he wanted to be. Most of the time, though, he was just full of bluster. And…he really loved us. Both of us.' Caitlin's voice cracked a little. She took a small breath while her eyes began to brim with tears. Pele pulled a box of Kleenex across the table and handed it to her. She dabbed her eyes and thanked him.

'Go on, Caitlin,' Pele said gently. Whatever she'd come to say needed saying, and he knew that the least he could do was give her the space to get it all off her chest.

She gulped, blew her nose loudly, and said, 'My mum was different from my dad. She didn't ever blow up like him or lose her temper. But she was always so distant. No matter what he did or how much he gave her, she never seemed really happy.

THESE THINGS TAKE TIME

It was like you were looking at a sketch of somebody, but the artist hadn't bothered to finish it.' Caitlin looked at Pele to check he was following. He nodded for her to continue. 'So, I knew all these things. Well, not knew them, really, but I suppose I was subconsciously aware of them. Then, I started secondary school. It was okay for the first couple of months, but then all the arguments somehow got worse. My mum's sadness spiralled, and she started to get angry, which was so unlike her. Dad always seemed hurt, like he just didn't know how to cope. So, he just worked longer hours and bought her more stuff that she didn't ask for or want. Then, one night, while I was upstairs, they forgot to whisper. Forgot to go quiet. They started to shout. That's when I heard your name for the first time.' Pele was clasping his hands together tightly between his knees as he listened. He looked up and held her anguished look.

'I'm so sorry, Caitlin. So sorry that you had to go through that. It's not something I would have ever wanted.' Caitlin gave him a sad smile through reddened eyes and carried on.

'A few days later, I got told I was moving school. I can't tell you how devastated I was. I cried and cried for days. Eventually, Dad came into my room and told me I didn't have to move and that he was sorry if he'd made me sad. And then I realised that was why you'd tried to move me out of your form. Later, when I moved up into year 8 and the other years, I realised why you never took me for English again. Not even our English GCSE top set, which you always took.

Pele rubbed his forehead as he listened to Caitlin recall the things he'd done. In his mind, he'd tried to protect her. But he now saw that his actions had ultimately confused and hurt her, compounding the misery she'd been experiencing in her home life. 'I'd see you around school, and you were always really nice to me, but often, you seemed like you were in some distant land, not in the present. Like a shadow of the person you were. And that's when I knew: you were just like my mum.' Pele got up at this and went over to the window. He looked out to the small garden at the back. Caroline had loved that little garden, but it was overgrown and uncared for now.

'I told your dad when I went to see him that I can't go back and change things. I wish I could,' he said, breathing out the words heavily. He turned to face her and asked softly, 'What do you want from me, Caitlin?' Caitlin turned slightly on the chair, placing the palms of her hands flat on her knees. She swallowed before speaking,

'What do I want? Why, I want the same thing that my dad wanted. If he could see a way through this mess and act selflessly, then why can't you see it too?'

'How could I even possibly do that, Caitlin?' Pele exclaimed.

'By not giving up on her,' Caitlin said firmly. 'Isn't that what you're supposed to do when you love someone? I remember when I came to see you about Moby Dick, and I told you I thought Ahab was nothing but a madman with a dangerous obsession that got him killed, but you told me he was much, much more. You told me that he lived life on his own terms, that he had so much spirit, so much fight in him, and even though he might lose everything, it was infinitely better to keep fighting than to ever just give up.' Pele cut in.

'But I gave up years ago, Caitlin. There's no more fight left in me. Some things are just not meant to be. A long time ago, I realised the truth that clocks can't be turned back, no matter how much we want them to be. Besides, your mum's going to need time to deal with her loss. Even if they had problems, a large part of her life was connected to your dad, and the mere idea of resurrecting something that was never meant to be is...'

'Oh, Mr Smith, you are so very wrong!' she interrupted. She exhaled loudly and held his forearm firmly. 'When I walk out of that door, I really don't want to leave behind some middle-aged man who's still living in the past and wondering about what could have been if only he'd had the courage to go and fight for his future.' Pele didn't, couldn't, reply to that as it was the very same conversation he'd been having with himself only thirty minutes earlier. They each stared at the other impassively for a few moments. Caitlin finally broke away and turned to pick up her coat. He watched as she buttoned it up, picked her bag up from the floor, sighed, and said, 'Goodbye, Mr Smith.' Pele only nodded, but before she reached the door in the hallway, something in him finally stirred, and he called her back.

'Caitlin. Please. Just a minute.' Caitlin stopped at the open door while Pele got up and grabbed a pad off the box next to the letters. He pulled a pen from his top pocket and quickly scrawled down some hurried sentences on the paper. Then he went down the hall and handed it to Caitlin. 'I don't know where the envelopes are,' he told her. 'Give your mum this. You can read it if you want. It won't make much sense to you anyway.' Cailin took the note from him, flicked open her bag and put it inside.

'I will, Mr Smith. I will. I just hope whatever it is, it's enough for you both.'

'So do I,' he replied.

Then she smiled at him and was gone.

The following Saturday, at around 1:30 pm, Pele took a walk.

He went out of his front door, down onto Grangeway and followed the main road to his old estate.

When he reached the entrance, he could see that the park was overgrown and covered in the sort of teenage graffiti that was exciting when you did it as a teenager but depressing when you became the age he was, as you became certain it heralded the downfall of western civilisation. He followed the tarmac path towards the swings and looked over. What he saw took him back in time. It wasn't the brown rust on the barely hanging chains or the chipped and rotted wooden seats that took him back. No, it was the woman wearing the Burberry scarf who was swinging her legs back and to on the end swing.

The very same swing.

She would have looked like an attractive middle-aged woman to anyone else. But Pele saw only the girl. The cherubic girl with the skinny legs and fringe that he'd fallen in love with in that very same spot so long ago.

She'd seen him now, and she smiled, calling over, 'Come to

give me a push?'

'A small push? Or are you still living dangerously?' he asked as he reached her side. 'I see you read the note.'

'Well, it wasn't so much the note that brought me here, to be honest. I was more intrigued that Caitlin told me I had to come because I was your whale. I figured she'd lost the plot. As far as compliments go, it's not the most flattering one I've ever had.' Her eyes were scrutinising his, and a smile was tugging at the corners of her lips.

'Oh, she's your daughter all right,' he said, laughing. 'The whale thing's a bit of an in-joke that I promise you is the very opposite of what you seem to think it means.' He moved in front of her and placed his hands on the chains to look into her upturned face.

'You know,' she said, 'when Stephen told me what he'd done, what he'd said to you, I was so angry. It took me a while to work through it all, to understand why on earth he'd done it. You know he gave me a lot of gifts, and in the end, I realised it was the most precious gift, the most generous gift he ever gave me. I thought that I couldn't do it. Take what he was offering me. I think mostly it was the guilt of not loving him the way he'd loved me that was so overwhelming. But I started to understand what it must have taken for him to do that, and I began to get past the anger; besides, there was one thing that I couldn't get past, and that was the simple fact that I've always loved you and I always will.' She reached up and gently touched his face while he placed his hand over hers and kissed it.

He turned round to sit on the swing next to her, still holding her hand, which she was grasping tightly like she might never let go.

They sat there for a long time, just rocking back and forth, holding hands, looking ahead, and not speaking.

They didn't need to.

They had the rest of their lives in front of them.

AFTERWORD

We have tried to make this copy of our novel as 'clean' from gramatical and spelling errors as we possibly can.

As independent authors the sums of money required by the diligent professionals who edit and check for these things are slightly out of our reach.

If you have in the course of reading this novel come across something which is clearly a mistake could you drop us an email with the sentence or area of the novel which is incorrect?

You can do this at:

thesethingstaketimebook@yahoo.co.uk

Alternatively if you have enjoyed it and would like to spend some time in the Highlands with us. Please let us know.

Thank you

Steve and Julie

ABOUT THE AUTHOR

Steve And Julie Carter

Steve and Julie live in the beautiful Highlands of Scotland. They are semi-retired, and when they are not writing, they run a small B&B and walk their golden retriever, George, in the surrounding forests.

BOOKS BY THIS AUTHOR

Love, Sex And Tesco's Finest Cava

Steve's first novel is a quirky Internet romance told from a male perspective.
This novel reached no1 among all Kindle romance novels in May 2011.

Finding Yourself In Seville

Steve's second novel is another quirky romance told from a male perspective based on his year attending Seville university in the 1990s.
This novel has been downloaded over 20,000 times.